THE NATOMA BRIDE

MATT BANNISTER WESTERN 15

KEN PRATT

Published in the United States by Wolfpack Publishing, Las Vegas

CKN Christian Publishing
An Imprint of Wolfpack Publishing
9850 S. Maryland Parkway, Suite A-5 #323
Las Vegas, Nevada 89183

cknchristianpublishing.com

Paperback ISBN: 978-1-63977-107-3
eBook ISBN: 978-1-63977-504-0
LCCN 2022946761

THE NATOMA BRIDE

Dedication

For my beautiful daughter, Jessica.
I love you.

Chapter 1

Audrey Butler could hardly control her nervousness. She had traveled by rail from Sacramento to San Francisco. There she boarded the SS Columbia and traveled by sea to Portland, Oregon, before boarding the Oregon Short Line Railroad east up the Columbia River Gorge to Walla Walla, Washington. Audrey had been riding in a stagecoach for three days over rough country and staying the night in tiny stage stops before climbing back into the smaller six-passenger Wells Fargo coach with three other passengers.

The well-dressed man sitting beside her was named Sal Gable. He was traveling to Boise City and claimed to be a gambler. He had refused to sit next to the elderly negro lady who sat across from them on the other bench seat. Her name was Jane Montgomery; she was departing the stage in the same town that Audrey was. It comforted Audrey to know at least one person in the new area she was moving to. Sal Gable didn't want to ride in the same coach as Jane and tried to get her thrown off the stage in Walla Walla, but the fourth passenger refused to let that happen and overrode Sal by threatening to bust Sal's jaw if he didn't shut his mouth. The fourth passenger was a large older man named Joel Fasana. He was a fatherly kind of man that made Audrey feel safe. He had a warmth in his kind smile that was reassuring beyond his Christian faith.

"Joel, how much further is it?" she asked. Joel had explained earlier that he had lived his whole life in Jessup County but had spent the past year living on the Oregon Coast. He was the only passenger familiar with the territory.

He understood the young lady was anxious to get to Natoma, but also her nervousness about arriving. Joel had raised six children to adulthood, four of which were girls. If any father understood a young lady's nervous jitters, fears, and excitement at the prospect of getting married, it was Joel; he had experienced it all with his girls. The trip had been long, but it was nearing the end for Audrey. She was a lovely young lady and he'd miss her company once the stage left Natoma for Branson. Joel was anxious to get back home as well. His dearest granddaughter, Hannie Longo, had been murdered several days before, and the funeral was waiting for him to get home. His son, William, had killed the teenage boy responsible for her death, but it didn't take away a single ounce of the pain. Joel's heart was broken.

"Oh, we're still a good two hours from Natoma. You'll know when we're getting close when we drop down into the valley. When you see the first wheat field, you'll know we're twenty, maybe thirty, minutes away."

"It's a stage stop, right? So we can eat?" Sal asked. He was a rude and domineering young man in his early thirties, with a self-righteousness that seemed to put him above the others. He was also a racist who had refused to speak a word or show any kindness to Jane.

"It is."

"Good. I can't wait to get out of the filth of this stagecoach," he said with a sideways glance at Jane. "I'm never coming back this way; I'll tell you that."

"Well, not having you around will definitely be our loss." Joel answered sarcastically. He didn't like Sal Gable.

Jane Montgomery asked Audrey, "You must be getting excited? You have only a few hours until you meet your groom."

Audrey nodded with an excited giddiness. She was a mail-order bride on her way to marry a man she had never met. "I am. I cannot wait to meet him. But I'm also petrified."

Sal dipped a shoulder as he leaned towards her. "If you're just looking for a man, you could stick with me. I'm not one to marry, but we could partner up."

Audrey wrinkled her nose without interest. "I'll stick with my fellow. I know we're going to have a good marriage."

Audrey had been talking about her fiancé since they left Walla Walla, but Joel had not questioned her about it. His mind was weary from traveling, with his being uncomfortable and the memories of his granddaughter. "Alan's last name is Butler?" he questioned. Joel had not mentioned that he owned the Fasana Granite Quarry or that he was familiar with many families around the county from making family tombstones over the years. He wasn't familiar with the Butler family from Natoma.

"No. That's my last name. I'm Audrey Butler. The man I'm marrying is named Alan Sperry. Do you know him?" she asked.

Joel answered with a quiet disappointment, "No." He *had* heard of Alan Sperry but figured he'd best not fill her head with all the bad stories he had heard. There was the possibility that Alan Sperry had changed over the years. He hoped so.

Audrey explained, "He works at a tannery and has a small farm. He takes care of his aging mother and widowed sister. Alan seems to be a wonderful man. He's older than me by over eleven years, but we seem to get along well and share the same values and beliefs as Christians. I prayed about it a lot and felt like this is what the Lord wanted for me."

Jane said, "The Lord certainly has plans for each of us. I have never been married…"

"Go figure." Sal interrupted without interest.

"But I don't regret it," Jane continued unphased. "I was a maid in a couple's home for a long time, and now that I retired, I am moving to help the young lady I raised with her newborn baby. It's a sad thing, but the woman I worked for doesn't have a relationship with her daughter, but I do. We have something in common, Audrey; we are both moving here to start our lives over again."

"Wouldn't it be neat if we were neighbors?" Audrey asked.

"It would, indeed." Jane agreed. She liked the young lady.

Sal Gable was tired of listening to the women talking. "Joel, isn't fishing kind of a menial job? It doesn't take much thought to throw a line in the water, does it?"

"Probably not." Joel said with a slight smirk.

"I asked before, but do you ever gamble, Joel? Roulette, poker, do you play your luck?"

Joel yawned, uninterested. "Nope. I work too hard for my money."

Sal rolled his eyes. "By your appearance, you don't have much."

Joel bet he had more money in the bank than the gambler would ever win in his lifetime. "Nope. But if I did, I wouldn't need a fancy gray suit like yours to let everyone know I had any."

Sal snickered and peered out the window. His suit was more silver in color than gray. The warm air of the July afternoon offered a little breeze to help cool the inside of the coach. Outside, the thick trees of the mountains and thickening underbrush from the lower elevations created a wall of green that was hard to see through.

Suddenly, the momentary silence was interrupted by shouts of unknown origin in front of the stagecoach, bringing it to a sudden stop. By the shouting of orders and threats of violence, the passengers quickly understood that the stage was being robbed.

"Set the brake and step down! Throw down the shotgun, or I'll fill you with lead!"

"Throw down the strong box!" another voice ordered.

The driver answered, "It ain't worth dying for, so take what you want. We aren't carrying anything of value except some mail."

"We'll decide that. Both of you get down and empty your pockets!"

Joel, noticing the two ladies were afraid, leaned forward and spoke softly to comfort them, "Stay calm, and everything will be fine. Understood?"

Audrey nodded quickly.

The passenger door was jerked open, and a man wearing a burlap bag over his face and burlap tied over his boots pointed a revolver at the four passengers. "Step out one at a time! If you have a weapon, lay it down, we won't hesitate to kill you. Hurry!"

Joel came out of the coach first, then helped Audrey step down before pushing Sal back to help Jane step out next. Sal stepped out last as they lined up under the eyes of four bandits. Burlap bags covered all four of the men's heads and boots. Not one of the highwaymen wore a fancy belt buckle or hat that could identify them.

Joel repeated softly, "You two ladies, remain calm. Nothing is worth dying for, so give them what they want."

One of the highwaymen cursed as he searched the strong box. "There ain't nothing here but mail. Take what you can, but I think we're the ones being robbed." He was angry.

Two of the bandits stood in front of the four passengers. One held a revolver, the other a shotgun. "Give me your wallets, money purses, and valuables!" one ordered.

Joel showed his rough and calloused palms to the robber. "Does it look like I have any money? I'm barely able to take the stage. Look, I'll show you," he pulled out his wallet and opened it. There was a five-dollar bill. "Take my last five dollars if you want." Joel knew there was always a chance of the stage being robbed, so he never dressed well or carried any money on his person. The gambler, Sal Gable, wasn't so wise and ended up reluctantly opening his billfold and losing eighty-four dollars, a gold pocket watch connected to his suit, and a gold ring with a square ruby.

Jane offered her handbag, and the bandits took ten dollars and her silver cross necklace. Audrey lost a butterfly broach with rainbow-colored wings that her mother gave her and four dollars from her money purse.

"You," a smaller robber said, jabbing the shotgun barrel into Joel's chest. "Are you meeting a woman today?"

Joel scowled. "No. I don't plan to."

"You're not getting married?" the bandit questioned further.

Joel was confused by the question. "No."

"Where are you headed to, then?"

"A funeral in Branson."

"Oh. Where are you from?"

"Astoria. I'm a fisherman."

The lad behind the mask nodded with satisfaction. "Then you're not coming here to get married?"

"No. Unfortunately, my business here isn't so pleasant." Joel replied.

"That's good." The highwayman ran the shotgun barrel up Joel's chest to under his chin and lifted his chin higher. "Because if you were the man coming to marry my grandmother, I'd kill you right here, right now."

"Well, I'm glad I'm not him."

One of the highwaymen with broad shoulders and a muscular build carried a sledgehammer out of the brush, and with a wide and powerful swing, the hammer fractured an oak spoke of the front wheel. Another swing and the spoke broke. He swung again and again until three of the wheel spokes were broken. He went to the other side and did the same. When he finished, he spoke to the driver, "Maybe you could limp slowly to the next town. Or maybe you won't make it today at all. Gentlemen, let's go!" he yelled. The four men ran down the road and around a corner where their horses were tethered.

The driver threw his hat in frustration. "We got six broken spokes and a rough downhill grade ahead. I'm not risking it. Mac, you'll have to ride one of those horses to Natoma and bring back two new wheels. We'll wait here. Sorry folks, but we're going to arrive at the next stage stop a few hours late."

"Well," Joel said contently, "I suppose since we have time, I might as well wander down to the creek and get a cold drink. Ladies, would you care to join me? It's just downhill; you can hear it running."

Jane declined, but Audrey was thirsty, and the sound of the running mountain water drew her like a bee to a flower. She also favored Joel's presence over Sal's. They cut through the brush down a bank thirty yards or so to arrive at a flowing stream. Both drank from the stream and sat on a fallen tree next to the water.

Audrey spoke sincerely, "Thank you for telling me to hide my money. I would have lost it all. Losing my mother's broach is hard enough."

"You're welcome. I wanted to tell you that if your marriage does not work out or you need some help, my name is Joel Fasana. I own the Fasana Granite Quarry in Branson. So, if you need help, don't hesitate to wire me. Okay?"

"I thought you were a fisherman." she said.

Joel winked, knowing he had misled the other passengers of his financial standing. "I fish for the fun of it. I retired a year ago, but I still own the business."

"You don't know Alan Sperry, though?" she asked.

"I've never met him. But the invitation stands; if you need help, don't hesitate to let me know."

Chapter 2

Sarah Pierce held her infant baby close to her heart while she and Nathan waited for the stagecoach to arrive in the shade of the Gregory Hotel's front porch. She was excited and impatiently waiting for the arrival of her childhood maid, Miss Jane Montgomery. Sarah had given birth to their first child a month before. They named the seven-pound baby boy Calvin James Pierce, after Nathan's older brother, Cal Pierce, who had been killed by Octavius Clark a year earlier near Windsor Ridge. They called their baby boy Little Cal.

Nathan was a proud father, which showed in his loving eyes as he watched his beautiful bride holding their son. He knew how important Miss Jane was to Sarah, so he built another room onto their home for Miss Jane. She retired and agreed to join the closest thing to a daughter she would ever have.

News had come that the stagecoach had been robbed and the two front wheels were broken.

Adam Bannister volunteered to take his wagon and meet the stagecoach to bring the travelers to town. The Pierce family, Annie Lenning, and Rory Jackson waited at the hotel for his arrival. Nathan would have gone with Adam, but Natoma had some bad characters, so he stayed with the women to keep them safe from the vermin that called Natoma home. The Sheriff, Zeke Jones, rode with Adam to collect information about the robbery.

Rory Jackson wiped a touch of perspiration from her forehead. "Oh, look, Annie, your best friend, is coming back."

Jannie Sperry walked towards them with her mother, Mattie, and two of Jannie's children. Her sixteen-year-old son, Tad, and her youngest child, four-year-old Eve.

Annie watched them approaching with no expression. "Great. I wish Adam would hurry up and get back here."

Rory grinned, revealing her bright smile. "I think I'll sit here and watch. You could invite her to one of our family girl nights. That might be fun."

"Hush up." Annie said, not nearly humored as much as Rory was. Jannie Sperry had been waiting with them for the stage earlier and seemed interested in Annie and her horse business. Annie didn't want to be rude, but she had no interest in becoming Jannie's friend or giving her a free horse just because she had plenty of them.

Jannie approached with a friendly grin. One tooth was missing, and the others were stained by coffee and neglect. She wore a homemade, simple

11

gray dress and walked barefoot on the dirt road. Her dark brown hair was straight and lifeless as it lay over her thin shoulders. She was not an attractive woman as the years of rough living, alcohol, and smoke aged her face beyond her thirty-two years.

Jannie's voice had a raspy edge as she spoke, "You know Annie, my father bought me a pony when I was about nine or ten. We ate it. It made tons of jerky when its foot rot got too bad. I've never owned a horse since. Are you sure you don't have one that you're about to butcher or something?"

Annie shook her head. "We don't butcher horses; I sell them. I could sell you a gentle mare for six hundred dollars. I can't go any less."

Jannie grunted. "I'm not rich. I could work it off, though. I could clean your home and watch your little ones. Just set me up in a room, and I could stay there on your ranch and work until it's paid off."

"There's nowhere to put you except maybe the bunkhouse, and it's full of men." Annie regretted mentioning it as soon as she said it.

Jannie's eyebrows rose with interest as her grin widened. "I'm okay with that."

"Unfortunately, the cleaning and watching my kiddos is Rory's job. I haven't got anything else for you to do. Sorry."

"Hmm." Jannie sighed.

Jannie's elderly mother, Mattie Sperry, wore her best dress, a long flowing purple gown with a pink flower pattern and black lace on the breast and shoulders. Her gray hair was neatly brushed into a bun while a rare friendly smile appeared on her weathered face. She joined the others in the shade of the covered porch.

"It's just too hot to stand in the sun. It's been two hours; I'd think Adam would be coming soon. I sure hope he doesn't think my boys did that robbery. Mort and Henry are driving wagon loads of bark for the tannery and are due back later from Branson. Alan is working for the Crawfords, and it couldn't have been any of my boys." Mattie volunteered. News of the robbery was alarming, and she figured everyone in town would suspect her sons and nephews. After all, her son, Alan, was just released from prison for robbing a stagecoach seven years before.

Annie replied, "No one is accusing them."

Mattie glanced at her with a concerned expression. "Your brother Matt will. This is the first robbery we've had in a long while, and Alan just got out of prison. I expect to see the marshal before too long."

Annie shrugged her shoulder nonchalantly. "Well, if Alan had nothing to do with it, then he has nothing to worry about. The Crawfords will vouch for him."

"I suppose." Mattie agreed with a series of comforting nods.

Nathan Pierce volunteered, "Highwaymen stalk roads all over the place. It doesn't mean they are acquainted with your family."

"What is your name? How are you acquainted with Adam?" Mattie asked bluntly. She had not yet met the young man with long brown hair and a trimmed beard about two inches long. He was a handsome young man with a square-shaped face. He wore a six-gun on his side.

"I am Nathan Pierce; I work on the Big Z Ranch. This is my wife, Sarah, and our boy, Little Cal."

Mattie's tone was cold, "Oh. I was curious how you seemed to know so much about my family when I've never met you. You're part of the Big Z bunch. Nice to know."

Jannie's green eyes roamed over Nathan from top to bottom. "I'm Jannie. I guess we met earlier today. You have a lovely wife and a beautiful baby. May I hold him?"

Sarah kindly shook her head. "He's sleeping comfortably, and I'd prefer he continues to."

"I understand," Jannie said. "I had four babies. This is my oldest, Tad. He is sixteen and nearly grown. I know what you're thinking; I don't look old enough to have a boy that old. Well, I was young. I still am. And this is my baby, Eve. She is four."

"Well, you are very pretty." Sarah said to Eve.

Eve ducked behind her mother's dress shyly. She was an adorable little girl with black hair and large brown eyes. Her skin tone slightly darker than her mother or brothers. Tad Sperry was a blonde-haired boy with Sperry green eyes like his mother's. It was well known that Jannie's two older boys had the same father, but the younger two children had different fathers. It was also well known throughout the community that Tad was a troublemaker and couldn't be trusted to close a gate, let alone not steal anything that wasn't nailed down.

Tad kept shifting his gaze towards Rory as she sat on a bench at the end of the porch. He longed to maneuver past the others and take a seat beside her. There were very few pretty women in Natoma, but Willow Falls seemed to have some of the prettiest women in the valley. He had never seen Sarah Pierce, and she was a very attractive blonde. Annie was a beauty in her own right, but Tad could not imagine a prettier lady than Rory Jackson. She and her father, Darius,were the only black folks he knew of. Tad knew Darius seemed like a friendly enough man, but he had never spoken to Darius himself. Tad had never spoken a word to Rory before either, but Rory had stolen his heart from the first time he had seen her. He was too afraid to talk to her because he didn't want to sound like a fool. Rory was the only woman that had that effect on him.

Jannie turned her attention back to Annie. "Kellie Crawford told me you traded a fine mare for her spirited Arabian. Do you think you can handle that beast?"

Annie lowered her brow with slight offense. "I already have. I don't want to break his spirit; I like it. But he will make a fine stud when my Arabian mares get here. I have two men bringing them from Central Oregon as we speak."

"You must be doing well in your new business then?" Mattie asked.

"It's alright."

"How much stock have you got? Have you sold

any?"

"I've sold twenty-three horses so far. I have thirty-three left, twelve more coming, and ten bred. It's what I've always wanted to do and the Big Z Horse Company is gaining momentum."

"That's wonderful. I wish my daughter was as enterprising," Mattie said with a disagreeable glance at Jannie. "The only breeding she does is herself."

Jannie was humiliated. She gave a defensive chuckle. "That's not true! I am starting a seamstress business of my own. Geez, Ma." She laughed with a flirtatious glance at Nathan.

Mattie ignored her with a slight huff and asked the others, "So, who are you all waiting for?"

Sarah answered, "A dear friend of mine. She is moving in with us to help with Little Cal."

"And you, Annie?" Mattie asked.

She directed a thumb towards Sarah. "Her friend. We all stick together on the Big Z, kind of like a bunch." She had not forgotten Mattie's words to Nathan.

Tad Sperry finally spoke, "Grandma is waiting for her new husband. That's why she is all dressed up."

"Hush it!" Mattie exclaimed with a harsh glare. "Why don't you go back to the house where you belong? I asked your mother to come along, not you."

"I just want to meet him." Tad replied. He was excited to see his grandmother's disappointed expression when she realized there was no man on the stagecoach coming to meet her. He had robbed the stage with his uncle Vince, cousin Jesse Helms and Cass Travers. It was his first experience being part of the Sperry-Helms Gang. No one else in the family was to know about it.

Mattie squinted irritably as she explained to Annie, "We're waiting for a friend." She turned her head with a sneer. "Tad, I told you to go home!"

"Fine." He walked away with a glance or two at Rory before he left.

Jannie suggested, "We girls should get together and have some fun sometime." She stepped closer to Annie. "I could find a ride to Willow Falls any-time."

Annie stepped to the side to create some space between them. "I'm afraid it's the wrong time of year for that."

"Are you that busy?" she asked Annie.

"I'm only here because it's Sarah's dear friend we're picking up."

"Here comes Adam, finally." Nathan said.

Adam drove his covered wagon with the elderly Sheriff Zeke Jones beside him on the bench seat. He stopped in front of the hotel's porch.

Joel Fasana jumped down from the back. His wide affectionate grin beamed when he saw Annie. "Annie, I didn't know you would be here to wel-come me." He helped Jane Montgomery down from the wagon's bed.

"Uncle Joel!" Annie exclaimed with surprise. "I didn't know you were on the stage," Annie said, walking briskly to hug him. "It's good to see you. I suppose you're coming home to the ranch with us tonight?"

"Well, I suppose I am." He helped Audrey down from the wagon. "How is that sister of mine?"

"Oh, Aunt Mary is fine. She'll be so excited to see you."

Sarah handed the baby to Nathan and went to Miss Jane with an emotional hug. She wept as she wrapped her arms around the elderly lady. "I'm so glad you're here."

Jane wept as well as she held Sarah tightly.

"Ohh, let me see that baby!" Jane said while wiping her joyful tears. She took Little Cal from Nathan. "He is beautiful. Good heavens! Look at those beautiful eyes." She grinned at Sarah as a tear slipped loose. "He looks like you. Sorry, Nathan, but he looks like his mama."

Nathan agreed. "I'm glad of it. Miss Jane, welcome to your new home."

Audrey Butler stood beside the wagon with Sal Gable, waiting for Adam to hand them their luggage. Audrey had hoped to be met by the man she agreed to marry, but so far, the only ones greeted were Joel and Jane. A strange scent was in the air, an aroma vaguely like rotting flesh mixed with cinnamon. "What is that awful smell?"

Sal waved back the way they came. "There's a tannery over there. Not much of a town, is it?" he asked, looking around. He was irritated about spending the night in Natoma instead of Branson. They were told the stagecoach would be fixed overnight and they'd be on their way in the morning.

A lady stepped out of the hotel to greet the guests.

18

"I have supper ready for our guests and fresh cinnamon rolls. Please come inside and register for your room."

Sal Gable raised his hands helplessly. "The thieves took all my money. I don't have any left, Miss." he replied and followed the lady inside the hotel to make arrangements for the night. He left Audrey standing alone by the wagon.

Mattie Sperry approached the lady that looked about as lost as a child left alone on a busy street. "You must be Audrey?"

"Yes. You are?" She was expecting a gentleman to be waiting for her. She was disappointed not to be greeted as warmly as Joel and Jane were.

"I am Mattie, and this is my daughter, Jannie. We came to welcome you to Natoma and take you home."

"Oh? Where is Alan? I figured he might want to meet me at the stage in case he wanted to send me back."

Mattie laughed. "There's not a chance of that. Let me take a look at you. My, you are pretty. Alan is going to be pleasantly surprised. Well, let's get your bags and get you home. I think you'll find your room is more than accommodating."

"We were robbed," Audrey stated with a troubled voice. "They took my mother's broach."

Mattie huffed. "Criminals are a plague to our society. I'm sure you have them in your hometown too. Are you okay? Did they mistreat you?"

"No. I was scared. Excuse me, but who are you?"

Mattie chuckled. "I'm sorry. I am Alan's mother.

He is working. The thieves didn't take your money, did they?" she asked abruptly.

"No. Joel told me to put it in my carry case, so I did."

"Good! Well, let's get you home and unpacked." Mattie grabbed Audrey's arm to turn her away from the wagon and walk her home.

"My stuff?" Audrey questioned. Her travel chest was full of her personal things and set on the road by Adam as he and Joel unloaded the four traveler's luggage.

"I'll send my boys right down to grab your travel chest. Trust me; you're in good hands."

"Audrey," Joel Fasana called. "Before you go, I want to introduce you to my niece. This is Annie Lenning. Adam and her own the Big Z Ranch in Willow Falls, which is about nine miles that way." He pointed down the road. He explained to Annie and the others, "Audrey is engaged to marry Alan Sperry. She traveled from Central California to do so."

Annie's brow lifted with surprise while her head rose upwards slowly. "Oh. Well, congratulations." there was no enthusiasm in her voice.

"Thank you."

Mattie touched her arm. "Come along, dear, we need to go. We need to get you freshened up before Alan comes home. He is going to be so happy to see you."

Annie called out, "Nice to meet you, Audrey."

"Yes, nice to meet you too."

Annie's teeth clenched together. "I don't think

that girl knows what she's getting into."

Joel took a deep breath and exhaled as he watched her walk away with Mattie and Jannie. "She's a mail-order bride. She's come a long way from home to be tied up with a man like that."

Adam grimaced. "Did you warn her about him?"

"No, Adam, I didn't. She said they'd been writing to each other long enough and that she felt compelled to marry him. She's a Christian girl and feels the Lord was leading her to him. I've never spoken to the man, so I figured she knows him better than I do."

Chapter 3

The two-story black house brought a wave of dread that swept over Audrey for reasons she didn't understand, but the closer she walked towards the front door, the more it felt like she was entering the belly of the beast. She didn't know what it was precisely, but a heavy cloud was forming over her spirit, and the light of the blue sky above wasn't penetrating the darkness closing in around her.

Two dogs, one a large brown and tan mixed breed, ran forward, barking aggressively at Audrey. The smaller one, a short-haired white dog, also came forward, but its tail wagged happily. The larger dog nipped at the hem of Audrey's dress.

Mattie kicked the dog in the ribs. "Go lay down, Duke! I'll kick your teeth out, you no good mongrel." The dog yipped quietly and circled Audrey nervously before offering an unfriendly growl behind her. Mattie forced a lukewarm smile before explaining. "Duke can be a bit unfriendly with strangers, but just give him a kick until he learns you are part of the family."

Jannie kicked the smaller dog when it got in the way of her walking. It yipped and hurried away towards the house. "Get out of the way then, you stupid dog!" She explained to Audrey, "I hate that dog. It belongs to my sister-in-law, Bernice." Her tone revealed a touch of hostility.

The house door opened, and a lady with red hair kept in a ponytail stepped out onto the porch. She knelt and picked up her dog. "Don't kick my dog again!" Her blue eyes burned into Jannie like a branding iron.

"The dumb dog got tangled in my feet. Sorry, for no fault of my own." Jannie explained with an ornery smirk.

"Girls, end it!" Mattie snapped impatiently. "Audrey just arrived and is probably skittish enough without you two fighting over a flea-ridden varmint. Audrey, this is your future sister-in-law, Bernice. She is married to my son, Henry. This fine young lady is Audrey, Alan's fiancé."

Bernice glanced at Mattie with a harsh glare and then glanced at Audrey. "Hello." she said with a hint of irritation.

"I want to meet her." Daisy Sperry said, and stepped past Bernice holding a naked baby in her arms. "Hello, I'm Daisy. Did Alan ever write about me?" Daisy was the youngest Sperry sibling at twenty-two years old. Like her siblings, she had straight dark brown hair that hung over her shoulders and back. Daisy was youthful and pretty with large green eyes that shined brighter and more lively than any others.

"Hello," Audrey said, taking notice of the flea bites on the baby's soft skin. "Yes. He said you were very sweet and a mother."

Daisy was pleased. "I have three children; Elliot is four, Walter is three, and this baby is my only girl, Alisha. The boys are out back playing. Jannie has four kids. She would have more, but she keeps having miscarriages." she offered.

Jannie was quick to rebuke her sister, "She doesn't need to know my business, nor does anyone else!"

"I'm just saying…"

"Well, stop it!" Jannie snapped.

Duke, the large brown dog, began barking at a wagon being pulled by two horses coming towards their home. Big Adam Bannister drove the wagon with Joel Fasana sitting beside him.

"What is he doing here?" Mattie questioned sharply.

Jannie was excited, "Maybe Annie wants to take me to her house for a girls' night."

Adam pulled the reins and set the brake. He stepped down from the wagon and paused to look at the dog barking at him aggressively. "Now, settle down, you. How will we be friends if you're not nice, huh? You're a good big boy. Yeah, I hear you." He turned towards Audrey, "You left your chest at the stage stop. I figured we'd better bring it to you. Natoma is not known for being the most honorable town."

"Thank you." Audrey said. She could not help the corners of her lips rising to see Joel and Adam again. Their arrival was as welcomed as a ray of sunshine on a rainy afternoon or a breeze of fresh air in a coal mine.

Joel stepped down from the wagon and approached the women. "Audrey, again, riding from Walla Walla with you was a great pleasure. I hope we get to meet again. Feel free to write me and let me know how you are. I wish you the best."

She suddenly hugged the older man. "Thank you, Joel." The temptation to ask if she could leave with him and Adam hit her like a fist in the stomach. It nearly took her breath away as a gut-wrenching emotion pleaded with her to ask. She resisted.

Nathan Peirce carried the large chest around from the back of the wagon. He had his flat-brimmed hat on over his long hair. "Could I take this inside for you?" he asked.

Mattie was quick to answer. "No. My boys will take it. Thank you for bringing it up."

"You bet," Nathan answered. He set the chest down. "It isn't too heavy."

Annie Lenning hopped out of the wagon and approached her brother Adam's side. "Welcome to our side of the country. It can be a little rugged, wild and dangerous sometimes, but we love it that way. Uncle Joel and Miss Jane told me that you are a Christian lady. If you go to church here in town, you'll meet Kellie Crawford. She's a dear friend of mine. You'll like her."

Audrey nodded with interest. "I look forward to

meeting her."

Jannie Sperry stepped close to Nathan. "You kind of look like Matt Bannister."

"No, Miss, I'm far more handsome." Nathan replied with a tip of his hat.

Annie continued, "Anyway, Kellie was taken prisoner by a rogue a few months back, and my brother, and Alan's brother, Morton, teamed up to save her. Ask Morton about it and introduce yourself to Kellie."

"I will. Alan didn't help?" Audrey asked.

Mattie quickly answered, "My dear, Alan wasn't home on that terrible day. We lost one of our own when that happened. My nephew Bo was murdered right up on the hill. I assure you, it is a difficult situation we don't like to discuss. If Alan had been here that day, my boys wouldn't have needed the good marshal's help. Well, thank you, Adam, for bringing that chest up here. We have a lot of introductions to do. It's best that we get to it."

Annie held out a hand to shake Audrey's and spoke intentionally, "I'm Annie Lenning of the Big Z Ranch. Everyone around here knows where it is. If you need anything, you let me know."

"I will. Thank you."

Vince Sperry came outside the house with no shirt to cover his flabby belly and chest. He was in his mid-twenties and just under six feet tall. Vince was well over two hundred pounds with a clean-shaven round face. He had the Sperry green eyes and straight brown hair that fell below his ears. His hands were stained with blood from butchering a chicken in the kitchen.

His chest puffed out when he saw Adam. "I thought something smelled like cow dung."

Mattie scolded him, "Hush your mouth! Adam and Annie brought Audrey's trunk up here. Why don't you take it to her room."

Adam slowly grinned. "It shouldn't be too heavy for a big boy like you. I loaded it by myself, and Nathan unloaded it just fine."

"Well," Mattie said, anxious for them to leave, "Audrey, let's get you inside and show you your room."

Nathan leaned against the wagon with a long piece of grass dangling from his mouth while he watched Vince struggle to carry the trunk into the house. He glanced at the bench seat where Adam and Joel climbed up to sit. "It just shows you that just because they're big doesn't mean they're strong."

Adam chuckled. "Vince wanted to teach me how to fight once at the bank. Morton saved me. Let's go home. Our good deed is done for today."

Nathan laughed. "Yeah, Morton saved you from breaking that man's neck."

Chapter 4

The house had a musty, stale smell of smoke, urine, and the stench of dirty cloth diapers piled in a basket in Daisy's room. Audrey wiped her nose as she passed Daisy's messy room to her own, down the dark hallway.

"Well, here you have it." Mattie said with a friendly tone. The room was at the back of the house. It was nothing more than a small room with a single mattress on a rusted iron bed frame. There was no window or anything to look at except the horizontal boards of the four walls.

"Thank you."

Mattie explained, "It's not much, but you stated in your letters that you were religious and preferred not to sleep with Alan until your wedding day. Alan sleeps in the barn, but don't worry. He is building a nice room in the hayloft for you two."

Audrey felt her head rise and fall with a slow nod. "Oh." The home was nothing like she was expecting, and the more she saw, the less appealing it became. "Would you mind if I took a nap? It's been a long trip to get here."

Jannie's mouth opened in awe. "Are you kidding me? This is the most exciting day. You're getting married!"

"Well, not today."

"I know that. But Alan will be home in a couple of hours. Aren't you excited? Mama's already got Daisy and Bernice, that's the ugly redhead that married my brother Henry, heating water for a bath. Don't you want to bathe and freshen up for Alan?" Jannie questioned.

"Stop fighting with Bernice," Mattie scolded. "She's doing what she was told."

Jannie rolled her eyes at her mother. "Only because she lives here. I suspect she and Henry will be moving out soon enough. She mentions it often enough."

"Hush it! Enough of that." Mattie held a hand out for Audrey to take. "Come on, dear, let's get you freshened up and looking like a princess for your handsome fiancé."

Audrey was perplexed. "In his letters, Alan made it sound like he couldn't wait to meet me at the stage."

"Well, love, he is employed by the Crawford farms, and sometimes working late cannot be helped. He wanted to meet you, but he was needed on the farm today." Mattie explained.

"I thought he worked at the tannery?"

"He got a better job." Mattie answered.

Tad Sperry wandered down the hallway rather meekly. "Miss, my name's Tad. Are you marrying my uncle?" They all knew a guest was arriving by stagecoach that day, but Tad assumed from an overheard conversation that a man was coming to marry his grandmother. Tad had thought it was the old man on the stagecoach. He would never have guessed it would be the lady. The arrival of Adam Bannister at the house was lucky because if his mother and grandmother had brought Audrey into the house, she would have recognized Vince's shirt immediately. He wore a green and red plaid shirt with dark green shoulders and large gold buttons with eagles on them. The shirt was one of a kind and made for him by Daisy the Christmas before.

Luckily, Adam's arrival spared their dirty deed from being known. Mattie and the family thought Vince had taken Tad hunting earlier when they hooked up with Cass Travers and Jesse Helms to rob the stage. It was the first time Tad had gotten to go along with the Sperry-Helms Gang, and he found it exciting. Tad had never killed his first man yet, but he was ready to if that old man was coming to meet his grandmother. There was no room in the Sperry home for a new grandfather. As it was, the moment of Adam's arrival gave Vince the time to strip his shirt off when Daisy went outside and buried it under his mattress. The last thing they expected was to be caught in their own home by one of the people they robbed.

Audrey answered somewhat awkwardly, "I am. I suppose I'll be your Aunt Audrey."

Tad spoke sincerely, "I heard your stage was robbed. That's why I want to be a sheriff when I get older. So, I can stop such crimes as that. We hate criminals around here."

"That's nice to hear. I'm not fond of them myself."

Mattie rested a firm hand on Tad's shoulder. "Will you go check the water over the fire and take it to the bath? Audrey needs to clean up after such a long trip."

He spoke loudly as he walked down the hallway, "Uncle Vince is sure being quiet, isn't he?"

Mattie did not hesitate to answer, "That's because he came outside undressed, and all that blubber bounced around more than Audrey did in that stagecoach!" Mattie was irritated that her son would make his first appearance as an undressed slob. It had embarrassed her.

Vince stood in the kitchen, cutting the chicken into squares for a pot pie. Feeding such a large family on a limited budget was a task, but they made do. Vince didn't have a full-time job and he preferred not to work too hard, so he found himself in the kitchen, cooking to help out. He hunted and often brought venison or elk home, but he was known as the laziest Sperry.

Tad wandered through the kitchen with a grin on his smug face. "What's the matter, Uncle Vince? Does a cat got your tongue or the lady?" he teased, knowing Vince was afraid of Audrey recognizing his voice from the robbery.

Vince pointed the knife at his nephew warningly. "Shut your mouth!"

Tad chuckled. "Nice shirt."

Vince grunted as he went back to cutting the meat. He had put a different shirt on. Like Tad, he thought the old man was his mother's special guest. It was agreed that Tad could kill any man coming to court Mattie. Vince wasn't a religious man, but if he were, he would say he was blessed that they didn't shoot the old man on the stagecoach. They had no idea he was related to the Bannister family, and just as bad, that old man was William Fasana's father. There would be no Sperry home left if a war broke out between their families, and killing Joel Fasana would have caused it.

"Vince, this is Audrey. She will be marrying Alan on Saturday. It's going to be a proper wedding." Mattie said, introducing Audrey.

Vince nodded. He spoke softly, "Miss."

Mattie scoffed with disgust. "Well, apologize for exposing your blubber. I doubt she's ever seen a sea cow before."

His cheeks reddened. "My apologies, Miss."

"It's nice to meet you, Vince."

"Bernice, come say hello to your new sister-in-law." Mattie called.

Bernice stepped inside from the back door, where a fire burned in the firepit, heating a cast iron bucket of water. She wiped the sweat from her forehead with her sleeve. She appeared annoyed.

"Hello. If you'll excuse me, the bath is almost ready."
She didn't wait for a reply before she continued
with her labors.

"She's rude," Jannie explained. "You don't have to
like her. We don't either."

"I do." Daisy volunteered from the family room
floor. She was changing the baby's diaper.

Mattie spoke to Daisy pointedly, "When Audrey
is done with her bath, I want you to jump in that
bath, and your kids too. When you're finished,
empty the bath water into the scrub tub, and I
want those stinking diapers piled up in your room
thrown into the scrub tub to soak overnight.
They're smelling the whole house up!"

"Yes, Ma, I will."

"I mean it, Daisy. I won't tell you again. Throw
those stinking things into the tub and let them soak
overnight. It's foul to walk by your room."

Outside, they showed Audrey a constructed
shelter beside the house with a tin bathtub inside.
It was half filled with warm water. She was able to
close the door and remove her clothing before stepping into the tub. Relaxing, she closed her eyes and
sighed. The water felt good, but the solitude was far
more pleasing. She had little privacy since leaving
her home, thirty miles outside of Sacramento. The
journey from Sacramento to Walla Walla was long,
but it did not seem near as long as the journey by
stage. She definitely could use a bath, but more than
that, she wished she could sleep until she awoke
refreshed.

The bar soap on the floorboards was coated with pubic hair and made her shudder to hold and wash off before using it. It wasn't that she had come from such a fine home herself, but she had always learned it was proper to make sure the bar soap used in a bath was kept clean. She despised touching each hair and pulling it free from the sticky soap only to rinse them off her fingers in the water she was bathing in.

She heard a strange sound, glanced to her left, and saw an eye peeping through a knot hole in one of the boards. She screamed, "Go away!" she covered her body, appalled to have been spied on.

Whoever it was ran behind the house.

"What? What's going on?" Mattie shouted as she came hurriedly. She yanked the door open. "What's the matter?"

Audrey covered her breasts. "Someone was peeking through the knot hole." Audrey pointed at it.

"I'll bet it was Travis. That little brat."

Bernice spoke pointedly, "Travis has been working with Henry all day. It was Tad. I saw him run away."

"That perverted little… I'll show him." Mattie walked away quickly.

Bernice laid a towel on a small table beside the tub. "Here is a towel."

"Wait," Audrey said. "So, you married into this family too?"

Bernice nodded with a bitter expression on her

attractive face.

"Do you have any advice for me?" Audrey asked nervously. It was only a matter of time before she met her husband.

Bernice shook her head silently and left, closing the door behind her.

"Well, at least Jannie and Daisy are nice." Audrey said to herself.

***

Mattie grabbed a willow switch, three feet long with leather wrapped around one end to use as a handle, with a thonged leather loop at the end to hang on a nail in the kitchen, and marched to the front of the house.

Tad was teasing his younger sister, Eve, with a garter snake. Eve was crying out in terror while he threatened to touch her with it. Tad spoke to her, "Stop crying like a baby. It's just a snake, a dangerous and biting snake. It's going to bite you! Aagh!" He touched her arm with the snake's head.

The little girl wailed loudly for someone to help her, but her cries fell on deaf ears. Usually, her brother Travis would come to her rescue, but he was not home.

"Eve, kiss the snake, or I'll drop it down your dress. Kiss it!" She tried to run, but Tad grabbed her by her hair and forced the snake close to her face. "Kiss it!"

She wailed, terrified of the snake.

"Do it now!" He squeezed his hand to make her

hair hurt more. Her tears and screaming didn't faze him. It only made it more fun to torment her.

The sound of the willow branch slicing through the air like a hummingbird's wings ended with a sharp crack as it slammed against Tad's back. He arched his back with a painful cry. The snake dropped and Eve ran with all her might towards the house, screaming. Her Aunt Bernice swooped her up in her arms into a comforting hug as she reached the front porch.

The menacing sound of the willow branch cutting through the air was repeated, followed by the branding of another long and narrow welt on Tad's back and legs. He had fallen to the ground, defenseless with each new stinging blow.

Mattie shouted, "I've told you before to stop peeking at the girls in the bath! How many times have you got to be told?" Mattie swung the willow switch again and again. "Audrey is not for you! She's a guest, and you have the gall to spy on her? I had ought to skin your hide, and if you weren't my grandson, I would! Don't do it again!" she shouted and whipped him a few more times. His cries were loud and painful.

"Good heavens." Audrey said, standing beside Bernice. She agreed the boy needed to be corrected, but she was appalled by the extent of the abuse.

Jannie stepped outside and ignored her weeping son. She angrily grimaced upon seeing her daughter being consoled by Bernice. "Give her to me." She took the little girl and set her on her feet. "You're too big to be carried. Why are you crying? Are you sad to see Grandma give brother a whipping?"

Eve shook her head with an unsure glance at Audrey. Tears saturated her little cheeks.

Bernice answered with disgust, "Your son was scaring her with a snake. He was trying to make her kiss it when I heard her screaming. Didn't you hear Eve screaming?"

Jannie laughed with a shrug. "She's four. What else is she going to do besides scream? She's always screaming about something."

Mattie walked back to the house with heavy breaths. "I think he learned his lesson about peeking on girls. Well," she forced a grin. "Shall we make you beautiful for the man of your dreams? Come on, Bernice; you can help."

She was uninterested. "I have vegetables to pick in the garden to help Vince with supper."

Mattie's eyes bored into Bernice, displeased. "So be it."

Chapter 5

Matt Bannister scratched his head. He had stopped by his cousin Karen Longo's home to check in on her and Jim, her husband. Their daughter, Hannie, had been murdered a week before, and the funeral was set for later in the week. As expected, they were morose and broken by the loss. While there, their youngest son Peter handed Matt a kitten to pet. While petting the kitty, Matt saw a large flea come out of the fur along its neck and disappear back into the kitten's coat. Ever since then, he had been scratching his head, it made him wonder if a flea had jumped into his hair. He contemplated going to the Monarch Hotel's bathhouse and using some of their best shampoo to ensure there wasn't a flea in his hair, but it was midday and too early to bathe.

"Maybe it's lice," Truet teased his friend. "You know they're too small to see from a distance, but they sure get around. I hear the school has an outbreak of them. Maybe little Peter gave you more than a kitty to hold."

"Shut up."

Truet licked his lips while the lines around his eyes formed with a light-hearted smile. "If you get one or two, they'll lay eggs in your hair, and before you know it, you have a small nation of lice declaring new ground. They'll run the flea right out if that helps. It's interesting how our scalp is its own environment for our insect friends."

"Tru, you're not helping." Matt scratched his head.

"You're making me itch." Truet scratched his short brown hair. "Phillip!" he yelled.

"Yeah?" Phillip Forrester hollered back.

"Will you run to the hardware store and buy a can of turpentine? I think Matt gave me lice."

Matt stood from his desk and tossed a pencil at Truet. "Oh, stop it."

Truet laughed as he watched Matt leave his private office.

Phillip grinned at Matt. "Do you want me to get the turpentine still?"

"No. I don't have lice, nor does Truet."

"You keep scratching that head of yours." Truet said, following Matt towards the table where a large pitcher of room temperature sun tea was.

Matt poured a glass of tea. "Go do something. See that wanted poster over there; go pack a bag and track that man down."

"None of those fellas are around here. The nearest one was last seen five hundred miles from here and thought to be going the opposite way. We have no immediate warrants or taxes to collect. The last I checked, we were pretty caught up at the moment. Am I right, Phillip?" Truet asked.

"At the moment, we are."

"See?" Truet asked. "Besides, I probably need to talk with my barber and see if he can see any lice. You're making my head itch. Don't visit David at the Monarch Hotel until you get your head checked. If you give him lice, that would be a nightmare for him." David Chatfield was a young man born with hypertrichosis, a rare disease that covered his body and face with long hair. He was stabbed a week before and was recovering in the hotel.

Matt gave an unappreciative glance at his friend. "Are you done yet?"

Truet laughed. "No."

"You're enjoying yourself, huh?"

"Yep. I find it funny how seeing a flea or talking about lice can make your head itch."

Nate Robertson scratched his blond hair. "I don't think it's funny. I had lice so bad as a kid that my parents shaved my head bald. I never wanted them since. I think they thrive in blond hair more than brown or black because they sure took root on my head."

Phillip answered, "They're harder to see in blond hair."

Nate continued, "I don't even know what they look like, and I don't want to know. Dang you, Truet!" he exclaimed and scratched the back of his head.

Truet laughed. "You better go get checked. Unless anyone has any disagreements, I think I'll go to the carpenter's shop and work on my newest project. I'm making a heart-shaped picture frame for that picture of Hannie that Karen has. I saw it on their table. I had William keep them busy while I measured it. I thought it would look nice in a white oak frame inlaid within a redwood heart. I plan on giving it to them after the funeral."

"That sounds nice. Go ahead and get to it." he said appreciatively to his friend, and then he caught a glimpse of someone outside the window that held his attention. Across the street on the other boardwalk, partly hidden behind a round support post for the awning, was a strange figure that sent an almost haunting chill down Matt's spine.

"Something wrong, Matt?" Truet asked, taking notice of Matt's expression.

Matt's attention never moved off the figure trying to remain concealed behind the post. The slim body stayed parallel with the post, ducking his head forward just enough to glance at Matt's office windows and duck back behind the post. "Truet, do you see that fellow trying to hide behind the post over there? Walk down a block, come back behind him, and bring him in here. You don't have to be friendly."

"Do you know him?"

"I believe so. Bring him in here and I'll make introductions."

Matt watched as Truet came up behind the figure, put his revolver to the back of the man's head,

41

and escorted him across the street. Nate held the door open as the strange-looking man was brought in with his hands raised. His right hand was amputated at the wrist.

He was a short and skinny young man in his mid-twenties, with dark red hair about neck length and a thin pale face covered with freckles. He had uncanny dark brown eyes that almost looked black, and his thin lips maintained a strange grin that never wavered as he stared at Matt.

"Marshal." he greeted Matt as he entered the office.

"What are you doing here, Dane?" Matt asked pointedly. There was no friendliness in his tone.

"Nothing." His odd grin widened as if humored. He wasn't wearing a gun belt, and his only weapon was a hunting knife on the left side of his belt.

Matt said, "Gentlemen, let me introduce you to Dane Dielschneider, from Prairieville. William and I found some trouble with Dane and his brothers down there last October; I believe it was."

"You took my hand." Dane said with a slight chuckle while lifting the stub of a wrist.

"William took your hand. What are you doing here, Dane?"

"We're getting supplies and things." His grin faded. "And Tiffany turned fifteen."

"And?" Matt asked, pressing him to continue.

"We're betrothed. I need to take Tiffany back so we can marry."

Matt snickered. "You're not taking her anywhere. You can get that thought out of your head.

Dane, I'm warning you right now, get your supplies and get back over the mountain to Prairieville. Don't be lingering around town or my office. Get your supplies and get lost."

"You left my family in a bad way. My brothers are dead, you took my hand, and Danetta's consumption worsened over the winter. She's not well and needs Tiffany to care for her and the girls. Tiffany knows she's betrothed. I came calling for her."

Matt's voice hardened, "Tiffany isn't going anywhere. Nor are you going to get anywhere close to her. Get out of my office, and I don't want to see you again, Dane."

A mysterious half Mona Lisa smile lifted his lips while he stared at Matt. "Don't you care about Danetta being sick?"

"That doesn't concern Tiffany."

Dane's unusually soft voice rose, "She's Tiffany's Mama! And being so, she gave Tiffany to me on her fifteenth birthday. I want my bride."

"I don't want to be mean, but I certainly will be if you don't leave my county. Tiffany isn't going to marry you, and there's not one man in this office that will let you get close to her, especially me. Goodbye, Dane. Truet, throw him outside."

Truet grabbed the back of his shirt, yanked him outside, spun around, and tossed him forcefully onto the street. He hit the hardened ground and rolled to a stop.

Dane slowly stood.

"Get out of my sight!" Truet shouted.

Dane grinned. "I'll see you all soon."

Truet came back into the office. "Can you explain him to me?" Tiffany was now an adopted part of Annie's family and would become Truet's stepdaughter if he married Annie.

Matt watched Dane walk away to join a large man on the other side of the street. He did not recognize the big man. "The only explanation I have for him is he's the product of Prairieville. He's not all at home upstairs."

Truet closed the door. "Tiffany will be here for the funeral in a couple of days."

"I hope he leaves before then. If not, then we need to motivate him to leave."

"Who is his big friend? Did you run into him down there?"

Matt shook his head. "I've never seen him before."

Chapter 6

Alan Sperry knew he had no friends when he was released from prison. He wasn't expecting a large homecoming party or opportunities to be given to him. He didn't have expectations, but he expected to be treated better than the Mexicans working for Crawford Farms. He was thankful for a job, but he resented being the only one hoeing weeds in the five acres of lettuce while the other employees got the better work. As a white man, he should have been given a better job than the responsibility of hoeing weeds. There was plenty of work to do, and plenty more he could be doing, than standing alone in a five-acre parcel of lettuce, hoeing weeds.

John Crawford rode his horse to the field and dismounted. He approached Alan with a careful eye on the work done. He stopped to bend over and tossed a large dandelion out of the row. "It's looking good. I figure another day and we can move you to the radishes and carrots. I came by to let you know it's quitting time. I'll see you in the morning."

Alan was discontent. "Do you think I can get away from hoeing and do some plowing, cutting, or something more work-oriented for a white man?"

John's brow narrowed. "What does that mean?"

"A child can hoe."

"So can a man," John said plainly. "I've done my share of hoeing. We all have. We have a lot of employees, Alan, and you're the newest, so you get to start at the bottom. If you're too good for it, collect your pay, and perhaps the tannery will be more to your liking."

Alan gritted his teeth. "That's where the women work."

"Your brother Henry works there. I understand Morton does too. If you want a job here, it starts with hoeing."

"We've known each other a long time, John. You know I can drive a wagon or do anything else."

"So can everyone that works for us. We're a busy farm with a lot going on. I need you where I need you, and that's how we work. Right now, I need this crop hoed. That's all there is to it. I'll see you in the morning."

Alan watched John walk back to his horse and step into the saddle. Alan snarled his lips and spat out a curse at John. Gripping the hoe tightly, he chopped a head of lettuce to pieces and then another with an enraged growl vibrating his throat. He swung the hoe in a wide arch to hoe another head of lettuce to pieces. "Hoe this field! Hoe that field! Hoe! Hoe! Hoe!" he yelled while he swung the hoe back and forth between two rows of lettuce, destroying several plants.

"Alan!" John shouted. He remained on horseback with a finger pointed at him. "I knew you wouldn't work out. You're fired! I'll have your earnings waiting when you get to town."

Alan scowled awkwardly. He had thought John was leaving and let the moment get the better of him. "I was just playing a little." he explained.

"Not on my dime. I'll be holding out a dollar of your earnings to pay for the damage you caused my crop. Get off my property, Alan, and don't come back."

"You're firing me for getting a little upset? I have the right to be angry. This is child's play, woman's work! Let me do the irrigating. I want to drive a steam-powered machine. Let me do something, not weed your gardens!" he shouted.

"I'll meet you in town with your pay. Start walking."

"Let me finish this row... I need a job, John."

John Crawford was a busy man and didn't have the patience or time to argue or make allowances for destructive employees begging to keep their job. "You had your chance. I'll meet you in town with your pay. Goodbye, Alan."

***

Alan had a mile to walk as he crossed the fields to the main road. He had reacted foolishly, but in the heat of the moment and frustrated, he couldn't help himself. There weren't many job opportunities in Natoma outside of Crawford Farms. There was the tannery, but they generally weren't hiring, and the Natoma Glove factory employed a good number of people too, but a lot of women. Without a job, money was slim, and slim living was an invitation to fall back into what he had once known, a life of lawlessness and robbery with the Sperry-Helms Gang.

He had spent seven years in prison, which was closer to hell than he wanted to admit to anyone. It had broken him. Survival wasn't an easy road to travel in the prison system, and he had done what he needed to survive. He fought to protect what little he owned, he fought to protect himself, and he killed to end a threat to his life. A fight in prison wasn't like a schoolyard fisticuffs where a bloody nose ended the scuffle and friends could be made of a bully. Behind the high fences and guarded dark walls, a fight could quickly end in death. Every fight started with the intent to injure, maim, or kill by any means necessary. It was a harsh world so far removed from the cares of Natoma. There, a man worried about staying alive and protecting himself from the wrath of the guards and other inmates. Here in Natoma, a man had the luxury of worrying about dandelions overtaking his lettuce patch or firing an overqualified employee for getting angry and hoeing a few heads of lettuce. Alan knew one thing, here on the Crawford Farm, John Crawford could act like a big man and order him around, but in the world, Alan knew, John would burst into tears, bawling like a baby while hiding in the corner, scared to death.

While in prison, Alan swore he was going straight and working for a living so he would never have to return to the hellhole called prison. He had promised himself his life of crime and violence was over and wrote to his wife as much to promise her he'd come home a changed man. Not long after, he received a letter from his mother stating that Racheal had taken his children and disappeared. No one knew where or how she left Natoma unnoticed. A few months later, he received a divorce notice in the prison mail.

The prison warden expected Alan to return and serve another sentence soon, perhaps even before the end of summer. Alan came home intent on proving the warden wrong. The first thing he needed was to find a job to make money and prove to his relatives and others that he was a changed man. He knew John Crawford didn't like him; he never had. Alan spoke to John's younger brother David Crawford about a job. David was more reasonable and a nicer man than John. David hired him, but John checked on him every day and waited for a reason to fire him, and now he had.

***

Alan saw David Crawford riding a horse towards home after work. David lived a few miles outside of Natoma. David pulled the reins of his horse. "How are you doing, Alan?"

Alan was still stewing in a pot of anger. "Your brother fired me."

David was surprised. "Which brother?"

"John. Who else would? I should've known he would. He has never liked me."

"Why did he?"

"Because he doesn't like me!"

"There had to be more of a reason than that. What were you doing?"

Alan was quick to respond, "Why am I hoeing? That's not man's work. There's nothing I couldn't do on the farm, and instead, I'm hoeing every day. You got Mexicans doing all the good jobs."

David peered out over a wheat field. "Everyone starts by hoeing, weeding. Do you ever read the Bible, Alan?"

"No." he said bitterly.

"*He that is faithful with a little will be given more.* Our parents based our whole operation on that biblical truth. Our employees have proven faithful with little jobs, so they are promoted to more important jobs. I'm sorry it didn't work out for you, Alan. But I can't override my brother. He's the boss, mine too."

Alan resigned. "Yeah, I know. I appreciate you giving me a job, at least."

"You're welcome. It was the least I could do. What are you going to do now?"

Alan shook his head, disheartened. "I don't know. Maybe I'll pack a bag and try to find Racheal. It surprises me that no one around here knows where she went or how she left. It's almost like everyone knows but is keeping it from me. Do you and Kellie know what happened to her?" His hardened green eyes glared at David accusingly.

"No. Racheal was just gone."

Alan scoffed quietly. "Yeah, that's what I keep hearing. The only thing that kept me going while in that hell was the idea of seeing Racheal and my kids again when I got out." His lips snarled. "And then I got the news she disappeared and then a divorce notice. I had no say in it."

"I can't imagine how hard that was."

"Does Kellie know where she is?" he asked.

"No. How Racheal left town was a mystery. To my knowledge, no one has heard from her since. I don't know if there was a stage that day or not, but I don't think anyone seen her leaving."

***

John Crawford met Alan in town and handed him five dollars for three days' work. Alan walked to Avery's saloon and ordered a drink. Before long, the sound of familiar voices lifted Alan's head as his two brothers, Henry and Morton, walked into the saloon. Both men had just returned from hauling bark from the mill in Branson to the tannery. "Avery, two of what we usually get and keep them coming. We just returned from a long trip, and we're thirsty," Henry Sperry said. He and Morton both wore their gun belts on their hips in case of trouble. "Make it three. I see our plow boy brother is sitting over here moping in the corner."

Alan lifted his head. "I'm not moping."

Morton sat down. "Sure, you are. How was your day?"

"I was fired."

"Already?" Henry asked. "It's only been three days."

"I know," Alan said, irritated. "That John Crawford doesn't like me."

"So? Why were you fired?"

"It doesn't matter."

"So now what?" Henry asked. "Do you want us to try to get you a job in the tannery?"

They were interrupted by their mother walking into the saloon. "Oh, I'm glad you boys are all here." Mattie Sperry said as she sat down at the table with her three sons.

"Ma. What are you doing here?" Henry asked. "This is no place for you."

"Travis told me where you were, and I figured Alan may have stopped by here. Stop drinking. I need you sober." She took Alan's drink and drank it herself.

"Sober? No. I plan on getting good and drunk."

"Oh, no, you're not. I have a surprise waiting for you at home." she said firmly.

"A surprise?" Alan asked with a raised brow. "When do I need to be sober to get a new shirt?"

"It ain't no shirt. Here, read these." Mattie said and handed Alan a stack of letters addressed to him.

"What's this? Are these from Racheal?" he asked hopefully while looking at the nice handwriting on the envelopes.

"No. They are from your fiancé."

"Who?" Alan asked, perplexed. He was already irritated, and the nonsense she spoke irritated him more.

"Shut up and read the letters." Mattie answered.

"Ma, what do you have going on?" Henry asked. He scratched the scar on his neck curiously.

"I'll explain in a bit. Let your brother read."

Alan questioned as he set the first letter down and opened the second, "Ma, who in the hell is Audrey? And why is she writing to me?"

"Read!"

"I am, and it's not making any sense. Who is she?"

"Your fiancé."

Morton and Henry laughed.

"My fiancé? I'm already married to Racheal."

"No, you're not. Now read."

"What is she talking about? I never asked her to marry me!"

Mattie's lips rose with a slow-growing mischievous smile. "You did. You just don't know it."

"What did you do?" Alan asked with a stern look at his mother.

"I put an ad in for a wife. Audrey answered my ad, and these are the letters that you need to read before you meet her. She's a very nice lady and will make a fine bride for you."

Henry chuckled. "What did you do, say my son is being released from prison and needs a wife?"

Mattie answered bluntly, "No. She doesn't know Alan was in prison and doesn't need to know that before the wedding."

Alan gasped. "She doesn't know me! What did you write to her? What did you tell her about me? Why is she so impressed with my heart?" His brothers laughed.

"I'm a woman. I know what other women want to hear. I pretended to be you and told her what she needed to hear to come here and marry you. I did my part. Now you need to do yours. And you need to be sober because she's a good, religious lady and expects you to be the same..."

"What?" Alan interrupted. "Ma, what did you do? I'm not anything like she thinks I am. And when is she apparently coming here?"

Mattie smiled, pleased with herself. "She arrived today. She's waiting at home to meet you."

"What?" Alan yelled. "Ma, you had no right to do that! Maybe I want to go after Racheal and bring her home. I don't love this woman. I don't even know who she is! Is she ugly?"

"No. Audrey is quite nice. Finish reading the letters, and then we're going home. She's anxious to meet you."

Henry's humored grin disappeared. "Ma, you deceived her into coming here to marry Alan?"

"No, I took the initiative to find him a wife. And I have. Now, I never want to hear Racheal's name spoken in our home again. She is gone, and so are your kids. It's time to replace them and move on. Are we clear?"

Alan grimaced. "Racheal..."

Mattie cut him off firmly, "She divorced you,

and you'll never see her or those girls again! It's time to move on and start a new family. You'll love Audrey." She looked at Henry and Morton, "And you two boys, do not mention this to Audrey. She thinks Alan sent those letters, and there's no need to tell her different. And do not mention prison. She's a fine lady, and she will be a wonderful wife for Alan."

Alan grinned as he read a letter. "Well, it says she loves me, so maybe I won't be sleeping alone tonight." He chuckled.

"Oh yes, you will. She is devout to the religious thing and won't consummate the marriage until the wedding night. You only have a few days to wait. She wants a church wedding, so we'll have one."

"We've never stepped foot in that church." Morton said.

"Well, it won't hurt us to do so," Mattie answered. "Come on, boys. Let's go home and meet Audrey. I think you're all going to love her. Oh, Henry, your wife is being rude. You need to set her straight when we get home, or I will take her to the barn and do it myself."

Henry responded frankly, "I imagine she disagrees with you deceiving that woman. I do too. What you're doing is wrong."

Mattie snapped, her eyes burning into Henry, "I don't care what you think! She's going to marry Alan, and everything will be fine."

Morton lifted his hands questionably. "You're serious? You wrote back and forth pretending to be Alan, and now she is here expecting to marry him?

55

I thought that was kind of funny at first, but it's not. That's a little bit like slavery, isn't it?"

Mattie's fierce glare bore unappreciatively into her son. "Morton, you've never been in love your entire sorry life. You have no idea what it's like to come home and find your wife and daughters gone. I am replacing what is missing in your brother's life, and now he can be happy. He'll have a wife!"

Alan flipped the last letter over to read the back of it. "Is she pretty, at least?"

"She's darling. Everyone loves her already, except for Henry's wife."

Henry rubbed his forehead in disbelief. "I don't have to ask her to know why. She probably likes that woman fine. It's what you're doing that she finds repulsive. I sure do. Ma, you can't deceive her like that. We need to tell her the truth."

Mattie's voice lowered as she warned, "If you say one thing to her, I will toss you and your family out of our house, and you'll never be welcomed back. I'm dead serious, and you two will not interfere with Alan's future. This will keep him out of prison and working! He needs a woman to be happy. I got him one!"

"Ma," Alan offered, "I was fired. John Crawford doesn't like me and won't give me another chance."

Mattie huffed with disappointment. "Well, don't tell Audrey that. We'll say you were being cheated out of your pay and quit. Let's go home and meet your wife. And you two," she pointed at Morton and Henry, "heed my warning. Alan matters right now. Not you!"

Chapter 7

Audrey dressed in a pretty but simple light blue dress with a white collar. She brushed her long wavy dark brown hair that had a touch of a red tint in the sunlight. She was blessed with beautiful hair that was pretty enough left naturally down or in a ponytail when alone, but Audrey coiled it into an attractive bun for meeting Alan. She dabbed a floral perfume on both sides of her neck as she gazed at her image in her hand-held mirror. She wanted to make a wonderful first impression when Alan saw her for the first time. She knew she wasn't considered beautiful, but she hoped Alan found her more attractive than her previous husband did. It was easy to become attracted to the personality behind the written word, but now that he would see her in person, she hoped he wouldn't be disappointed.

Audrey was twenty-nine years old. She was taller than most women, not exactly thin, but not heavy at about a hundred and fifty pounds. She had a square-shaped face, narrow blue eyes, and a delicate nose slightly broadened at the end. Her thin lips made her mouth appear too small for her face, but her smile was always bright and quick to show her white teeth. All her life, her sisters had some good-natured teasing that Audrey couldn't smile and keep her eyes open at the same time because her eyes narrowed into a thin line when she laughed.

At twenty-six, Audrey lived in her parents' home without a suitor interested in her. Those who inquired of her soon discovered they were not as interested in her as they might've thought. The question of why often plagued her, but she could never quite find an answer. There were certain realities in life; one of them was her parents getting older and eventually passing away. Fearing she would become an aging spinster with a cat or two to keep her company, Audrey decided to answer an ad for a bride while she was still relatively young.

The gentleman whose ad she answered lived in California. Grant White, a man in his forties who claimed to be a minor of good fortune. They corresponded for a short time, and Audrey eagerly accepted his marriage proposal. She said a tearful goodbye to her parents and sisters in Colorado and boarded a train for Sacramento. It was frightening, but she was sure the Lord's providence was with her and would lead to a blessed marriage and future family.

Grant White met her at the train depot with a vase of beautiful flowers of various colors. She had hoped for a church wedding in the white dress neatly tucked away in her trunk, but Grant took her to the courthouse, and they married that same day.

Audrey had been taught that a lady's honor was preserved for marriage and believed it would be a special moment. After quickly marrying him in a courthouse, Grant rushed her to his hotel room to consummate the marriage before taking her thirty miles outside of Sacramento to a filthy shack in an unnamed mining camp. It didn't take long to understand she had made a wrong decision. Grant had some unmentioned qualities: gambling, womanizing, and drinking. What he did have was absolutely nothing in common with her, and he couldn't care less about her or what she thought. It ended when she woke up one morning and discovered a note on the table leaning against the same vase he had given her at the train depot, but this time, the vase was filled with ugly dry grass and a dead thistle. The note stated that Grant was looking for greener pasture because she was about as lively as dead weeds.

The frightening part about answering an ad for a wife was not knowing if the gentleman was honest or not. Her mistake in answering Grant's ad was she rushed to marry him without getting to know him. She understood now that it wasn't the Lord's leading, but her craving to be loved and have a family, that immediately accepted Grant's proposal and moved to California. That was her error and one she regretted wholeheartedly and vowed never to repeat.

Suddenly single, Audrey lived in a boarding house in Sacramento and paid her keep by doing the cooking and cleaning. A few men that stayed there seemed to take an interest in her, but it was clear they were looking for nothing more than a bedwarmer. That was something that she would have no part of before a wedding ring was placed on her finger. She went to church and hoped to meet a fine gentleman there, but again, finding a single man interested in her was a bit more than she could ask for. At twenty-nine, the fear of never finding a husband was becoming a fact of life, more so than a fear, and she again peeked at the matrimonial ads. There were a few men she inquired about and corresponded with, but Alan's letters touched her in a personal way that no other man's written words did. She could tell by his phrasing of words that he cared more about getting to know her as a person than he did about her cooking skills or body shape. Alan's letters moved her in ways she'd not expected; they touched her heart. They were sensitive and kind and spoke of his desire to have someone to love and hold on those rugged Oregon days and nights. With such honest emotions penned on paper, all other correspondences with other would-be suiters stopped, and she wrote exclusively to Alan. After months of deeper conversation through the mail and much prayer, she was ready to accept his wedding proposal.

The vase of dry grass and thistle that Grant White had left for her was a wound that cut deeper than a slap or harsh words could have. It was a vision of how he saw her: worthless, ugly, boring, dried up like grass in a late August drought. That was in central California, and now she was in Oregon, ready to try it again. They say a fool doesn't learn from their mistakes, but she had been careful and taken her time, and she was sure Alan was the man the Lord was leading her to, despite her first impressions.

Alan explained that he lived in a small town within a beautiful valley, in a large home he shared with his mother and siblings. He told her many things, and although they weren't a lie, they weren't what she expected. She didn't know what she expected, a dream come true perhaps, but that wasn't what she found waiting for her.

Now the time was drawing near to meeting Alan face to face, and she was growing more nervous. She sat on the edge of her bed with folded hands and bowed her head in prayer. "Lord Jesus, my nerves are rattled. You have given me a safe passage here, and I thank you. Thank you for keeping me safe during that robbery. I pray you might bring justice upon those thieves and, if possible, return to me what was taken. Jesus, I'm afraid to meet Alan. What if he doesn't like me? I'm afraid he might think I'm like dead weeds too. I think that affected me more than I know. Jesus, how can I feel so led by you and be so worried that I'm making a mistake at the same time? If this is not your will, then make it known to me before I make another mistake. Jesus, you are my only hope and my dearest friend. Lord,

I may be a fool, but don't let me make a bigger mistake if it is not your will."

There was a knock on her door. "Dear, come on out and meet Alan." Mattie said through the door.

Audrey felt a warm smile appearing as the timing could not be more perfect. "Thank you, Jesus." she said quietly.

**

"Hello." Alan's gaze roamed over Audrey like a stockman appraising a prized heifer. He had seen prettier women; Henry's wife, Bernice, was prettier, but Audrey would be his wife soon, and the idea of sharing a bed with her appealed to him.

She laughed uneasily. "Finally, we meet. It is a pleasure to meet you, Alan." Audrey's gaze wasn't disappointed in seeing him for the first time. He was tall, thin, and dressed in shabby work clothes, but he was clean-shaven, with short brown hair and handsome in a rugged manner. He had large penetrating green eyes like his mother's that Audrey found adorable.

"Well," Jannie thundered, "give her a kiss. She came all this way to marry you!"

Audrey snickered shyly. "There'll be a time for that later."

Alan didn't know what to say. "Remind me, where did you come from?" Alan asked, trying to play along with his mother's ruse.

"Sacramento. You know that!" Audrey exclaimed with a humored grin. Her eyes were brought to narrow slits of blue. Her teeth were bright, healthy, and white.

"Of course. How were your travels?"

Her grin faded quickly. "Ugh! Our stagecoach was robbed a few miles from here. Thank goodness no one was hurt. It made for a long trip, though."

His forehead wrinkled curiously. He wondered if his gang had done it without his consent or if someone else was maneuvering into his territory. "I suppose it would."

Mattie put an arm around both of them. "Why don't you two go for a walk and talk? It's been a long time coming."

"Yes, I think we will." Alan said awkwardly.

Mattie kissed him on the cheek happily. "Good. You two get." When they walked outside, she watched from the window until they were a safe distance away, and then she turned around to glare at her daughter-in-law, Bernice. "You start treating her like a friend instead of a moldy cake!"

Bernice was disgusted. "What you're doing to her is wrong, and I won't play a part in it. I imagine Henry won't either."

Mattie's lips twitched. "This is my house, and if you're going to live here, you will do as I say! You keep your mouth shut and treat her better than you are. You're making her feel uncomfortable. Knock it off, or you can divorce my son and move out!"

Bernice took a deep breath. She would've liked nothing better than to move out if she could. "Like Racheal?"

"Racheal's name is no longer spoken here. Ever!"

Mattie shouted. "Audrey is here now, and she isn't leaving. Get used to her, Bernice, or get out!"

***

"A vase of dead grass, huh? Did you ever write that to me?" Alan questioned. He had quickly scanned through the letters in the saloon but had not been interested in what they said beyond key phrases that caught his attention. He didn't know what she knew about him either, except that his mother told him that Audrey had no idea that he was in prison, had an outlaw past, or had been married or had children. She warned him not to mention any of that to Audrey until after they were married, when she'd be good and pregnant.

"Yes. I told you all about that. Don't you remember what you wrote?" Audrey asked.

He chuckled to cover his lack of knowledge. "Sure, I do." They walked casually along the road towards town.

She repeated the words he had written that she memorized, "*The morning dew refreshes the gentle blades of grass every morning. The only dead grass was pulled up by the fool who left a vase behind.* I took that as a profound answer, because it shows an understanding of what makes a relationship work. Especially a marriage. I took that to mean a person needs to be uplifted and encouraged daily. Is that what you were meaning?"

He nodded affirmingly. "Yeah. That's what I meant. It takes two, you know."

"Right. Grant never understood that. He just wanted someone to do the chores and be happy about it. But I'm a sad case of hoping for more from marriage than just surviving."

Alan felt a sense of jealousy spark within him. "Who's Grant?"

"My ex-husband." she responded with an odd expression. She had written two full pages about her experience with Grant White. She was surprised that he didn't recognize the name.

"I knew that. I'm just overwhelmed that you're here." Alan explained quickly.

Audrey nudged him with her shoulder as they walked. "I'm glad I'm here. I wasn't so sure at first. Your mother and sister weren't exactly who I was expecting to meet me at the stage stop."

"Who were you expecting?"

She grinned with a soft chuckle. "You! Silly."

"Oh yeah. I had to work."

The road leading to the town was their half-mile-long driveway. A thick forest surrounded it as they built their homestead against the mountain's base. Audrey found the singing birds, the sound of a running creek, and the scurrying chipmunks and squirrels crossing the road or along overhead tree branches to be a paradise all on its own. She could not help but to feel a bit giddy to be near Alan in such a peaceful and dreamlike creation of God's nature. "Alan, what are your plans once we get married?"

He grinned. "Honeymoon. That's what I look forward to, unless you want to run into the trees and skip the wedding part?"

She slapped his arm playfully. "Beyond that. I mean, are we going to get our own place?"

"We'll have our own room. I'm making a room for us in the barn."

Her joyful smile slowly faded. "I thought your family was joking about that."

"No." He shrugged, sensing she was displeased. "Would you rather live in the house?" He had no idea how to answer her or what she wanted to hear. "We could, but everyone will hear us newlyweds at night?" He snickered like a deviant fourteen-year-old boy who had just stolen the teacher's exam answers.

"Alan!" she exclaimed with a shocked grin.

"Well, it's the truth. We're going to be busy making a family for a while. Ten or twelve boys, a few girls, and a lot of tries in between."

She gasped. "I don't know; that's a lot of children. I suppose we'll need a whole barn to raise such a herd of children in. With that many children, we'd never hear if a fox gets into the henhouse." she joked.

Alan answered reasonably, "The henhouse isn't in the barn."

"Huh?" she asked. "Oh, look, I can see your town. Will you walk me by your church? I'd like to see where we are getting married. Have you spoken with your reverend yet?"

He stopped, not wanting to continue downhill into town. "My ma may have, I don't know. Since we're getting married anyway, how about we hop over into them trees and get started on that family?"

Audrey wrinkled her nose with distaste. "I think not. Seriously though, you need to introduce me to your reverend so I can talk to him. I wrote you that I am a Baptist, but you never said if you were too, or a Presbyterian, Methodist, Episcopalian, Catholic, or exactly what. What denomination are you?"

Alan shook his head, not knowing the difference between any denomination. "Um, the church just says the Natoma Christian Church on the sign. I don't know. I guess just Christian. It has a cross and bell tower, you know."

She chuckled. "What is your favorite book in the Bible?"

"What is yours?"

"I love the Gospels, but Romans is probably my favorite New Testament book. I love the trail of redemption down the Roman road. But I also love the Old Testament and the story of David in particular. I love how human he is. Don't you?"

He nodded. "Yeah."

"What is your favorite verse?"

"Um… the one that says something about being faithful in the little things and more will come or something like that. I like that one." He was suddenly glad to have run into David Crawford on the way home from work. He didn't know any Bible verses, nor did he know any books within the Bible. He was pretty sure the Bible was a book itself.

Audrey corrected him, "The verse actually says, *he that is faithful in that which is least is faithful also in much: and he that is unjust in the least is un-*

just also in much. I think that is a very good favorite verse. It kind of sums up a person's character, kind of like the verse that says,

A good man out of the good treasure of his heart bringeth forth that which is good, and an evil man out of the evil treasure of his heart bringeth forth that which is evil: for of the abundance of the heart, his mouth speaketh. Is that why it is your favorite?"

Alan turned his head away from her and rolled his eyes. "Of course. How about we turn back towards the house? I'm getting pretty hungry and supper should be about done."

"Sure. You can introduce me to your reverend tomorrow. I thought we could marry on Saturday if the reverend is free. Do you think you could get off work early tomorrow so we can discuss our plans with the reverend?"

Alan shrugged his shoulders. "That shouldn't be hard to do." He stopped walking and turned to face her. "Audrey, we've been writing back and forth for a while, right? And I know we'll be married, so how about a kiss?"

She giggled bashfully. "I don't know. We just met."

"Oh, I see," he said with a flirtatious grin. "Are you going to disappear in the morning and leave weeds and dead grass in a vase for me? Am I that unattractive to you?" He chuckled as his hands rose to her sides, just barely caressing the side of her dress.

"No," she laughed. "I think you are quite handsome. Luckily for me, you're not as scary looking as your brother, Morton. He frightens me. I suppose the question is, am I unattractive to you?" Despite the cover of a playful countenance, her eyes revealed a fragile vulnerability that couldn't be hidden.

"I wouldn't want to kiss you if you were ugly. I'm very pleased. What do you say? Can I kiss my fiancé for the first time?"

"Here on this road? It's not very romantic."

"Well, you mentioned the roman roads, and I'm guessing they weren't too pretty either. This is our road that ends at our farm, the Sperry Road. I guess you could say it leads to my heart and the rest of my life if you follow it. I can't think of a better place for our first kiss."

She smiled bashfully. "In the church, on our wedding day, perhaps."

"Come on. You agreed to marry me; the least you could do is kiss me before the wedding. We've waited a long time." Alan licked his lips expectingly.

She chuckled uneasily. "Alan, don't you think it's a little soon? I just met you."

He bit his bottom lip with a tight grin. "No." he laughed. "You came all this way, and I've been waiting a long time. We obviously like each other, and I know my words were true. I'd be honored if I could kiss you. As my fiancé."

She gazed thoughtfully down the dirt road, contemplating. "Okay, but only a small one."

"Fair enough." Awkwardly, she looked into his green eyes, and their lips met in a soft kiss. It was broken quickly as she pulled away, turned her head, and covered her mouth with her hand.

Alan playfully scoffed with severe disappointment. "That was not a kiss, Audrey. That was like my daughter giving me a peck on the lips."

"Daughter?" she was surprised. "You didn't tell me you had a daughter."

"I didn't?" he questioned.

"No. I thought you were a bachelor?"

Alan's heart began to pound as a sense of panic overtook him. "I am." He had to think quick because he remembered he wasn't supposed to mention his ex-wife or daughters. With the first little kiss out of the way, it was going too well to blow it now. "I meant if I *had* a daughter, that's what she would do. I don't have one." It was a true statement; he had two daughters.

Audrey's brow lowered questionably. "Wait. Do you have a daughter or not? I'm confused."

"No. I'm a bachelor." He touched her sides with his hands. "How about another kiss?"

She pushed his hands down and away from her. "I want to take this slow. Alan, can I tell you something? My first husband wanted too much from me immediately, and I had no choice. He was rough, and then he was done with me. I don't want to make the same mistake again. Do you understand?"

"I suppose so. So what you're saying is what? You don't want to do anything?"

"Not right away. I want to get to know you and for you to get to know me before we agree to marry. I think it's the only wise thing to do."

Alan shrugged his shoulders, slightly annoyed. "You already agreed to marry me. I don't see a problem with a kiss or consummating our marriage now that you're here."

Audrey swallowed nervously. "Grant forced himself on me, and I didn't want him to. Alan, I was saving myself for my husband, and I wanted it to be special. He robbed me of that opportunity. It wasn't nice or special and didn't mean a thing to him. I won't let that happen to me again. I hope you understand."

"So, you're not interested in a romp in the woods?"

She appeared hurt. "No. And I must say I am surprised to hear you say that. As a Christian man, I wasn't expecting that to be a large concern before our wedding. After we are married, then it is appropriate, but not until. I'm disappointed that you would ask me that."

He chuckled. "I was teasing. I can wait as long as you can. Let's get back to the house and have some dinner."

"It might take me a while to get used to your sense of humor. But thank you for understanding. It's important to me to be as wholesome as I can be."

"Me too." He watched her fondly. "How about another kiss? A wholesome one, you know, that lasts longer?"

She laughed lightly. "Not today."

Chapter 8

The chicken and dumplings Vince had made for dinner were more watery than any other chicken and dumplings that Audrey had ever eaten. The dumplings were too doughy, and Audrey doubted the chicken was cooked all the way through as her stomach was upset. Everyone else seemed fine, but she felt sick and prayed she wouldn't vomit. The privy, she discovered, was filthy and had a foul odor.

She sat in a cloth armchair with ripped armrests in the family room with Alan, his youngest sister Daisy, her three children, Tad, Travis, and Mattie. Henry and Bernice had taken their children to their room for the night. Morton, Vince and Jannie had gone to the saloon after dinner. Another brother named Jack had gone to Branson to visit their brother Mark who worked in the silver mine. It was the topic of conversation.

Mattie spoke to Alan, "Jack is growing up. I

think he is sweet on a dancer and wants to be able to provide for her. He might leave us and start working in the mine to be closer to her."

Alan swatted a fly off his arm. "I saw Mark when I went to Branson last week. He didn't say much." It was the first time he had seen his brother in over seven years. Their relationship faltered long before that, though.

Mattie spoke with no emotion, "Well, he doesn't have much to do with us. I'm okay with that. He's never helped us much anyway. Enough about Mark. Audrey," she said, "I need to tell you, this is a dangerous town for a young lady to venture out into alone. There are bad elements around here, as you discovered on the way here. Bandits, highwaymen, and rapists roam the streets day and night, so please do not go wandering to town alone. Make sure Alan, one of the boys, or I are with you at all times. Everyone knows not to mess with our family, but you are a stranger and will undoubtedly be victimized. So do not leave this house without an escort. I would hate for anything to happen to you, dear."

"Is it really that bad?" Audrey asked. "That explains why Adam and Joel brought my chest up here when they did. Alan's going to introduce me to the reverend tomorrow and look around the church. I'm going to ask the reverend if he will marry us on Saturday. I believe that will give us enough time to know if we really want to marry each other or not."

"Of course, you'll want to marry Alan," Mattie said reassuringly. "Alan will make a fine husband.

And you fit right into our home like a glove. You'll love it here with us. We may not be the perfect family, but we're a good family and take care of our own. Around here, that's the cardinal rule we live by. Isn't it, Daisy?" she asked her youngest daughter.

Daisy nodded with a yawn. "Yes. I'm excited to have you as my new sister."

Audrey rested her hand on her tummy as her stomach rumbled uncomfortably. "Me too. I have two sisters in Colorado, but it will be nice to have a new little sister." Audrey liked Daisy already.

"Are your parents still alive?" Daisy asked.

"Yes. They are living with one of my sisters and her family."

"What did your father do for a living in Colorado?" Mattie asked.

"He was the reverend of a Baptist church. He still is. I notice you don't have a Bible handy. Maybe you'd like me to read a chapter or two of the Gospel of Luke. That's what I'm reading currently. Luke and Second Chronicles. I also read five Psalms a day and one chapter of Proverbs. Would you all like me to read for you?"

Tad Sperry stood uninterested. "I'm going to my room. Come on, Travis." He and Travis walked out of the room towards the back of the house.

Mattie forced a small smile while she sewed a torn sleeve on a shirt. "Hearing some of the good book won't hurt us any at all on a Tuesday night."

"Great. Let me grab my Bible, and I'll start with the Gospel of Luke. We always need to hear what Jesus said first in our lives, right?" She scowled and put her hand on her stomach as it gurgled loudly.

"Are you all right, dear?" Mattie asked.

"I'm feeling sick to my stomach."

"Why don't you go lay down? We can read the good book anytime."

"I think I'll go out back for a minute or two. Excuse me." She took a deep breath and went out the back door towards the privy.

"Vince's food must not have agreed with her. I told you not to let him cook, Ma." Alan said.

Mattie waited for Daisy to take her children to bed and then said quietly, "Alan, she wants to go to church tomorrow. Do you know who the reverend is nowadays?"

"No. I don't know who the reverend is, Ma. But I have a plan, and we won't have to worry about that after tomorrow."

"Good. The last thing I want is for her to interact with the community. Do you like her, Alan?" Mattie asked.

He nodded. "I do."

"Did I do good?"

"You did good, Ma. I think she'll make a fine wife."

***

Half an hour later, Mattie sat in her wooden rocking chair, sewing a patch onto the torn knee of her grandson's pants under the light of a lantern. She listened to Audrey read from the Bible with half interest. Alan sat on the davenport with his arms

75

crossed over his chest, listening.

Thirteen-year-old Travis came running through the house frantically with sixteen-year-old Tad right behind him with a right fist tightened and ready to hit his brother.

"Grandma!" Travis yelled as he ran past the rocking chair and grabbed the back of it, jerking the chair forward as he ran by and slowed down to tattle. Tad tackled Travis to the floor, face down, and started hitting Travis in the back with his fist as Tad's mouth snarled with gritted teeth in anger.

The quick jerk of the chair had driven the needle into Mattie's finger. She cursed loudly. "Alan, stop them!"

Alan grabbed Tad by the hair and yanked him off Travis roughly. Tad swung a right fist at his uncle, but it was blocked. Alan's voice turned fierce, "Better stop while you can, Tad! I'm not Vince. I'll snap your head right off!" He pushed Tad down onto the davenport.

Travis stood with tears burning in his eyes, breathing hard, red-faced and embarrassed. He pointed at Tad accusingly, "He stole the knife I lost! It was under his mattress!"

"Ah, shut up! You lost it. I found it. It's mine." Tad argued.

"No, it's not! Uncle Morton gave it to me for Christmas! It was the one Grandpa gave him when he was little."

A baby began to cry towards the back of the house. Bernice Sperry could be heard griping about her child being awakened from her bedroom down the hall.

Mattie stood angrily and slapped Travis across the face with her right hand, followed by her left hand. His cheeks reddened more. "Shut your mouth! The children are sleeping!" she hissed like a venomous snake with glaring unmerciful eyes.

"What did I do?" Travis asked, not understanding why he was being punished when his brother stole his third-generation knife.

"Look!" Mattie squeezed the tip of her finger, and a drop of blood came through the needle prick. "I'm trying to patch your brother's pants, and you made me prick myself with your carelessness. Give me your finger!"

"Grandma, I'm sorry..."

"Give me your finger!" Mattie took hold of Travis's finger, squeezed the tip until it was red, and then forcefully jabbed the needle deep into his fingertip. He jerked his hand away, crying out in pain. It bled a lot more than her needle prick.

"That hurts, Grandma!" he shouted.

Mattie scolded him, "Stop your damn bawling like a baby! Act like a man, or I'll take you out back and beat those tears right out of you. And you don't run from your brother again. Do you hear me, boy? It's the Sperry Rule. We don't run from anyone. We don't quit, and we don't lose! We fight until we win! Am I understood, boy?"

Travis nodded as he wiped his eyes. "Yes, Ma'am."

"Good! Because if I catch you running away from anyone again without a fight, Travis, I'll beat your legs right off you! Am I understood?"

"Yes, Ma'am."

Tad sat on the davenport, enjoying his brother's scolding. He pointed at Travis and said, "He still has my knife, Grandma."

"Give him the knife, Travis!" Mattie ordered.

"It's mine! Uncle Morton gave it to me for Christmas."

Tad argued, "You lost it. I found it. Isn't that right, Grandma?"

She nodded. "Give me the knife." She held out her hand expectingly.

Travis, angered about being wronged, put the knife in her hand.

Mattie lifted his chin to look into his eyes. "There ain't nobody that's ever going to give you anything in this life. You have to fight for whatever you get, and since you're a running coward, the knife now belongs to Tad. He fought for it. You ran like a little girl. You know the Sperry Rule." She handed the knife to Tad.

"That's not fair," Travis complained. "He knew it was mine when he found it."

"The only fairness in this world is being strong enough to take what you want. If you want that knife, take it from your brother, but you do it in the daytime, not this late at night. Ain't that right, Alan?" Mattie asked.

He turned his head towards the front door as the sound of laughter came from outside. He nodded in answer. "It's the only way we Sperry's know."

The door burst open as Morton and Vince helped Jannie walk into the house. She leaned heavily on them, obviously drunk. Vince held a mostly empty bottle of whiskey in his hand. He laughed. "I think she's had a bit too much, Ma." He and Morton set her in a wooden chair just inside the door. Jannie's head hung heavily, and she struggled to keep her eyes open. The smell of liquor filled the room. She wore only her simple homemade gray dress with no shoes exposing her filthy feet.

"Take her to her room," Mattie stated irritably. "I thought I told you, boys, to watch her."

Vince's loud husky voice boomed, "She disappeared with some stranger waiting for the next stagecoach east when we weren't looking. They were talking, and then they were gone. I forget his name, but he lost most of his money in that stage robbery today," he laughed. "So, I bought him a drink or two. Jannie took some of my poker money, bought a bottle, and they disappeared for a while. We found her on the hotel steps trying to pull a sticker out of her foot. She's in love again."

Mattie stated with a bitter scowl on her lips, "I'm sure there's another grandchild on the way. Get her out of my sight!" She waved her hand towards the bedrooms with disgust.

Vince and Morton grabbed Jannie's arms to help her to stand. "Wait…" Jannie slurred the word. Her head remained downward, her breathing quickened, and she grew pale and clammy.

Mattie sputtered, "Travis, get your mother a bowl!"

"Huh?"

"Get your mother a bowl!" Mattie shouted.

Jannie made a choking sound, followed by a stream of vomit that spewed out of her mouth onto the wooden floor. Her brothers Vince and Alan laughed as she continued to lean forward and empty the contents of her stomach on the floor. The contracting of her stomach forced air out of her with a foul stench that could make a goat cringe as the remains of the foul dinner mixed with a large quantity of liquor spread across the floor in a large watery puddle. Jannie would have fallen into it if it wasn't for Morton holding her up. He wasn't as amused as his brothers.

Audrey covered her nose and mouth and turned her head with disgust. She had vomited her supper outside near the chicken coop for the birds and dogs to enjoy, but the sight and foul odor made her sick to her stomach all over again.

"Get her out of here!" Mattie yelled. "Damn it, Travis, when I tell you to do something, do it! Don't stand there like a dim-witted fool saying, 'Huh?' Now, get a bucket of water and a rag and clean your mother's mess up."

"What about Tad?" he whined. Tad was sitting on the davenport laughing at his mother.

Mattie glared at Travis bitterly. "I told you to clean it up! Get it done before I grab my switch and whip the complaining right out of you. I'm going to bed. Get it done!" She spoke to Audrey. "I apologize for my family. Our nice Bible reading time was rudely interrupted. Tomorrow we'll look at that church. Goodnight, Sweetheart. Alan, could you open my bedroom window? It's jammed."

"Sure, Ma." he left the family room behind his mother. He had a pretty good idea that she wanted to know his plan for the church or had one of her own. They both knew they'd never been to the church for a Sunday meeting and couldn't very well act like they were church members in front of the Reverend.

Tad stood, snorted, sucked a wad of mucus into his mouth, and spit it into the vomit. He looked at Audrey with his tongue running along his cheek. "I don't like my brother." He left the family room with an elbow into Travis's ribs as he carried a bucket of water towards the family room.

Audrey left her chair and got down on her knees. She asked Travis, "Do you have another rag? I'll help you."

"I'll get one. Thank you."

Together they started scooping, washing, and cleaning the disgusting vomit off the floor. Morton Sperry walked into the room and knelt with a rag to help them. He gazed upon Audrey, "Miss, you don't have to do this. It isn't pleasant work. I'll help Travis."

She spoke tiredly, "I don't mind helping Travis, and it needs to be done. Those babies will be playing on this floor tomorrow morning."

"Uncle Mort," Travis said, "I lost that knife you gave me for Christmas and Tad found it. He hid it under his mattress, knowing I've been looking for it, and he won't give it back. I took it, and we got into a fight."

Morton spoke irritably, "He probably stole it, to

begin with. Don't worry. I'll get it from him."

"Grandma says I have to fight him for it."

Morton leaned back and shook his head. "It doesn't end, does it?"

"What's that?" Travis asked.

"The Sperry Rule. That's part of the reason Mark has nothing to do with this family. Let's just get this cleaned up. By the way, Miss. I'm Morton. We met earlier, I know, but I don't know what else to say." He chuckled uneasily.

"I'm Audrey. It's nice to meet you, Morton."

"Over a pool of puke. I suppose it is the perfect place to meet me." He chuckled with an affectionate nudge to his nephew.

Chapter 9

Dane Dielschneider and his friend, Bill Cooney, entered the Green Toad Saloon and stood against the bar while ordering a drink. Dane's dark brown eyes scanned the paintings of nude women and signs along the wall behind the bar while he waited. A knife with a large note stating, "The knife that killed the Leather Man," was pinned below the sheath tacked to the wall.

John Gibbs brought two drinks and set them down. "Welcome to the Green Toad. I haven't seen you two in here before. My name is John Gibbs. I'm the proprietor of this saloon."

"What's the Leather Man?" Dane pointed his left hand towards the knife.

"Oh. A child killer that murdered a young girl last week. That's the knife that killed him. I bought it from the kid that witnessed him in the act and took his rightful revenge. It has blood stains on the blade if you want to see it. It'll cost you a dime, though," said John.

He knew quite well that the Leather Man did not kill young Hannie Longo, but in the interest of making conversation and earning a little money for looking at the knife, he was more than willing to twist the truth.

The knife didn't have any bloodstains when he bought it from Nick Griffin for five dollars, but a touch of red paint, watered down and allowed to dry, tinted the blade a pinkish color where the stains could be seen.

Dane put a dime on the counter. John pulled the knife out of the mounted sheath and handed it to Dane. The feel of a weapon that killed a man felt good in Dane's hand. The leather grip was more comfortable to hold than his own knife's buckhorn handle. He admired the weapon expertly as he looked at the faded red stains on the steel blade.

"I'll trade you knives." He set the knife on the bar and pulled his buckhorn knife from the sheath on his belt with a six-inch blade. "Mine has deer blood on it."

John laughed at the offer. "I don't think so. This knife killed the notorious Leather Man." He replaced it in the sheath on the wall. "Unfortunately, the kid that killed the Leather Man got into a fight with William Fasana on Sunday and got shot. He's dead now too."

Dane's teeth clenched together. "William Fasana. What if my knife killed William or Matt Bannister? Would you trade then?"

John chuckled. "Sure. But if you tried going after

either one of them, I'd be putting your knife on the wall with a note stating that this knife belonged to the world's biggest fool. Kid, if I were you, I'd go back to the farm or wherever you're from and leave the killing talk to men more capable than you."

Dane's eyes narrowed into an awkward stare that didn't blink. "Maybe your right, except I'm no kid. Do you know where Tiffany Foster is? I want to find her."

"I've never heard of her. Sorry."

"Sure, you have. Matt Bannister and William Fasana brought her here from Prairieville last fall."

"It doesn't ring a bell. I remember hearing about the marshal and William going there and getting into some trouble, but I've never heard anything about a girl."

Bill Cooney spoke slowly, "Maybe she isn't here. No one knows her."

"She's here. I'll bet they changed her name." The deep laugh from the back corner where a group of men were playing a game of poker caught Dane's attention. "That's Jack Sperry. Come with me." he said to Bill. He neared the table and stood about four feet back, holding his drink with a half grin and staring silently.

Ritchie Thorn glanced at him irritably. "Do you have a problem, Red?"

Dane's lips lifted just a touch. "Not with you. Jack, how are you?"

Jack Sperry looked at Dane, not immediately recognizing him. "Well, I'm fine. Who are you?"

"I know your cousins in Prairieville, all of them.

I met you in the Blazing Bull Saloon in Prairieville. I'm Dane Dielschneider."

Jack's brow lifted. "I knew your brothers, but I can't say I know you. Sorry to hear what happened to them."

"If your cousins joined with us, I'd still have brothers. But the Crowe brothers didn't do anything to help us against the marshal and William Fasana."

Jack shrugged uncaringly. "Maybe they were just smarter. Matt Bannister's reputation wasn't made by running away or being stupid. Isn't that where you lost your hand?" he asked, looking at the stub where Dane's right hand used to be.

Dane nodded.

Joe Thorn collected the cards on the table and straightened the deck. He held them out towards Dane. "Do you want to shuffle the cards?" He laughed. His brother Ritchie, Bruce Ellison, Bobby Alper, and Jack laughed.

Dane's odd grin faded slowly. "Sure. Put them in my hand." He stuck out the stub of his right wrist.

Joe shook his head with a laugh as he shuffled the cards. "Are you sure you didn't miss the wagon train when the freak show left town?"

Dane's lips pressed together tightly. "Freaks are strange."

"You don't say?" Bobby Alper laughed.

Jack asked frankly, "What do you want, Dane?"

"Nothing. This is my friend, Bill."

"Hello, Bill!" Ritchie yelled loudly before taking a drink.

"Well, crap! We didn't know you had a friend named Bill!" Joe Thorn shouted with mock enthusiasm.

Dane's grin grew as he stared slowly at each man at the table. "Yes, I do. I'm looking for my fiancé, Tiffany Foster. Do any of you know where she is?"

"Wait," Bruce Ellison said, "Didn't we just go through this last week when that freak, the Leather Man, was searching for his wife?"

Joe Thorn laughed loudly with a slap to the table. "We did!"

Ritchie asked through a humored grin. "Let me guess, Red, did a couple of big and bad silver miners steal her from you?"

Dane didn't understand why they were laughing. "No," he said softly. "Matt Bannister took her away from me last Fall. I don't know where she is, but I'm taking her home when I find her."

Joe's laughter faded. "You mean that girl Matt brought back?"

"Yes. Do you know where she is?"

"Well, yeah. She's at the Big Z Ranch. She lives with Matt's sister. Billy Jo told me about her."

"Where's that?" Dane asked pointedly.

Jack Sperry answered, "Hey, you'd best go home. You don't want to go on that ranch if you're not welcomed. You'll be nothing but a red spot on the ground."

"I'll be fine. Where is the ranch?"

Joe answered, "Willow Falls. But she may be here in town already. Hannie Longo's funeral is in a couple of days, and I'm sure she'll be there with the rest of the family. I'm hoping Billy Jo and my sons come back myself. Maybe you can find her at the funeral. But I'll warn you, if you interrupt the funeral, I'll take care of you myself. We all work with Hannie's father, and none of us here will tolerate anyone interrupting it. That family has been through enough. Got it?"

"She's coming here? Where here?" Dane asked.

Ritchie Thorn answered, "Think about it. What last name is she related to? The Bannisters. Good luck."

His words struck a nerve that angered Dane. "She's not related to any of them! She is promised to me. Matt took her from me, and I came to take her back."

"Like Ritchie said, good luck. We'd like to return to our game if you don't mind."

"I don't mind." He remained, staring at Jack like an infatuated twelve-year-old girl.

"It looks like you got yourself a suitor, Jack." Ritchie Thorn said with a laugh.

"What?" Jack shouted at Dane abruptly. His patience was running out.

Dane grinned. "I know you. We met at the Blazing Bull Saloon."

Jack's brow lowered as he shrugged slowly. "So? I don't know you. We're not friends, and I don't want to know you. Get away from here before I throw you out the window!"

"Bye, Bill!" Ritchie yelled.

"See you later, Bill." Bobby shouted with a chuckle.

Jack glared at Dane with growing aggravation. "Leave now!"

"Bye, Red." Joe said.

Dane's lips curled upwards awkwardly. "I'll see you later." He and Bill walked back to the bar.

Chapter 10

The Bella's Dance Hall band's fiddle player played a lively tune while a wide circle of dancers danced the heel-toe polka. Matt Bannister had heel-toed, slid into the center of the circle with each new partner like the other twenty couples, and slid back out again. Clapped right, then left hands, knees, and hooked elbows and swung each lady around, releasing her elbow to hook elbows with his new partner, where the dance repeated itself until he ended with his original partner, Christine, which brought an end to the dance.

He couldn't help but grin, despite the lines of sweat that ran down his face. He wiped the sweat with the sleeve of his arm. Christine was dressed in a bright yellow dress with a pink and light blue floral pattern, with a matching yellow bow pinned to the bun that held her coiled-up hair. She was as beautiful as a spring morning, and her soul's joy could light up the darkest of rooms. Beads of perspiration spotted her forehead and nose, but the affectionate smile on her lips revealed a love so strong and true for him. It filled him with a joy that couldn't be satisfied with a bow and a curtsy. The feeling must have been mutual as Christine's arms went around his neck as his arms encircled her to hold her close. Silently, his lips pressed against hers as their eyes closed with an affectionate kiss on the dance floor.

Their lips parted, and Matt stared into her eyes longingly. "I love you."

"I love you, Matthew Bannister." She touched his cheek with her hand as she broke the embrace. "You're going to get me in trouble again." Christine said, unconcerned with Bella's rule about displaying affection during working hours.

He chuckled slightly as he licked his lips. "I won't apologize for kissing my lady. No rule can stop me from doing that." He took hold of her hand to escort her to the bar and buy her a customary glass of champagne. Matt knew it was merely pink lemonade to keep the ladies hydrated and sober, but other men purchased the customary drink, believing it was pink champagne. Some of the ladies intentionally acted a little intoxicated towards the end of the night to encourage their potential suitors to buy them more champagne. The ladies earned money not only from the dance tickets they were given but also from how many drinks were bought for them.

Christine dabbed her forehead with a napkin to remove the beads of perspiration while waiting for her glass of pink lemonade. "Are you going to stay after closing? We could go up on the roof, watch the stars, and talk for a while." She knew too well that Matt's heart was broken from the murder of his young cousin, Hannie Longo. The funeral was in a couple of days, and although Matt had said very little about it, she knew it weighed heavily on his heart.

"I would like that." He wiped his forehead with his sleeve again. The dance hall was quite warm on a July night, with so many people crowded within the ballroom without having just danced for ten minutes of constant moving, swirling, and changing partners. It impressed him how used to it Christine was because comparatively, she sweated very little compared to him. It was the same with all the ladies and men, though.

A tap on Matt's arm got his attention. Dane Dielschneider stared at him with his dark brown eyes and a strange smirk on his lips, merely standing a foot away. "She's your fiancé." He stated while waving a finger at Christine.

"She is." Matt answered, slightly spooked by his sudden appearance and eerie presence. Dane's eyes were as cold as glass and never seemed to blink near as often as other people.

"Introduce me." Dane said. It came across more as an order than a request.

"Why don't you step back a bit? You're too close to me." Matt's tone was increasingly unfriendly.

"It's crowded." Dane said in his soft voice.

"It's not that crowded. Step back." Matt said sternly.

"Okay," he resigned and took a step back. "Now, introduce me."

Christine, wanting to avoid an ugly scene from starting, reached her right hand out to shake cautiously. "I'm Christine. I haven't seen you before, have I?"

Dane cast a victorious glance at Matt before focusing on Christine. He reached his left hand out to shake. "I'm afraid that's the wrong hand. I can only shake with the hand I have left. My left." He chuckled while shooting a sideways glance at Matt with a slight twitch of his narrow upper lip. "I've never touched a more beautiful woman." he said while shaking her hand. "Your hand, I mean. Matt's lucky."

"Thank you." she replied, trying to pull her hand back. He held it just a moment longer than she was expecting.

"I have a dance ticket. I would like to dance with you." He reached into his shirt pocket and pulled out a ticket he had stolen from another man's pocket.

Matt spoke frankly, "I don't think that's a good idea. Go find another dancer." He scanned Dane's belt to make sure he didn't have his knife on him. It had been removed before being allowed into the ballroom.

Christine touched Matt's hand softly. "It's fine. Mister... I didn't catch your name."

"I'm Dane." His lips lifted into a creepy grin.

"Dane. I'd be honored to dance with you. But I have another gentleman that I must dance with first." She took his ticket and put it in her pocket. "I'll come to find you right before the dance starts."

"I'll be waiting for you." He turned to Matt. "I look forward to dancing with your betrothed." His grin widened expectantly.

Christine turned to the next man she was to dance with and walked out onto the dance floor with him. Matt leaned against the bar, taking notice of Dane watching Christine intently. Dane turned towards Matt. "Are you going to tell me where Tiffany is or not?"

"No."

Dane's head lowered while his lower jaw extended outward to rub his upper lip with his lower teeth. "She's betrothed to me. Danetta said I could have her when she turned fifteen. I need to take her home."

Matt took a deep breath as the band started playing. He spoke loudly, "Get away from me, Dane. Go home and find somebody else."

The corners of Dane's lips rose just enough to become unnerving. "I tried to be nice."

"Me too. Go join your friend over there before I throw you outside." Matt nodded to Bill Cooney, who watched them alone at a table.

"That's my friend, Bill."

"Go sit by Bill then!" Matt said sharply.

"I will. Tell your betrothed where I am. I bought her."

"You bought a ticket, not her. You have a strange way with words, Dane."

"The ticket cost my money. I bought a dance

with her, so for the time we dance, she belongs to me. Not you." Dane explained.

"Go sit down before I lose my patience." Matt warned.

Dane's eyebrows rose. "You'd hit a man with one hand?"

Matt nodded affirmingly. "You, I will."

Dane snickered and walked away to join his friend at the table.

***

Matt and William Fasana had gone over the mountain to Prairieville to investigate the murder of Louis Eckman, a California railroad tycoon. The Prairieville Sheriff, Chuck Dielschneider, had several deputies, including his brothers, Troy and Devin Dielschneider, and Matt's old friend John Grey among others. Circumstances turned bad, and Matt and William were attacked while staying at the Grand Lincoln Hotel. Several men died that night, including two of the three Dielschneider brothers. Chuck survived the night with a bullet in his back but passed away a week later. William saved Matt's life by putting a bullet through Dane Dielschneider's hand, which was amputated.

Tiffany Foster's father, Dallen, was married to Dane's older sister, an unscrupulous woman named Danetta, that had Dallen murdered by her corrupt brothers. She had become the widowed stepmother of Tiffany, and had apparently promised her strange youngest brother that he could marry Tiffany when she turned fifteen to be rid of her. Matt had rescued Tiffany from a horrible home and brought her back to Willow Falls, where she had been living with Matt's sister Annie on the Big Z Ranch. Annie legally adopted Tiffany, and now she was a part of Matt's family.

It was spooky to have Dane lurking around Branson, thinking he could marry Tiffany. It made Matt uncomfortable, and a part of him wanted to beat Dane senseless, tie and gag him, and send him with a one-way ticket back to Prairieville on a stagecoach. Dane appeared harmless, but he was not the helpless little man that so many thought he was. He was quiet, perhaps not too bright, and most dangerous of all, he was unpredictable. He was like a venomous Copperhead snake hidden among fallen leaves waiting to strike. If it were a coincidence that he'd be in Branson the week of Hannie's funeral, it would be hard to believe the timing. However, it was harder to think that Dane somehow learned Tiffany was a part of Hannie's family and would be attending a funeral in Branson. Whether coincidence or something more nefarious, Tiffany was coming to town for the funeral, and Matt had every intention of keeping Dane far from her.

***

The dance ended, and the gentleman dancing with Christine escorted her to the bar to order a glass of pink champagne. Unlike Matt, the gentleman was out of breath as he wiped the sweat off his face.

"Thank you, Miss Knapp, for the dance. It's always a pleasure."

"You're welcome, Mister Woods. Thank you for the champagne."

Lionel Woods was a large and heavy man in his fifties, a widower, and a good man in the community. He spoke to Matt appreciatively, "I sure envy you. You be good to her, young man."

"I will." Matt's attention went to Dane as he pushed himself into their conversation.

"Remember me? I gave you a ticket. You're a good dancer; I liked what I saw." He breathed through his mouth while he stared at her.

"I remember. I'm talking to Mister Woods at the moment, though. I'll come to get you right before the band starts playing." Christine's words were kind. Matt's glare was not.

Dane walked four feet away, only to stare at her with an awkward half grin as if insidious thoughts were going through his mind.

"Well, I see you have an anxious suiter impatiently waiting." Lionel mentioned.

Christine giggled. "I do." She glanced at Matt and noticed Matt watching Dane irritably. "Are you okay?" she asked.

He nodded slowly. "Yeah. I don't like him."

"Oh. It's just one dance. Speaking of which, I need to go." She held out her arm towards Dane to be escorted out onto the dance floor. To Matt's disappointment, the band played a waltz intended for single couples. He liked dancing with Christine to a slower-paced waltz than a faster dance such as the heel-toe polka. He watched as Christine took Dane's left hand in hers and placed her right hand on top of his shoulder to keep the acceptable distance of six inches between them. Dane's right stub of an arm was placed on her side respectfully as they slowly moved in a circle across the floor. As the dance continued, Dane's stub casually enclosed on her back, and she would step back to keep the acceptable distance between dance-host and customer. To Matt's annoyance, Dane kept trying to close the distance while Christine expertly maneuvered to keep it at a minimum of six inches.

As the dance ended, Christine released his hand and removed her hand from his shoulder. "Thank you for the dance." she said with a customary smile.

Dane's eyes though already dark, turned even darker, and his left hand went around her while his right arm jerked her into him abruptly. "Where's my kiss?" he asked, and tried to force his mouth to hers.

Christine's right hand came up and caught his chin with the space between her thumb and index finger and sharply pushed his head upwards and back to create enough room for her left hand to press against his throat, releasing his grip on her. She quickly pushed against his chest with both palms with all her force to get him away from her.

"How dare you?" she yelled angrily.

Dane snickered. "You kissed Matt. I bought a dance too." He was grabbed from behind and spun around quickly to see Matt's angry expression just before a fist, as solid as a brick, connected with the side of his jaw. Dane hit the ballroom floor quickly and lay there stunned for a moment. He had been hit and never seen it coming. A vice-like grip took hold of his red hair and pulled him unmercifully off the floor, facing a ballroom of guests and dancers watching in awe of the fury on Matt's face.

Matt did not say a word as he took hold of Dane's right arm and yanked it upwards behind his back until Dane was bent over while at the same time pulling Dane's hair backward to control him firmly. Matt guided him across the floor at a hurried pace and into the entry by the stairs. Matt intentionally rammed Dane's head into the door jamb abruptly while Bella's husband Dave held the door wide open. Matt walked Dane out of the dance hall and threw him down onto the hardened street.

Matt shouted, "Get out of this town and don't come back! Do you hear me? Get back to Prairieville, Dane! I don't want to see you again." His chest rose and fell angrily.

Dane sat on the ground and rubbed his jaw. He unexpectedly grinned. "You killed my brothers, and I lost my hand. You stole my betrothed bride." His grin faded into a hateful scowl. "You have no authority in town. You'll see me around. Your payment is due in full." He snickered.

Matt nodded his head slowly. "Go home before you end up going home in a box." He turned to go back inside.

Dave told Dane, "You're no longer welcome in this establishment. Don't come back."

Bill Cooney met Matt at the door. Bill's size took

up the door space. He looked at Matt and motioned toward Dane. "Dane's my friend."

Matt's face was as hard as a stone. "Are you going to do something about me hitting him?"

"No." Bill said softly and stepped out of Matt's way.

"Find a better friend." Matt advised as he walked inside the dance hall. He found Christine with Bella and a few other ladies at the bar. "Are you okay?" Matt asked.

"Yeah, he didn't hurt me. He tried to kiss me." she said with disgust. "Who is he?"

"Dane Dielschneider. The last of the Dielschneider brothers from Prairieville. He's here because he thinks he's going to marry Tiffany."

Christine's eyes widened. "You didn't tell me that!"

"I didn't have a chance to."

Bella huffed. "And that is why I don't want you girls smooching on your loves during working hours. The other customers might think they can too."

Chapter 11

The moon lit the sky, creating a faint light as he moved within the shadows of the woods, keeping a good distance from town and the risk of being seen. The hour was late, much later than expected for anyone to be awake. It was two hours before dawn when Alan Sperry stepped out of the woods and into the cemetery behind the church, holding two bottles filled with kerosene and a rag stuffed in the openings. The cemetery had a ghostly appearance in the moon's silvery light. The tombstones stood in rows like forgotten soldiers awaiting the sergeant's instructions. Under the upright wooden and granite markers rested family plots with names Alan Sperry knew, including his brother Dwight and his cousin Barry Helms, whose tombstones stood as cold and unmoving as all the others.

The white church was a symbol of peace and hope in the small community set on the far edge of town. There were other white buildings in town, but none were quite as bright as the church with the large brass bell in a proud belltower that rang every day at noon and every Sunday morning to remind the community it was time to go to church.

Alan remembered being a ten-year-old boy when the church was being built. He had stolen candy from the mercantile and ran behind the church to sit and enjoy it. The new reverend in town, a gray-haired man named Reverend West, witnessed him steal the candy and followed him to the church. Reverend West grabbed his arm and whipped his hind end and lower back with his leather belt before roughly manhandling the ten-year-old back to the mercantile to be humiliated in front of the owners and other customers. It was Alan's first experience meeting a kind and loving reverend and the last time he wanted to.

Reverend West now rested under a block of granite shaped like a cross in the cemetery. Alan could see the cross in the moon's light, approached it, and set the bottles down to urinate on the cross tombstone as a personal message to Reverend West.

The stars shined brightly on the clear night, and the crickets sang in an unceasing harmony, creating a peaceful sound that was an invitation for a few frogs to join in as well. Alan stood on the good reverend's grave, slightly uphill from the church, and gazed around the sleeping town and fields. It was a beautiful view on a splendid night. It wasn't nearly cold enough for a fire, but he wasn't there to warm up. He was there to stop Audrey's persistence in having their wedding in the church. Like a wart

Alan once bit off his hand; the answer to the problem was as simple as getting rid of it. Alan picked up the bottles and continued to the church's far side where the windows faced the eastern skyline. He set one bottle down, lit a match to light the thin fabric, and flung the bottle through the window towards what Christians called the altar and prayer bench. The bottle broke, and the kerosene caught fire as it spread across the floor. He lit the other bottle and threw it through the same broken window towards the entrance door and watched the bottle break against the door and ignite the flames.

The sound of the shattering glass of the window was loud enough to attract attention if a home was nearby, but the houses were mainly on the other side of town, along the creek. Alan watched the fire spread within the church from the window with a pleasurable expression on his face. Aware that the orange flames were casting a glow, Alan left the side of the church, walked back through the cemetery to the forest, and sat down to watch the fire grow brighter. Smoke began to billow out of the broken window and the front door.

The flames ended any hope of a church wedding and the need for Audrey to meet the Reverend that presided over the church. But more than that, the burning church was the last living memory of Reverend West and his influence on their town. It was the only church in Natoma, and it would be nothing but ashes before long. Reverend West would be forgotten, and Audrey would have no reason to leave the Sperry home now.

After twenty minutes, flames were leaping out the windows when the first yells of "fire" awakened the town residents. With the fire being discovered and the sun beginning to rise, Alan slinked further into the trees to make his way home unseen. He took one last look at the flames, feeling an exhilaration he had not felt since his first bank robbery.

Alan entered the back of the barn to avoid waking the dog. He climbed into the loft and lay on his bedroll as the sun was beginning to brighten the eastern horizon. The news of the burning church would reach his home soon enough, and he may have to fight the flames, but he no longer had to listen to Audrey talk about getting married in the church.

***

Audrey was awakened by the sound of baby Alisha crying and the tired groans of her mother not wanting to wake up, followed by an angry bang on a distant wall and Mattie shouting at Daisy to let her one-year-old nurse. For a moment, there was silence, and Audrey could feel herself falling like she tripped down a well into the pleasant paradise of sleep when another child began to cry. The house was a maze of rooms built onto rooms as closely as they could be without insolation or separation, other than the plank boards that built a wall. It became apparent the night before when she could see the lamp light through the cracks in the boards of the next room. There were no tongue-in-groove walls or walnut shells, newspaper or sawdust insolation poured between two walls like other homes. She now understood why Alan slept in the barn's loft. There was not a sound that didn't carry into the next room. There was no privacy. She could hear Vince snoring three rooms away and every word spoken in Jannie's room.

Audrey sat up on the edge of her bed and rubbed her face. Her bed was not comfortable, but she had been so tired that she slept well. Audrey turned up the oil lamp beside her bed and prayed silently before picking up her opened Bible that was set on the floor. A Bible left open was inviting and called to her to read it each morning.

A soft knock on her door startled her. She had slept in her dress because she was not comfortable enough to sleep in her nightdress. "Yes, come in." she answered, while laying her Bible on the bed and standing.

The door opened respectfully. Morton Sperry spoke behind the door. "Miss, I saw your light on and wanted to let you know I brought the eggs in and Bernice is making breakfast if you'd like some. The women around here aren't early risers, so if you are, make yourself at home. I hope you slept well." he added awkwardly.

"Thank you, Henry. Tell Bernice I'll be out there as soon as I finish my devotions."

"I'm Morton," he said softly. "May I ask what a devotion is, or is that a woman thing I don't need to know about?"

"Morton?" she was surprised. He was a cruel and

105

mean-looking man. "I'm sorry, I thought you were Henry. You can come in." she said, looking at the opened door.

His rugged face with steely green eyes peeked around the door. "I don't want to bother you, Miss."

"My name is Audrey, and we're going to be related, so please call me Audrey. You must know what devotions are. It's just devoted time to reading the Lord's Word, prayer, and listening in silence for his voice."

Morton's brow lowered. "Whose voice?"

Audrey mirrored Morton's perplexed expression. "God's. Don't you listen for the Lord's voice, Morton?"

He shook his head. "I didn't know he had one. I don't do the whole Bible thing. Anyway, Henry and I are leaving for work. Have a good day."

"Have a nice day at work, Morton." She said as he closed the door gently. She had judged him fearfully when they first met. His neck-length brown hair, green eyes, and a thick goatee gave him a menacing, mean, and cruel appearance. She feared him because he appeared like a man who would rip her head off for saying the wrong word. Perhaps she judged him wrong as he *did* help clean up his sister's vomit the night before.

She prayed for him to hear the Lord's word in his heart and learn, in his words, to do the whole Bible thing. He may have appeared meaner than a rabid dog, but he had been nothing but kind to her so far. It was the same thing for the rest of the family as well. They were not what she expected, but they had welcomed her into their home and made her feel most welcome, aside from a few moments of fighting amongst each other.

She peered in a handheld mirror and brushed her hair into a ponytail for the day. She brushed her teeth with a bowl of water she had used the night before and then carried the bowl of water to the kitchen.

"Good morning." she said to Bernice as she tossed the used water outside the door.

Bernice sat on the family room floor, changing the cloth diaper of Daisy's daughter Alisha. She did not look pleased. She gave Audrey a sideways glance and went back to changing the diaper.

Audrey could smell the eggs and bacon set on a plate on the counter. "May I have some of your eggs and bacon?"

Bernice nodded affirmingly. "Yes."

Audrey took an egg and two pieces of bacon off the food tray and carried a plate into the family room. There didn't appear to be a dining room or dinner table where they sat together. "Thank you. I'm afraid Vince's dinner didn't sit well with me."

Bernice looked at Audrey tiredly. "He's a horrible cook, but he likes to think he's great at it."

"That's Daisy's baby, right? I'm still trying to memorize who belongs to who and who everyone is."

"I understand. There's a growing herd of children here." Bernice picked Alisha up and held her close to comfort the little girl. Bernice set her full attention on Audrey. "I don't want to sound rude, but why are you here?"

Audrey almost choked on a piece of bacon. "Excuse me." She covered her mouth while swallowing a half-chewed mouthful. "I agreed to marry Alan. I thought you knew that?"

Bernice turned her head towards the back of the house when she heard a door open. "I suppose I did. Congratulations." It didn't sound sincere. "Do you like children?"

"I love children." Audrey answered with a loving smile for Alisha.

"Good. You need to like them around here." She handed Alisha to Audrey. She spoke softly, not to be overheard, "The Sperry girls are terrible mothers. I get so aggravated with them. This is Alisha. She's almost one."

"Where is her father?"

Bernice shook her head warningly. "Don't ask about their fathers. I can promise you one thing, and that is this; they aren't around here anymore. It is a subject you don't want to bring up. You may not have any children yet, but living here, you'll become a mother to Daisy's and Jannie's younger ones. Jannie's oldest, Tad, is a lost cause, but Travis is a good boy so far. Henry sure has hope for him to be a good man."

Audrey's expression offered a joyless frown. "I hate to think of any child as a lost cause."

Bernice nodded in agreement. "So did I, until I came here."

The heavy footsteps of Mattie coming into the kitchen got their attention. She smiled at the ladies as she poured a cup of coffee. "Morning. Bernice, you need to stop taking care of Daisy's problems. She can get up with that baby. She'll be scrubbing diapers today." Mattie said with a determined nod. "How did you sleep, dear?" she asked Audrey while sniffing the air.

"Good."

"Glad to hear it. It sure smells like something's burning." She opened the front door and sniffed. "Yep, someone is burning something out there. I can see the smoke plume. The Crawford's must be burning a brush pile or something today." She closed the door as the scent of burning wood filled the family room. "So, what are you two girls talking about?"

Bernice appeared uneasy. "Children. Audrey loves children as much as I do."

"Excellent. Audrey, will you and Alan be trying for a child right away? I have plenty of grandchildren, but I'm never against plenty more. Alan is my oldest living child, and I'd sure like to see him settle down, marry, and have a few children of his own."

Audrey shrugged with a hint of a bashful smile. "I don't know. He says he wants ten or more, but we haven't talked about it seriously yet."

"I knew Alan would want some. He's been waiting to fall in love and have a family all his life. I'm so glad he found you," Mattie said appreciatively, "or should I say you found him?"

"I believe the Lord's providence brought us together."

"Yes," Mattie agreed, "I believe that too. Well, we

have a big day ahead of us. We need to discuss wedding plans. I don't have a big guest list, and I know Alan wants a small and private wedding. He isn't a people person, you know."

Audrey bounced Alisha on her lap. "I'm learning about him, and hope to learn more. I'm fine with a small wedding. I just want it in the church."

Chapter 12

Henry and Morton Sperry had noticed the thick smoke plume rising into the sky as soon as they stepped outside their home. They walked hurriedly to town to see what was on fire before they began their workday at the tannery. They were stunned to learn the town's only church was engulfed in flames.

Harry Yablonski, who owned the Heather Creek Tannery, was working with other men and women in town, carrying buckets of water from the creek to pour on the dry grass around the church. The grass had caught fire, and they worked to extinguish any risk of the flames spreading to the nearest structure. The threat of their town burning to the ground was their greatest concern, but there was a hay field not far away that reached the forest, and with the July heat, it was prime burning material. There was no time to stand and watch the church burn; they all knew the importance of stopping the fire's progression. The cemetery's grass caught fire and burned a few wooden grave markers before the townsfolks could get enough buckets of water on the hill to stop the flames from reaching the forest. If the fire spread to the town, fields, or woods, there would be little the townspeople could do except flee their homes and watch it all burn. There was not one person in the community whose livelihood didn't depend upon stopping the flames, and the community worked together for that single cause.

Morton and Henry didn't need to be asked; they immediately joined with the others to contain the flames. The sparks that rose into the sky added to the anxiety, but there was no breeze, and most sparks burnt out before they settled to the ground. The bell tower that once rose proudly above the church collapsed, and the bell rang a final time as it fell into the flames. The sound of the bell's final ring momentarily stopped the work as a thousand sparks rose like fireworks into the sky.

The Reverend, Micah Penny, wearing dark pants and a dirty white shirt, wiped the sweat from his forehead with his sleeve. He could see the ladies of the church crying, and the faces of good men that he knew were crushed to see the bell tower fall as if it was what they were fighting to save. "Brothers and sisters," he hollered, "we will hear the bell ring loud and proud again. We can rebuild the church, bigger and better than before. We needed to add on anyway, didn't we?" He laughed to break the solemn mood. "For today, let's just save the rest of what we love about living here."

"Amen!" someone called.

When the flames died down and were no longer a threat, the damage done was to the church and a surrounding area of grass that reached the cemetery. No one was hurt beyond a few minor burns and the wooden grave markers that could be replaced.

Harry Yablonski approached the two Sperry brothers. "We did it. We stopped it from spreading."

"Thankfully." Henry said. He wasn't quite as broad-shouldered as Morton, but Henry was still muscular. He had short brown hair and a trimmed goatee. His green eyes shined brighter than his brother's and held a certain joy that the other Sperry's were lacking. Henry's life started as a bitter outlaw, but after meeting Bernice, he began to change and now worked an honest job to support his family. Like his older brother Mark, Henry's wife and children were his priority in life. "We still have half a day, we can get some work done."

Harry Yablonski replied, "The tannery can wait. I want you two to keep carrying water to cool the coals. We need to know how the fire started. Reverend Penny said there was nothing inside that could have started that fire. Not a candle, not a lantern. Nothing. Help these men remove the debris and see if you can find what started it. We may find nothing, but maybe we will. Reverend Penny suspects someone did it intentionally."

Another two hours of throwing water on the remains cooled the coals enough for several men to begin removing rubble to search for a cause. It didn't take more than forty-five minutes to find a broken bottle near the door and another near the altar.

The town sheriff, Zeke Jones, held a piece of one of the broken bottles. It was evident that someone had thrown two firebombs into the church. There were no witnesses, nor could anyone think of someone with a grudge against the church or Reverend Penny. Sheriff Zeke Jones was disgusted that someone would burn the church. He shrugged his shoulders. "There's no way to know who did it. If anyone hears a rumor or something, let me know. I'm sorry, Reverend. I suppose church is done with for a while around here, huh?"

Reverend Penny answered, "No. We'll have a church service this Sunday at the same time. That fire is not going to end church services."

Morton Sperry stood on the street with the others, listening. They were all covered with soot, dirty and sweating from their labors. The ladies in town had made several pitchers of tea and lemonade for the men. Morton held a glass of sun tea in his hand. The reverend's words confused him. "Micah, your church burned down. I'm not trying to be funny, but do you expect to rebuild it before Sunday?"

Reverend Penny chuckled. "No. Morton, the church is not a building. It is the hearts and souls of the congregation, the believers. We can have a church service right here on the street or down at the creek. In a home or a dirty barn." He pointed at the burnt rubble. "The church building is just a place we meet. The heartbeat of the church is Jesus, and He doesn't live in a building; He lives in the hearts of the believers. Even if we had a great big church building with all the height, brickwork, and glamour like some of those churches in the big cities, without Jesus being the centerpiece of the congregation, it isn't much of a church. We'll meet down at the creek this Sunday, behind Oliver's house. He won't mind. Come join us and you'll see what I mean."

Morton wrinkled his nose. "I'm not a church-going man, as you know. But I am sorry to see your church is gone. If I hear anything about it, I'll let you know."

Reverend Penny shook his hand. "Morton, you and your family are always welcome to join us anytime. My door is always open."

Morton nodded towards the rubble. "Your church doesn't have a door anymore."

Reverend Micah Penny laughed. "I said, *my* door. You're always welcome to talk or eat at my house."

They had worked hard enough that Harry Yablonski told them to go home for the day. The two brothers walked on the road towards their home. The coolness of the shade of the trees was a refreshing retreat from the heat of the flames and the labor of carrying heavy water buckets as fast as they could.

Morton volunteered, "I think I'm going to strip down, sit in the creek and wash off."

Henry had more profound thoughts on his mind. "I didn't want to say anything in town, but I have a feeling Alan started the fire."

"Why would he do that?" Morton asked with a perplexed expression.

Henry stopped in a nice shaded spot and faced his brother. "You can't tell me you support what

Ma's doing to that lady. Audrey thinks she's been writing to Alan all this time, and it was Ma. Alan is not right in the head, and you know that. None of us have been perfect saints, but Alan is like nitroglycerine; he can blow up anytime. He's going to hurt that woman, and it's going to be Ma's fault for bringing her here. It makes me angry! I would tell Audrey to leave. Hell, I'd pay for her stage ticket back wherever she came from if I could. But Ma made it clear to Bernice and me that she'd kick us out of the house and off the property if we said anything. I have children, Morton. I'm stuck between a rock and a hard place. All my money goes to providing for our family. Which is a trap I can't get out of because I'm afraid Jannie's and Daisy's children will go hungry if we leave." He gave a discouraged exhale.

"I don't understand what that has to do with the fire. Why do you think Alan started it?" Morton asked.

"Audrey is a very devoted Christian and wanted to marry in the church. She wanted to see the church and meet the Reverend today, and Ma promised to take her. Ma has never stepped inside that church for a Sunday service or knows Reverend Penny. It would ruin Ma's whole charade if Audrey discovered she was being lied to. I think Alan burned it down to end that threat. It wouldn't surprise me if it were Ma's idea. We weren't raised in a very honest family, Mort."

Morton lowered his head thoughtfully. "If he did burn the church, I will bust his chops. He could have burned everything around here, including our home."

Henry rubbed the scar on his neck. "Alan's our brother, and I love him. But he reacts without thinking about the consequences of his actions and then wonders why you're mad at him. I don't trust how Alan looks at my wife, and I sure don't like how Ma set Audrey up to be Alan's fiancé. I think it's wicked! Bernice hates Ma for it."

"I knew Bernice was sickened by it. It's easy to see."

"Mort, It's getting to the point where I wonder how long it will be before Bernice takes my children and leaves me. She has family she can go to, you know. I must get my wife and kids out of that house, Morton. Vince is too lazy to work, Jannie is worthless, and Daisy is trapped caring for her children. You and I support them all. And now Alan is home, and he obviously can't keep a job. You know he's going to get the gang back together and end up dead or back in prison. And you haven't said one word about Audrey yet. Please tell me you disagree with what Ma and Alan are doing."

Morton was heavy-hearted. He sat on a stump beside the road and wiped the sweat from his black, soot-covered face, smearing it. "I think it's wrong. I wish we grew up in a better family like the Crawfords or damn near anyone aside from the way we did. It's not normal. Everyone with our bloodline are criminals, except for you and Mark. I saw Mark when we went to the circus in Branson. He still wants nothing to do with Ma or Alan. He's getting Jack a job at the silver mine to break free of here and go straight, which I am proud of Jack for doing. I hope he leaves the Sperry-Helms Gang behind him and never looks back. I'm never going back to it, but I don't know what I'm going to do. I suppose a part of me wishes our place would burn down so we could put it all behind us and move on. I understand your frustration, Henry, about feeling trapped here because I do too." He paused as a feeling of helplessness filled him. "I agree; we can't let Audrey marry Alan. He'll just beat on her and abuse her like he did Racheal. I regret many things in my life, but one of my biggest is allowing Alan to hurt her over and over again while I did nothing to stop it."

Henry knelt to toss a nail off the road. "Then let's not let it happen again. Alan has a long way to go before proving that he can be trusted to feed the dogs, let alone marry someone. Ma is babying him like a child since he's come home, and it isn't going to end well."

"Bernice wants to leave you?" Morton inquired.

"She doesn't want to leave me, but she is sickened by what Ma is doing to Audrey. And like most wives, she wants to have a place of our own where we can raise our children without Tad picking on them or Ma yelling at them or Bernice."

Morton stood. "I'll see if I can reason with Alan, and maybe he'll end the engagement and do what's right. That would save us all a headache or two."

Chapter 13

Matt walked into the Monarch Hotel and paused when he saw his cousin William Fasana standing at the curved reception desk talking to a well-dressed man in a silver suit. Behind the counter, Pamela Collins finished checking the gentleman into the hotel.

William's eyes peered past the gentleman to Matt. "Did you know the Wells Fargo Stage was robbed outside Natoma yesterday?"

"No. I haven't heard a thing." Matt replied.

"This is Sal Gable. He was a passenger as well as my father. They were robbed coming down the mountain, and the thieves broke the wheel spokes with a sledgehammer. Adam picked up the passengers and took my pops to the ranch. I imagine he'll come to town with Aunt Mary and Uncle Charlie. Lee sent his driver to Willow Falls today to pick them up for a more comfortable ride into town. Sal says the Natoma sheriff couldn't find the bandit's trail." William was angered to learn highwaymen robbed his father.

"Was anyone hurt?" Matt asked the man in a silver suit.

"No. They didn't hurt anyone. They had their faces and boots covered in burlap, and I didn't see any horses. There were four of them. They took a good portion of my money." Sal stated.

William suggested, "It was probably the Sperry-Helms Gang."

"Sperry?" Sal questioned.

"Yeah, a family of bandits." William explained.

Sal's lips widened just a touch. "I met a lady last night named Jannie Sperry."

"I wouldn't brag about that." William chuckled.

Matt appeared to be irritated. "Zeke Jones, the Natoma sheriff, should have wired me about that. I guess I'll be taking a trip to Natoma. It's been pretty quiet around there for a while, and now that Alan Sperry is out of prison, we have our first stage robbery. Coincidence?" he asked William.

William wrinkled his nose. "My money is on the Sperry-Helms Gang. Do you want me to go with you to confront Alan when you go?" William knew quite well that he couldn't go if he wanted to. The stitches holding the six-inch slice across his stomach together from Nick Griffin's knife hadn't healed enough for him to be that active.

Sal Gable questioned, "Alan Sperry? There was a woman on the stage who was coming into town to marry him, I think. Her name was Audrey. She is a pretty woman for a mail bride. She liked what she knew of him."

William offered, "I hope she knows what she's getting into. His old wife, Racheal, left him because he's a brutal man. They had a hell of a time getting her out of that house once she was in too. I hope his new wife fairs better, but he's returning to his former trade, and one way or another, he won't be around much longer. Sal, if you had a hankering for her, she'll be back in the mail catalog by the end of the month."

Sal chuckled. "I offered, and she turned me down flat. I don't think she liked me."

Matt's brow lowered questionably. "William, can I talk to you in private?"

"Sure, come into my room."

"That's not very private." Matt said as he followed William into his room, which David Chatfield was occupying to recover from surgery after being stabbed several times by Nick Griffin.

David set the book he was reading down as they entered. "Hi, Matt." he said with a welcoming grin to have a visitor. He was lying in bed in an enclosed room day after day, and it got monotonous. David had a rare disease called hypertrichoses that covered his entire body with long brown hair, including his face. He was sixteen years old and part of the Chatfield & Bowry Amazing Circus and Sideshow. His older sister, Nancy, was staying in a different room of the hotel to watch over him.

"Hi David, how are you?" Matt shook his hand like always.

"Bored, but I'm doing well. The doctor says I

should recover fully in four or five weeks and be able to go back home."

"That is good news. If you'll excuse me." He turned to William. "This room isn't very private."

William shrugged his shoulders unconcerned. "Whatever you have to say to me can be said in front of my little brother here." He pulled the hair on David's chin. "What's up?"

Matt spoke to David, "Whatever you're about to hear is not to be repeated to anyone. David, you may not know what I'm talking about, but if you say something to anyone and it gets back to the wrong person, lives can be endangered. That goes for any conversation I say is private. Understood?" His stern expression left no question about the seriousness of his words.

David nodded his head slowly. "Yes, sir."

Matt put his attention on William. "What do you know about Racheal leaving the Sperry home? Who had a tough time getting her out of there?"

William grinned and bit his bottom lip. It was a slip that he had never intended to let out. "Matt, you listen too well. You do understand if I tell you and it gets back to the Sperry family, there will be some killings, right?"

Matt responded sarcastically, "Says the man who publicly stated that he knew about it. Sure, William."

"Seriously." He gave a severe glance at David. "That means you too. And I'm serious, David. I know I can trust you, so never repeat what you're about to hear to anyone or I'll bring a couple of fleas in here and let them go." he said with a wink. "No, it could endanger some of our own family."

"What does that mean?" Matt asked.

"I'll keep this simple. Talk to your brothers Lee and Adam. That's all I can say."

"That's it?" David asked, disappointed. "That's the secret I can't tell anyone. Talk to Lee and Adam?"

William nodded. "Shh! Not so loud."

Matt chuckled. "Okay. I'll ask Lee about it. I came by to let you know your old friend Dane Dielschneider is in town. He seems to think he is taking Tiffany back to Prairieville."

"No?" William chuckled. "Did you smack him around and tell him to go home before he gets hurt?"

"Basically. Dane saw me kiss Christine on the dance floor last night and tried to kiss her too."

William laughed loudly and grabbed his stitches as the vibrations hurt.

"I don't know what to think of him." Matt stated flatly.

William offered through a grin, "Don't waste much time thinking about him. Tiffany will be kept safe by all of us. Even though I look forward to seeing Dane," his broken heart showed in his expression, "I hate funerals, Matt. If he shows up at Hannie's, I'll shoot him just for the hell of it."

"I don't like funerals either. Especially this one."

"Yeah," William agreed softly. "I miss Hannie a lot. I miss how she'd scold me for making a bad joke." He blinked a few times to force the moisture away. "Well, that Sal Gable is a gambler. So, we have a poker game later tonight. I will take what little money he has left and send him to Rose Street to make some more for me to win tomorrow. He was on his way to Boise City to hit some mining towns but heard we do pretty good here. He may be around for a while."

"That will be fun for you. David, I'll be back soon to visit for a while."

***

Matt opened the door to David's room and paused. Dane Dielschneider was standing with his friend Bill Cooney at the receptionist's desk, talking to Pamela.

"What are you doing here, Dane?" Matt asked with no friendliness in his voice.

Dane turned around. He did not seem surprised to see Matt come out of the room. "Checking prices. The Lucky Man's Bunkhouse is not very comfortable. I like to be comfortable. You know what used to be my hand needs comfort." He grinned.

"Can you afford it?"

"It seems like, no."

"Then maybe you ought to leave." Matt said firmly.

Dane intentionally looked around the interior of the hotel. "It's a beautiful building, and there is a restaurant. I suppose since it's a public building, I can look around. There is no law against that, is there?" His fixed grin never changed.

William came out of the room with a welcoming smile on his face. "Well, if it isn't little one stub in person. How's the hand?"

Dane's grin slowly faded. "You would know." he said as William stepped to the counter and leaned against it, facing Dane.

"Would I? Oh yeah!" William slapped the counter with an animated strike of memory and a loud laugh. "I shot your hand off! It was a hell of a shot, wasn't it? I still brag about that. Pamela, listen to this, little red here was stalking up behind Matt with a knife in his hand, I was on the porch roof of a hotel and blew that knife right out of his hand from what, Dane? Maybe thirty or forty yards? Maybe fifty? How far was it, Dane?" He waited for Dane to answer.

Dane stared at him with a blank expression as if in a trance.

Pamela's eyes widened in the uncomfortable position of being told such a story in front of the person it was about. It was clear by Matt's and William's tone of voice that they didn't like the young man.

"I know, I forget too." William continued after a moment. "Matt, what was it, fifty, maybe sixty yards?"

"More like twenty." Matt replied simply.

"Ugh!" William grunted. "Your eye sights bad. Anyway, Pamela, it was a great shot! I doubt even Adam Bannister could make that shot as quickly as I did with his trusty rifle. And he was a sniper during the war! Unfortunately, I was using a .44 Winchester rifle, and it blew so much of his hand off, they just cut the rest off and called it good." He lowered his voice and spoke sincerely to Dane, "I notice you carry your knife on the left side now."

Dane's face had reddened to match his hair. "My right-hand doesn't grip it so well anymore." He lifted the right arm where his hand used to be.

William chuckled. "Well, Dane, I wish I had your hand stuffed and mounted to keep as a trophy. I hear you came courting for Tiffany. Let me tell you something; it will be a mistake for you to go anywhere near her. If you do, I might put a bullet through your other hand, and then you'd become little two stubs. Worse, you'll have to ask your buddy there to wipe your backside every time you use the privy. You two would become very close indeed." His tone turned serious. "Don't even say her name. Just get back home."

Dane motioned towards his large friend. "That's Bill. He's bigger than you."

William eyed Bill and looked back at Dane, unimpressed. "Should I be scared?" He tightened his shoulders, coiled up his arms, and shook his body frightenedly with all the mockery he could muster. "Ewe wee, I'm scared." He dropped the sarcasm and spoke plainly, "If you're going to eat, go do it. If not, get out of here. The restaurant is the only public part of the hotel; the rest is private. And little one stub, if I see you again, I may not be so nice."

"I'll see you later." Dane said to William and left the hotel.

"You are so mean." Pamela said to William.

William nodded agreeably. "Sometimes. If he comes back in here, let me know."

***

Matt entered the Branson Home & Land Brokers office and noticed a new painting on the wall near the receptionist's desk. It was a painting of a train pulling four passenger cars exiting a tunnel through a high cliff along a river. The office wasn't overly large, the reception desk was set in a lobby with seating available on a davenport and a few leather back chairs. The fine wood paneling of the walls, artwork, and a few plants made it a pleasing and comfortable atmosphere. There were two offices and a conference room beyond the lobby. If there was a negative to entering Lee's office, it was the sour expression of the receptionist Lois Reynolds.

Matt sat in a comfortable leather-back chair across from his brother Lee's oversized desk.

"Lee, how did you get Racheal free from the Sperry farm, and where is she now?"

"I don't know what you're talking about." Lee said. He was surprised by the question.

"Bull. William told me you had something to do with it. Now that Alan is out of prison, it is better for me to know than not. I heard a mail bride came in this week for him."

Lee sat quietly watching his brother. "Alright.

Racheal and I ended our courtship. We weren't as compatible as we thought, but we were good friends. Alan moved in like the vulture he is, and Racheal married him on her own accord. Alan treated her like a piece of property that he could buy or sell at his whim. He prostituted Racheal to his friends or travelers passing through town when he needed money. If she refused, he'd beat her black and blue, which he would do without cause too. He broke her nose, ribs, and arm at different times. Alan did all kinds of things to make Racheal's life a living hell. She had been cut off from the world, including her family.

"Regina and I got married and lived our life. One day, John and David Crawford came in here and handed me a letter from Racheal, begging for help. We all met at Adam's house and devised a plan to get her out of the Sperry home and Natoma. We knew we had to hide her where the Sperry-Helms Gang couldn't find her. We knew her life, and ours would be in danger if they found out. No one wants a blood feud between families, so we kept it as quiet as possible and told no one what we were doing. We got messages to and from Racheal through her sister-in-law, Bernice, who would make contact with Kellie Crawford. That is how Racheal got word to me initially. Bernice would meet Kellie at the store, glove factory, or wherever at certain times and places to pass notes that were to be read and thrown into the fire.

"One day, just like any other, Racheal took her children outside for a walk on the Sperry property,

128

which she was not permitted to leave. They cut through the woods, and John Crawford met them, hid them under a wagon-load of corn stalks, and took them to his barn for a night. The next night they were moved through the fields to David's barn. David took them to meet Adam outside Willow Falls, and he brought them here. I kept them in the hotel for a week before we put them on a stage to Utah. From there, a train to Sacramento and then a ship to Portland. Racheal now goes by the name Shirley Hotchkiss and owns a sewing, mending and, women's clothing shop on 7th Street. We all decided she needed to survive and make a living. We all raised some money and bought her a house and a business in Portland. Racheal changed her name, the children's last name, and has a new life. John and David Crawford were just as much to thank for that as Adam and I were, more so even; they took the greatest risk. We all agreed, never to mention it outside of one another. My wife knows about it, but John Crawford's doesn't; there was too much at risk to tell her, Annie, or anyone else. Now you know."

"How is Racheal doing?"

"Very well, as far as I know."

Matt rubbed his beard thoughtfully. "I won't mention it to anyone."

"Matt, if Alan has a new mail-order bride, you might talk with Alan's sister-in-law Bernice Sperry. She is the one that helped Racheal get out of their home. Bernice and Racheal were good friends. The Sperry mother and Alan's siblings were the ones that trapped her there after he went to prison. Morton and his gang tore the town up and beat Racheal's brother nearly to death, looking for Racheal. Morton even came here to threaten me. That's about it. If there is a new bride for Alan, I feel sorry for her already."

"After the funeral, I'll be going over there to investigate a stage robbery. Now that Alan is back, those are starting again."

Lee narrowed his eyes pointedly, "You be careful of them. And remember what I told you last week. You tend to think people are your friends; Morton Sperry is not your friend. Make sure you have someone to watch your back. Take me if you need to. I wouldn't mind putting Alan in the ground myself. I owe him for what he put Racheal and those girls through."

"I don't think I need you this time, but I'll keep your words in mind. William said you sent James with your coach to get Aunt Mary and Uncle Charlie for the funeral. That's nice of you. Uncle Joel will be coming with them. He was on the stage that was robbed."

"He wasn't hurt, was he?" Lee asked with concern.

"No. It will be nice to see him, though."

Chapter 14

Morton Sperry watched his brother Alan carefully as he sat in a padded chair in the family room while Henry explained that the smoke in the air was from the church burning to the ground. They may have lived a half mile or more outside of town, but it was uncanny how no one in their home had made the walk to town to see what was burning.

"Grandma said the Crawfords were burning brush." Travis said with disappointment.

"The church is gone?" Bernice asked, shocked.

"It's nothing but ashes and rubble." Henry answered.

"How did it catch fire?"

"Arson. Someone torched it with firebombs."

Alan's jaw dropped open, shocked. "Wow. This town is getting more and more unrighteous all the time."

Tad Sperry rubbed between his toes while sitting on the floor. "Firebombs, huh?"

Morton spoke plainly, "Whoever did it is stupider than a chicken. They could have burned the town down or started a forest fire that could've burned our home down. If it weren't for the folks in town carrying water from the creek, we wouldn't have a home anymore. Whoever did it is stupid!" His eyes burned into Alan accusingly.

Tad shrugged. "It would have been a heck of a fire to see the town burn down."

Morton was irritated. He spoke heatedly to his nephew, "Who will feed you if the town burned down? You better start thinking, boy. The only people who provide around here are those of us who work. And I'm telling you all right now, I'm not spending my life providing for you all. You and Vince need to get a job."

Vince scowled. "I work."

Tad snapped at his uncle, "I'm joining the gang."

Mattie shouted from the kitchen, where she was heating some oatmeal for lunch. "No one is joining an outlaw gang around here! I won't have any criminals in this family. Any more talk like that, young man, and I'll wash your mouth out with soap!" Her eyes cut into Tad like a dagger. She shifted her head to Morton with a cold scowl. "And you, you better watch your talk too. We all do our part around here."

Alan spoke to Audrey, who sat on the davenport. She looked uncomfortable with the sudden shouting. "Audrey, unfortunately, we can't get married in the church. I suppose we can do it here. I don't know that we need to wait until Saturday. I can bring the good reverend here later today to marry us."

She shifted in her seat. "I'd like to meet the reverend, but he may not feel like meeting anyone today." she answered.

"I doubt he would." Morton agreed.

"Hogwash," Mattie interjected. "A marriage might be exactly what he needs to make him feel better. Alan, why don't you go to town and see if he can come by for dinner tonight? I'll throw some goods into a pot, and we'll have a fine stew and fresh bread."

Alan's lips pulled back just a bit. "I will."

Audrey suggested, "I can go with you."

Mattie quickly answered, "No, doll, I would like to spend today with you. You can help me with supper. With this herd of Sperrys and the reverend, we have a lot of food to prepare."

Audrey remembered the dinner the night before and figured she had better help in the kitchen. "I'd be happy to."

"Well, I suppose I'll go find the good reverend." Alan said. He stood and left the house.

Morton put his attention upon Jannie, who sat against the wall with her youngest child, Eve, on her lap. Jannie wasn't feeling good from the night before and waited for the oatmeal to finish. "Jannie," Morton snapped, "Audrey, Travis, and I cleaned up your puke last night. That's enough! You should return to work at the glove factory and start helping around here."

She scowled and spoke softly, "You're not my father."

"You're almost thirty-three years old with four kids. It's not fair to Henry to work every day to support your children."

"He doesn't!" she exclaimed with a rude stare at Morton.

"Who does then, Jannie?" Morton asked. "Ma watches over those kids more than you do."

Mattie scolded, "Morton James! What has gotten into you today? I just said we all do our share around here. Leave her and everyone else alone!" she shouted.

"Fine, I will." He walked out the back door and crossed the backyard to the barn.

***

Alan was saddling one of their horses to ride into town when Morton entered the barn and asked, "What reverend are you going to find?"

Alan chuckled like a schoolyard kid. "Reverend Cass Travers. He'll find a Bible somewhere to carry."

Morton rested a foot on a stall board as he leaned on it. "Alan, you can't do this to her. Audrey believes she's marrying a man that doesn't exist."

Alan grinned. "Oh, I exist. She's almost as pretty as Racheal, isn't she? Ma did alright."

"No. Ma didn't. It's wrong, Alan. You need to be straight with Audrey and let her go back to wherever she came from. All you're going to do is ruin her life."

Alan lowered the stirrups to fit his long legs. He

faced Morton and raised his brow to speak frankly, "Little brother, as long as she shares my bed, I don't care. Once we are married, she can't divorce me. It's against her god's law." He snickered as he circled the horse to the other stirrup.

"Racheal was a Christian too. It didn't stop her."

Alan's face hardened like a stone as he glared over the saddle. He spoke heatedly, "You guys let her go. Not me! I was in prison where you should have been too. All of you! Cousin Barry and I took the blame for you, and I was with him when he died. Racheal's leaving is on you and the others in there who I went to prison to cover for!" he exclaimed while pointing towards the house. "I was counting on you to watch over my family for me, Morton. It's only fair to replace what you all lost because you owe me! Ma is doing her part to make up for your failure. Audrey is here to stay."

"Bullcrap. I don't owe you a thing. I wish I had knocked you on your ass the first time you laid a hand on Racheal. Alan, I won't stand by and let you lie, deceive and marry Audrey. I'm telling her the truth if you don't. I'm giving you until tomorrow to be honest with her."

Alan walked back around the horse and lifted his hands questionably. "Do you think you can beat me, little brother? You know the Sperry Rule."

"I don't want to fight with you, Alan. Think about it. You couldn't handle three days of working. How are you going to handle a wife?"

Alan spat on the ground. "Working for John Crawford is a lot different than being married. I'd know; I was married. Hell, Morton, you've never even seriously courted a woman."

"No, I haven't. But no matter how lonely I ever got, I would never do what you are doing to Audrey."

Alan grinned with a shake of his head. "Mort, you're wasting your time talking. Audrey loves me. We're getting married, and that's all there is to it. The truth will come out little by little, and she'll adjust to it."

"Truths like you burning down the church?"

Alan nodded. "Yeah. What choice did I have? The reverends never met me. How can we be church-going people if we've never been to church?"

"You could have burned everything around here down. Did you think about that?"

"It turned out fine, so forget about it."

"If you try to marry her, I'll tell her and the sheriff that you burned the church down."

Alan stepped quickly towards his brother. "I've been sitting in prison for seven years. I deserve this!" he shouted. "Stay out of my way and keep your mouth shut. Or we won't be brothers anymore. If I return and she doesn't want to marry me, you had better have your gun belt on because you'll need it. I'll kill anyone that interferes with my life, including you." He quickly climbed into the saddle with a stern glare at Morton before riding out of the barn.

Chapter 15

Morton walked into the corral and leaned on the wooden fence to peer over the hill towards Heather Creek. He listened to the water from a small waterfall upstream as the stream rippled over the streambed below. Living in the Sperry home, the only rare thing was finding solitude. He sometimes took his horse for a long ride to escape the chaos and commotion of his house. Henry's words about supporting the family had struck a nerve. It was true. He had never felt any differently; his responsibility as the eldest son still at home after Alan was sent to prison was to provide for his family, and he robbed, stole, and killed to provide for them. It was true. If his crimes were known and proven in a court of law, he would be in prison too. Morton knew he was not a good man. He wanted to be, though.

It was disheartening to labor so hard to save the town from fire, knowing many of the townspeople suspected someone in his family of starting the fire. The feeling was made worse now that it was confirmed. And the reason behind the fire was just as terrible as causing it. He was ashamed to be part of the Sperry family.

"Are you praying?" Audrey's gentle voice asked, pulling him from his thoughts. She was quickly beside him inside the corral. She leaned on the fence like he was. "I'm sorry to interrupt if you were. I can leave."

He shook his head with a slight glance at her. "I don't pray."

"No? Looking at the beautiful little creek down there and the beauty of this place, I'd think you'd at least thank God for creating such a beautiful place to live."

He scanned the scenery appreciatively. "I suppose I should."

"For not praying, you seemed upset about the church burning down."

He took a deep breath in through his nose and exhaled. "Just because I don't go doesn't mean it didn't belong here. Many of the town folks go there. They're good people, and they don't deserve that."

"I wanted to get married in the church." she said sadly.

He nodded quietly.

"You don't like me much, do you, Morton?" she asked.

"Why would you ask that?" He turned his down-turned head towards her curiously.

"Just a feeling. You, Henry, and Bernice don't seem as friendly as the others. I hope you don't think I'm taking your brother from you."

Morton chuckled. "I like you. Unfortunately..." he trailed off.

"I'm engaged to your brother?"

He hesitated to answer.

"Wait! I didn't mean it as you might think," she said with widened eyes. She tried to explain, "I meant it like..."

"Yeah," he answered slowly with a touch of humor in his eyes, watching her struggle to explain. "Can I give you a bit of advice?"

"Yes. Please." she laughed.

"Go home. You're too good for this family. I'd appreciate you not telling anyone I said so because it would cause problems. But it's true."

A warm and sincere lifting of her lips created a soft smile. "I appreciate that. But I fell in love with Alan. His letters just, how should I say? They were like poetry to my ears and delight to my heart. I couldn't resist him. He's a little awkward now, but I'm sure once he relaxes, that person I fell in love with will come out. He's a gifted writer."

"Oh yeah? Maybe you should have him write another note to you. You know, a small little love note about why he wants to marry you or something like that while on a picnic or sometime when you're alone."

Audrey laughed. "Do people in love around here usually write letters to each other while having a picnic?"

He shrugged. "I wouldn't know. I've never been in love or on a picnic. It was just an idea."

She was surprised. "You've never been in love? Not even as a teenager?"

"There weren't many girls my age around here. Most of the women I've known weren't worth knowing. There was one young lady I wouldn't have minded to court, but she married someone else. She wouldn't have been interested in me anyway."

"You can always put an ad for a wife as Alan did. It worked for him."

He shook his head with a slight chuckle. "No. I doubt many men are lucky enough to meet someone like you."

"Ohh. You're making me blush."

"I don't mean to."

"Are you okay? You appear troubled."

He nodded while looking at her. "You're observant, good. Keep your eyes open and stay observant."

She chuckled uneasily. "What does that mean?"

He met her eyes and spoke sincerely, "It means I think you need to go back home. This is not where you belong."

Her brow narrowed with a touch of anger. "Am I not good enough for your brother? You know, I'm getting tired of being rejected everywhere I go. Am I that unattractive?"

He was surprised she'd ask such a question. He thought she was beautiful. Morton gazed into her pretty blue eyes. "Not at all, Audrey. I think you're a very beautiful lady. I admire everything about you. But..."

"But what?" she demanded.

"You deserve better."

Again, a warm and sincere lifting of her lips revealed a soft smile that expressed her heart was touched. Her voice was soft and gentle, like the footsteps of a spotted fawn walking out of a forest. "Thank you." She turned her head towards the creek and continued, "But I've fallen in love with Alan. I think he is right. The sooner we get married, the sooner he'll relax and be the man he is in the letters. I just think he is so nervous right now."

"I'm sure he is." Morton couldn't hide his disappointment. "As I said, stay observant and don't let your love blind you. I'm just trying to be your friend." he said and started to walk away.

She turned towards him. "Morton, do you want to pray with me?"

He offered a sad, ever so slight decline. "I don't pray."

Audrey tilted her head empathetically. "It looks like you could use some prayers."

"I'm sure I could."

"Then I'll pray for you."

He took a deep breath and exhaled. "I really wish you would." He knew she would not understand what he meant, but he wished she had come to town interested in getting to know him. From what he knew of her so far, he found her to be perfect in every way.

Chapter 16

Cass Travers glanced up from milking a cow. He sat on a T-shaped milking stool and wore a pair of faded bib coveralls. "You must be kidding me. You want me to pretend to be the reverend and marry you?"

Alan nodded excitedly. "She doesn't know the difference."

"You burned the church down, didn't you?" Cass accused.

"No one can prove if I did or didn't." Alan said with a shrug of his shoulders. He had met Cass in the past two weeks when he came home. Cass was a member of the Sperry-Helms Gang with a lethal reputation that was well earned. He lived on the Helm's Dairy and milked cows to earn his keep and make a little money. He and Jesse Helms had become close friends over the past few years. Alan liked Cass immediately.

"It wouldn't be a legal wedding. I'm no minister."

"That doesn't matter. Jannie can use her fancy writing to make a marriage license, and if we all sign it, it'll be good enough."

Cass grinned. "I heard you were a cunning man. More so than your brother, Morton. Alan, I'll make you a deal. I'll marry you and that woman, but I'm getting real sick of milking cows. Jesse and I robbed the stage and got very little after splitting the money with your fat, lazy brother and idiot nephew, Tad. I'm not working with that little twit again. I might shoot him, but I won't work with him. I didn't come back here to be a permanent employee at Helms Dairy. I despise milking cows." he hit the cow in the gut with a hard fist. "Jesse is loyal to your family line; I'm not. Get some banks lined up to rob, or I'm leaving for good. Get one good bank job lined up within a week, or I'll tell your bride it's all a hoax before I leave."

"I just got home from prison. Give me a chance. There's a bank in Willow Falls that we've never robbed..."

Cass gave a short chuckle with a disappointed shake of his head. "You're going to have to do better than that! The Willow Falls Bank is where the Helms Dairy banks! I say we hit Loveland like we planned last year. Maybe another town on the way, before sparking into Idaho and hitting some banks there before coming home. I don't want to waste my time with suicidal plans. Willow Falls, Alan? Seriously? If it wasn't Matt Bannister and his deputies breaking our doors down, it would be your uncle Gerry. I'll do my best to play the part of a reverend, but she might see through me. I know very little about that stuff. I know robbing banks, and that's what I came here to do, not milk cows or dilly dally with robbing mail carriers and poor stagecoach passengers. The Sperry-Helms Gang used to have a spine. It's gone soft and yellow."

Alan spoke irritably, "Morton's spine has turned soft and yellow, not mine. Give me a chance, and I'll prove that to you. But first things first, you're now a preacher. She won't know the difference. Just talk her into marrying me, do the ceremony the preacher's way, and I'll take care of the rest. We'll head to Loveland next week."

Cass stood from his stool, allowing it to fall over, and shook Alan's hand. "Okay. Now you're talking my language. Morton changed after hanging Pick. I don't know what happened to him, but he's lost his fire to lead. Jesse is as mean as a rattlesnake, but he can't plan a robbery to save his life without Morton's blessing. That aside, your bride is bound to find out the truth eventually."

Alan shrugged carelessly. "After we're married, it won't matter because she'll be my property, and I'm going to make sure she knows I own her. Come to the house dressed in the nearest you have to a suit, preferably black. And don't forget to bring a Bible with you. Jannie will have the license ready."

"Shall I bring the rest of the family, the Helms clan, to celebrate?"

Alan couldn't help the wide lopsided grin that took shape. "No. I don't want anyone there. I'm taking her straight to the top of the barn when the wedding is over. You ought to see her, Cass. Tall, built for childbearing, not that I want more children," he added quietly. "But it will be fun to try."

***

"It's a pleasure to meet you, Miss. I'm Reverend Cass. That's my first name, by the way. We mountain folks are a bit less pretentious than you city folks. We don't do things exactly like you, folks, so bear with us if it seems strange. I don't have all the training, schooling, or education your city ministers probably do. But, the good news is, we make do." Cass Travers said. He was sitting in the family room in a ripped padded chair, speaking with Audrey and Alan, who sat on the davenport facing him. Behind them, he could see Tad and Jannie in the kitchen grinning at him while they tried not to laugh. Mattie sat in her rocking chair while Vince sat in a wooden chair. Daisy had her little ones outside playing so they would not interrupt the adults talking. Henry and Bernice walked their children to the creek to play in the water. They had no interest in participating in the ruse. Morton had gone to the river with his nephew, Travis, to do some fishing.

"I understand," Audrey said. "I was sorry to hear about your church burning down. That is very sad."

Cass nodded in agreement. "Well, that's what we have collections for. And any offerings you want to donate, I'll be glad to take to build a new one. I guess until I do, I'm on vacation, right? Well, after your wedding ceremony anyway. So, shall we get started?"

"I think so," Alan said with a childlike grin. He nudged his shoulder into hers playfully. "Then we can get busy making a family, right?"

Jannie laughed with delight. "Oh yeah! Knocking out babies left and right."

Audrey's cheeks reddened slightly by Alan's comment. She ignored him. "Reverend Cass, aren't you going to continue church services despite the church burning?" she asked.

"I suppose we could." He shrugged. "Why? Do you want to go?"

"Well, yes. Doesn't everyone?"

His brow furrowed. "I don't know. The church just burned down today."

"What is your church denomination?"

"Denomination?" he asked with a puzzled expression. Cass had no idea what she was talking about.

Her shoulders lifted questionably as she explained, "Presbyterian, Lutheran, Baptist, you know, what your church believes? What denomination is your church?"

Cass grimaced. "Aren't they all about the same? Mormon, maybe?"

Mattie interrupted, containing her irritation at Cass for sounding like an idiot. "Darling, I told you it's a Christian church. Reverend Cass doesn't claim one denomination over the other. He believes it's not fair to saddle a free church with a title that whittles its beliefs to fit into a particular mold."

Cass pointed at Mattie. "Exactly." He nodded.

Audrey wasn't satisfied with his answer. "Who do you believe Jesus is?"

"Well," Cass arched his back to stretch the muscles. "He's Jesus."

"Yes, but who is he? What makes him important?" she pressed.

Cass chuckled. "Miss, what's with the questions? I came here to marry my friend and you. I'm leaving town for a while, so if you want to be married, we need to get it going."

Audrey had a bad feeling in the pit of her stomach. It wasn't caused by bad food like the day before or sickness, but a stirring within her soul that gave her a hesitance to allow the mountain preacher to marry them. The marriage license was a handwritten paper Jannie wrote out, misspelling several words, and was far from a State of Oregon legally binding and sanctioned license. Even for a backwoods town like Natoma, it wasn't an official, legally binding document.

Audrey spoke plainly, "There are plenty of false teachers that don't know the Bible well enough to know what they are teaching. Some teach to please the ears of the congregation. I'm sure that helps with the tithes and offerings, but compromising the word of God for lies is wickedly wrong. So far, you haven't been able to answer one of my questions, or you are purposely avoiding them. I'm skeptical of letting you marry us."

Mattie exclaimed, "Audrey!"

"What?" Jannie shouted, surprised. "He came

here to marry you!"

Cass laughed lightly. "Miss, we don't care about denominations. We're mountain folks. We just preach and teach what the Bible says. Nothing fancy, nothing like you're used to, I'm sure. The fact is, I'm the only one around here that can marry you, whether you like me or not. So shall I do it, or shall I leave?"

Mattie was displeased. She spoke frankly to Audrey, "If you love Alan as you say you do, then marry him."

Alan took hold of her hand. "Audrey, this is our only chance. Don't break my heart already. You'll make me feel like dead weeds in a vase."

A deep frown entrenched itself deeper in her expression as evidence that his words stung her heart. She knew the pain of being rejected too well.

Cass grinned at Alan. "Dead weeds in a vase?"

Audrey answered softly, "It's what my former husband gave me when he left me."

Cass laughed heartily. "That's a good idea. I like that."

"Reverend Cass!" Mattie exclaimed with a scalding glare. "Shall we get the wedding started?"

"Yes," Cass agreed. "Let's stand up and get this marriage rolling."

Alan stood quickly. "Come on." He pulled on Audrey's arm.

"Wait," Audrey said, refusing to stand. "Reverend Cass, I apologize if I came across as rude. But I'm not prepared to marry Alan today. Are you free tomorrow?"

"Tomorrow?" Alan gasped. "We can get married right now. Why wait? What's the difference between right now and tomorrow? We're going to be married anyway." His voice rose irritably.

She understood his frustration, but she was determined to wait. "I'm sorry, but like you said, what's the difference between today and tomorrow? We can wait a day to make it more special than right now. I'm not dressed for a wedding."

Alan spoke heatedly, "You don't need to be dressed. The dress is coming off afterward anyway!"

"Baby time!" Janie shouted enthusiastically.

Audrey grimaced, repulsed by his choice of words. "Is that all you're interested in? Because it's all you talk about. What's in the heart comes out of the mouth, Alan."

Jannie volunteered, "It's all I'm interested in."

Mattie spoke to Jannie harshly, "Hush it!" She took a deep breath and talked to Audrey calmly, "Darling, Alan is excited to marry you. He's been waiting a long time. Forgive him for being impatient. That is fine if you want to wait until tomorrow to prepare yourself."

Alan was angered and threw up his hands irritably. He spoke loudly, "Tomorrow it is! Why not wait one more day? It's not like we could get married right now and be done with it! Come back tomorrow, Cass. My fiancé needs to be prettied and all dolled up to say the words, *I do*." He cursed. "I'm going outside." He walked out the back door and slammed the door behind him.

Audrey was taken aback by his temper. "I won't marry a man that has a bad temper. I won't do it."

"I don't have a bad temper," Cass said lightly. "If you choose not to marry him, let me know. You're quite attractive."

"Reverend Cass," Mattie spoke pointedly through her teeth, "please come back tomorrow at five. We'll have a wedding then."

"Fine. I'll be back tomorrow." He chuckled before leaving.

An uneasy silence filled the room. Mattie's irritable sigh was plain to hear. "Audrey, you had a good opportunity to marry Alan. We can do it tomorrow, but you will marry him without any excuses. Are we agreed on that?"

Audrey hesitated. "Yes. But-"

"Good!" Mattie interrupted and stood from her rocking chair. "My son has waited his whole life to be married and finally met a woman we want to make part of this family. Don't betray his love and, in the process, ours."

Chapter 17

Bill Cooney was a quiet man that was hard to rile up, but when someone did get him riled, Bill was a fist-fighting bear of a man. He stood six foot two and was as broad-shouldered and strong as a bull. Bill got caught up in Dane's sister, Danetta's, flirtatious web and soon moved in with her. Bill was a simple man, not too bright, but as faithful, hardworking, and courteous as a man could be. He wasn't handsome by any means. He had black hair that fell to his mid-neck and a patchy black beard that was reminiscent of a map of an island chain in the south pacific. Bill's face was pockmarked by a severe case of smallpox in his youth, and his nose was slightly bent to the left from a lucky right fist years before when saloons and drinking were a way of life. He had since quit drinking and remained sober, not for religious reasons but to be able to keep a job. He worked for a farmer outside of Prairieville and had a good reputation as an able-handed and dependable employee. Danetta Dielschneider was his woman now, and they were engaged to marry when he returned to Prairieville. Danetta knew Dane would not be safe traveling alone and sent Bill with her only living brother to bring Tiffany back home.

Dane Dielschneider knew Bill would do whatever was asked because, quite simply, Bill would do anything to please Danetta rather than suffer her wrath.

Dane leaned against the support post of an awning across from Bella's Dance Hall, watching quietly. He scanned every inch of the construction, looking for a way to sneak through an upstairs window. It could be done, but not with all the people on Rose Street. He had been forbidden from ever going back inside, but if he played his cards right, there was a slight chance he could change the owner's mind. There was one thing he knew: a wad of cash money spoke a language of its own. He'd need more money than he had, though.

His expertise at pickpocketing and thieving had been greatly diminished by losing his primary hand. His left hand had to do all the work now, and he'd gotten better with it, but he wasn't quite as smooth or swift with his sleight of hand. The best idea he had was to sneak into the rooms of the dancers while they were busy dancing. He knew no one was upstairs, and the ladies probably kept a stash of money. The problem was getting up there unnoticed.

Dane spoke thoughtfully, "Bill, you can go back

in there, I can't. You're a big and strong man. I know how to get a lot of money for us to take home. A lot of money. But I need your help. It would be enough money for you to buy Danetta a real wedding ring, with a diamond, and a dress for her and the girls. They'd like that, right?"

"Yeah. They'd like that. Are you going to sell your horse?" Bill asked curiously.

Dane grinned with a slight scoff. "No. I want you to go into the dance hall and start a fight with someone at the bar. Make it a big fight where you hit two or three men and all their attention is on you. Destroy the place. I need that man to move away from the stairs. I'll meet you behind the building when you get kicked out."

"I don't want to fight anyone." Bill said through a yawn.

"Danetta will be mad at you if I get arrested. I'm the only brother she has left. Just think of how happy Danetta will be when you give her a wedding ring and have new dresses for her and the girls. She will be so excited, and you'd make her happy. Or we can go back with your hands empty and tell her what could have been, but you were too scared to help me. All you have to do is start a fight and keep fighting. I'll do the rest." He turned his head so his dark eyes could stare evenly at Bill.

Bill thought for a moment. "I might get in trouble. She wouldn't like that either."

"I'll have enough money to bail you out of jail in the worst case. But they'll just throw you out like they did me. It's no big deal, start a fight, keep fighting, and I promise we'll leave here richer than we've been in a long time. If you don't want to do it for me, then do it for Danetta. Think of how happy she'll be."

Bill nodded. "All right. I'll do it."

"Bill, I need you to cause a scene. A big scene so no one will notice me."

***

Bill entered the dance hall and maneuvered to the bar. He pushed his way to the front and ordered a drink. He debated about drinking it, because whiskey used to put him in a fighting mood, and he had given it up for a reason. He was supposed to cause a scene that would hold everyone's attention. He held the shot glass of whiskey in his hand and scanned the men around him for the right man to hit. He settled his sights on a much smaller man, who weighed about a hundred and forty pounds, talking with one of the dancers.

He approached the young man and tapped him on the shoulder. "This is for you." he said, handing the shot glass to the young man.

"Thank you." He drank the shot glass in a single gulp. "I owe you one."

"No," Bill spoke over the music that played. "That was an apology."

"For?" the man questioned over the music.

"This." Bill grabbed him by the collar, jerked him forward, and picked the young man up over his head. The young man yelled in terror as Bill carried him three steps towards the bar and threw the man over the bar and into the wood shelves that held various bottles of alcohol and clean glasses. The shelves collapsed, creating a loud crash as the many bottles and glasses fell to the floor behind the bar along with the young man. Bill turned and hit the closest man to him in the face, followed by another. Like a madman going wild, Bill swung, kicked, elbowed, and flipped men off his back that tried to grab him. One man jumped on his back, and Bill rammed the man's back into the bar to release a choke-hold, while three other men tried to wrestle Bill to the ground. Bill sank his teeth into an arm, causing a man to scream, and quickly release his grip on Bill.

Like a mad bear surrounded by hunting dogs, Bill swung and gave it his all to grab, throw, hit, kick and headbutt anyone that dared to challenge him. Everyone in the ballroom was drawn to the fight as more men moved in to help secure the beast of a man. Numerous men outnumbered Bill, and still, he caught a quick glimpse of Dane successfully scurrying up the stairs like a cockroach hurrying across the floor. His job was accomplished, and he could walk away, but the customers' fury for ruining the bar and starting a fight wouldn't be so easily forgiven. The fight was started to create a distraction, but now he was fighting to protect himself. A chair slammed across Bill's back which jarred him forward with the pain. Angered, he turned around wild-eyed and stepped quickly towards the man with a chair.

The sound of a gunshot pierced his ears and he froze. His eyes widened, and he gulped nervously as a streak of fear streamed up his spine when he saw Bella's husband, Dave, pointing a revolver at him.

Dave was furious. "You better stop right now! Sit down in front of the bar until the sheriff or marshal gets here. Gaylon, go find a lawman!"

Bill slowly raised his hands. Breathing hard from his exertion, he asked, "Do you want me to leave? I'll go and won't come back."

"You sit down!"

Bill tried to sit slowly but fell onto his backside and leaned against the bar. Then, he noticed that he had a fat lip that was bleeding slightly. It was worth buying Danetta a new wedding ring and pretty dresses for her and the girls. They'd like that.

***

Upstairs, Dane found a hallway with rooms on both sides that were both; empty and unlocked. He stayed away from the rooms facing Rose Street because of the windows, but the ones built over the ballroom and those with windows facing the alley and Chinatown at the far and back sides of the building were fair game. Each room had treasures but way too many to carry. He wondered which room was Matt Bannister's fiancé's, but he didn't have time to search through everything in every room to find hers. He searched for money and jewelry that could be quickly sold. Little closed boxes on the desks, bedside desk drawers, and cigar boxes in the closets proved to be a common place the girls stored their money. He took all the paper money that he could find, ones, fives, tens, and twenties, along with coins that continued to fill his pockets as he went room to room.

One room in particular that faced Chinatown proved to be the actual treasure, as the lady kept hundreds of dollars in a wooden cigar box under the bed. It was a small gold-colored padlock that caught his attention. He used his knife to pry the tiny screws holding the latch out of the wood and opened it. He nearly shouted when he saw the box full of paper money. Like a cat with rabies attacking a chihuahua, his hand hurriedly grabbed a handful of money, shoved it into his pant pockets, and quickly repeated until the box was bare. Having searched the rooms until he was in the last room, he knew the fight at the bar had long since ended. He had heard a gunshot, and he hoped Bill wasn't dead, but with the money he had found, Bill's death was still worth it. Tiffany couldn't resist him now that he had money and some expensive jewelry for her.

With the fight over, the guard protecting the staircase would be back at the entry, making it impossible to descend from upstairs unseen. Dane had to think quickly to escape the building unnoticed, as he had not considered it earlier. He ripped the two bedsheets off the bed and carefully tied them together using his one good hand, teeth, and right arm. The two sheet lengths were not long enough, so he pulled the sheets from two other rooms and tied the six sheets together. Dane struggled to secure one end of the sheets to the bed frame, but once tied, he pulled the bed across the room and tossed the sheets out the window facing Chinatown. Slowly, carefully, he slid down outside the building to the ground.

He counted out forty dollars to put in a separate pocket and went to the front of the dance hall. He opened the front door and was stopped immediately by Gaylon Dirks, who stood guard.

Dane explained with a friendly grin as soon as the guard stopped him, "I know. I know. Trying to kiss that dancer was a misunderstanding. I didn't know it was against the rules. I'm new here. Can I speak with the man that kicked me out, please? Just for a moment."

Gaylon Dirks refused to let Dane wait inside while he called for Bella or Dave to speak with him. The commotion at the bar earlier had almost brought the night to an end, but despite the broken bottles of alcohol, there were plenty of bottles that remained intact and enough unbroken glasses to make drinks with. Bella and Dave helped the bartender clean up the mess of broken glass and kept the drinks flowing, refusing to close down the bar, which was a primary source of their income.

Bella and Dave stepped outside of the dance hall to speak with Dane. "I told you not to come back here." Dave said irritably. He was already in a bad mood.

"I know. Listen, it was my first time being here.

I saw the marshal dance with a woman and kiss her at the end of the dance. I thought it was part of the price of a ticket, but I learned it isn't. Please, I have money." He flashed the wad of dollar bills. "It won't happen again. I just assumed every dance came with a kiss." he explained innocently. "Maybe you could reconsider and give me another chance? I won't try to kiss anyone again."

Dave wasn't convinced. "I don't like you. Matt told us who you are. We don't need any trouble. Wasn't it your friend who destroyed our bar a while ago?"

"Bill?" Dane asked curiously. "I don't know. I haven't seen him since we argued earlier this afternoon, about one o'clock. He was in one of his bad moods. Did he do something?"

"He started a fight and ruined our bar."

Dane exhaled sharply with an empathetic shake of his head. "I didn't know. Where is he now?"

"The sheriff's deputies took him to jail. He settled right down when he saw my gun."

"As he should. I hope no one was hurt."

Bella looked at the money in Dane's hand. "Since your friend cost us a lot of money, how about you pay for the damages? Then you can come in. But if you harass any of our girls, including Christine, you'll wish you hadn't."

"He's going to pay me back." Dane said irritably as he handed the forty dollars to Bella. "But I'd be happy to." he said with a strange grin. There was a lot more money in his pockets, hundreds if not more than a thousand dollars. "Do you have a dancer named Tiffany by chance?"

"No. And I mean it. You'll join your friend in jail if there's any trouble."

"After our fight today, Bill is no friend of mine. He can rot there for all I care."

Chapter 18

"Matt, do you want a drink?" Lee Bannister asked. He stood at his private bar in his home, making drinks for whoever wanted one.

"No, thanks. So, Uncle Joel, Uncle Charlie, and Aunt Mary went over to Jim and Karen's house. Are they staying there, at the Monarch Hotel, or here while they're in town?"

Annie Lenning rolled her head to a tilted position with a perplexed expression. "The hotel. Derr-err, you sound like an eastern city kid coming to the ranch and asking if the brown heaps in the horse stalls are dung. Of course, they're staying in the hotel. It's more luxurious than home."

Matt grinned. "I suppose so."

"Definitely. Use your wits, brother," Annie said. "Aunt Eleanor will be here tomorrow. She's coming with Uncle Luther and Billy Jo. On the Fasana side, I don't know who is coming to town. I hope Cousin Wanda comes from Montana. I'd like to talk to her again."

"I haven't seen Aunt Eleanor in years." Matt said of his aunt that lived in Astoria.

"Oh, I'd say at least fifteen, right?" Annie quipped. Matt had run away from Willow Falls and the family when he was a teenager and didn't come home until fifteen years later.

"At the very least," Matt agreed. "I haven't seen her since she left here to go to college. I was what? Ten, maybe?"

"Somewhere around there." Adam Bannister agreed. He took a glass from Lee's hand. He yawned as he continued, "Do you know the plan for tomorrow, Lee? There is going to be a lot of people at Hannie's funeral."

Lee delivered the drinks and sat beside his wife, Regina, on a red davenport with room for two. "The Slater Mining Company rented the Branson Community Hall for Jim and Karen to have the memorial reception. After the funeral, we'll meet there for food and drinks. Tomorrow night, I closed the restaurant and lounge to have a private area for just family. Since most of the family from out of town will be staying there anyway, I figured we'd meet there. The kitchen staff will provide food and drinks for us."

"Who else is coming that you know of?" Annie asked.

Lee put an arm around Regina's shoulders affectionately. "I'm not sure. I told Roger and Pamela if anyone shows up for the funeral related to Hannie, give them a room. I hope we have enough rooms because I don't know Jim Longo's family or how many of them are coming." Lee shrugged. "I don't know. We'll make room somewhere."

Annie questioned, "I heard you have a freak from the freakshow at the hotel healing from something? The hairy man or something?"

Lee nodded. "Yeah. He won't bother us. He's still pretty sore from having surgery."

Annie nodded towards Tiffany Foster, who sat on the floor flipping through the pages of a book about African animals she found in Lee's library. "Tiffany says she likes hairy boys and wants to meet him."

"No, I didn't!" her head popped up quickly, causing Annie to laugh.

Matt spoke, "His name is David, and he is a great young man. He is covered with long hair and looks different, but trust me, he is no different than you or me. David has a great sense of humor, which has helped him deal with witnessing Hannie and another man being murdered. There are two ways of dealing with something as horrific as what he saw; one is holding it within, and the other is talking about it. We've talked about what happened quite a bit. He and William have become good friends, which also helps William."

Regina laughed. "It's so cute. David will tease Lee about stealing me away from him, but he's very shy when I'm there."

Annie stated, "I hope I can meet him. The only freak I've ever known is Matt." She turned her head towards Matt. "He's pretty freaky."

Mellissa Bannister sat beside her husband, Albert. She held a glass of milk in her hand. "I have not met David yet. I have been meaning to, but I wanted to wait until he was a little more healed. Do you think he'd mind if we met him tomorrow night?" she asked Lee.

"You could charge admission." Annie suggested with a chuckle.

"That's horrible." Mellissa said, not at all humored.

Albert thought it was funny and received an elbow from Mellissa for laughing.

Tiffany wiped her forehead and stood with the book. "I'm going to take a walk up the hill. It's so hot in here."

"Okay, don't be gone long." Annie stated.

"No," Matt said quickly. "Tiffany, I need you to sit down for a minute."

"Why?" she asked.

"I didn't want to tell you this right now, but Dane Dielschneider showed up in town. He's looking for you."

"What?" Tiffany asked with a horrified expression. Her chest began to rise and fall heavily as a wave of anxiety filled her.

Annie asked Matt with concern, "What does he want?"

Matt was hesitant to answer. "Well, he thinks since his sister, Danetta, told him he could marry Tiffany when she turned fifteen, that he can. He wants to take her back to Prairieville and marry her."

Tiffany's mouth dropped open as the fear she suddenly felt was revealed in her expression.

"Well, that's not going to happen." Albert said simply.

"Hell no, it's not going to happen!" Annie snapped.

"Who is he?" Regina asked.

Matt told Tiffany, "I'd prefer you not go outside alone. You don't have anything to worry about, but I did want you to know."

"Matt, he's..." Tiffany paused nervously. "He's sneaky. Dane's like a spider; you never know he's there until he just is."

"I don't want you worrying about him. If you are with family, you are perfectly safe. He is no threat to you. Do you know his friend named Bill?"

She shook her head thoughtfully. "I don't know. There were a few men named Bill."

"He's big, black hair and beard. His face is kind of blemished with pockmarks. Does he sound familiar?"

She nodded. "Bill Cooney. He was friends with my father. I don't know why he'd be with Dane. They weren't friends, I don't think."

"They appear to be now. Dane said Bill was Danetta's new fiancé."

She rolled her eyes in response.

Annie spoke to Tiffany, "Maybe you should stay indoors tonight."

"I will. Can I go sit on the porch and cool down?"

"Of course. Stay close." Annie said as Tiffany stepped outside.

"Is she not feeling well?" Regina asked.

"Oh, it's just *that* time. She is fine, though."

"Where are Steven and Nora?" Matt asked of his younger brother Steven and his wife, who had followed Adam and Annie to Branson in their wagon.

"Visiting a friend of Nora's. You know Steven, Nora rules the roost," Lee answered. "He's still henpecked."

***

Steven Bannister took a deep breath and exhaled slowly to avoid letting his wife hear his heavy sigh of boredom. He and Nora had walked across Branson to the home of Greg and Sue Hess. Greg was an accountant that worked for the Seven Timber Harvester Company and made a good living for his family. They had a nice home four blocks downhill from Lee's on the upper social side of Branson. Sue, his attractive wife of seven years, had never conceived, so their large home was empty aside from them.

"You're more than welcome to stay here. There's no need for you two to stay with family or at a hotel. I know you can't afford to and we have spare bedrooms. Stay here with me, Nora." Sue invited. Sue was a childhood friend of Nora's in Branson before her parents bought the Mercantile in Willow Falls and moved her there.

"We'd love to," Nora answered. "Wouldn't we, Steven?"

"No," he answered with a shake of his head. "You

can stay here if you want, but we already have a room at the hotel. Our things are there and..." he explained with a touch of sarcasm to Sue, "we can afford it because it isn't costing us a thing."

Nora rolled her head and then her eyes with agitation. "We're always with your family. You can see your family tomorrow at the funeral. You don't need to spend every night with them too."

Greg looked at the clock on the wall and asked, "Steven, how about we wander over to the Monarch Lounge, have a drink, get to know each other, and let these two beautiful ladies visit?"

Steven had not met Greg until that night, and so far, they had said very little to each other. It wasn't that Steven was shy, he certainly was not, but it appeared Greg did not have much interest in talking to a poor blacksmith from Willow Falls.

"I'm going that way anyway. Why not?" Steven told his bride, "If you want to spend the night here, I will bring your clothes and things over for you, but I'm going to stay at the hotel."

"Why? Don't you want to stay with me?" Nora asked.

"I do, but we already have a hotel room."

Greg laughed. "Come on, Steven. Let the girls talk. Let's go get to know each other."

Nora waved a hand at him disappointedly. "Fine. Bring my things over here. I want to stay and visit Sue."

Once outside, Greg grinned. "You seemed bored to death in there."

"Pretty much." Steven agreed.

"Have you ever been to Bella's Dance Hall?"

Steven answered, "Not when it was open. I went there with Matt to talk to Christine once. She helped me get a dress for Nora."

"Christine, now there is a beauty. Your brother's the envy of the town with her. You're going tonight, and you don't mention it to Sue. I'll buy you a drink or two if we have a deal?"

"Don't tell Nora is a better request. She'd rip my hide up and down both sides if I danced with another lady. Just knowing I went there would leave her in a frenzy."

Greg laughed. "Then you're just my kind of guy. Bella's it is. You're going to have fun tonight, Steven. I guarantee it."

Chapter 19

Matt Bannister walked into Bella's Dance Hall as it neared closing time, which was midnight on a weeknight. The disadvantage of having a fiancé that worked and lived at the dance hall was if he didn't get to visit with Christine before the dance hall opened, then the only time she had to visit was late at night. Matt had spent the evening visiting with family, but a day without seeing Christine was a day that didn't seem complete.

Gaylon Dirks, the security guard, met Matt with a handshake. "We sure could have used you earlier. That big brute friend of Dane's darn near ruined our bar. He threw Mike DeBeers over the bar, into the shelves, and knocked everything down. He started hitting people and causing quite a commotion. Dave finally stopped him by shooting into the floor. Truet's going to have to fix that for us. That brute was like a raging bull with rabies or something. It was pure chaos for a bit."

"Really? He seemed like an easy-going man to me."

"Not tonight. Dane said they had argued earlier today because Bill, that's the big fella's name, was in one of his moods. I don't know what that means, but that's what Dane said."

"What was Dane doing here?" Matt asked sharply.

"He's still here. He explained what happened last night and apologized. Bella let him back in." Gaylon laughed. "Your brother is having a good time. Your brother's been kicking his heels up with Sherry, and dang, he even has Bella buying him drinks. He's got her laughing harder than I've ever heard before."

"Where?" Matt asked. It wasn't the laughter of those watching or even Steven's voice that caught Matt's attention. It was the heavy stomping of Steven's boots on the dance floor with such force that it was heard over the band playing. Steven was on the ballroom floor dancing with Sherry Stewart, but while the other dancers, including Christine, danced a waltz in a uniform circle, Steven and Sherry were inside the circle, dancing alone. Steven was slightly stooped over and stomped heavily with his boots, one foot then the other, while his arms swung back and forth in front of him like an ape.

Steven, clearly intoxicated, stared at Sherry with his mouth ajar and his lips puckered while yelling over the band, "Ooof, oof. Come on, Sherry, be a monkey with me! Oof oof... Scream it! OOF! OOF!

Be a mon-kaay! Be a mon-kaay!"

Sherry laughed hysterically while she halfheartedly mimicked his dance moves.

"What's he doing?" Matt asked with a perplexed expression.

Gaylon chuckled. "He's dancing like a mon-kaay. He sure is having fun."

Matt could see Christine dancing in the circle with a gentleman. She'd glance at Steven with a concerned expression while others seemed humored. The gentleman she danced with wouldn't recognize her concern, but Matt did.

A humored smile lifted Matt's lips as he watched his brother. "Gaylon, is he drunk?"

"Oh, yeah. Between Greg Hess, Dane, and Bella buying him drinks and dance tickets, your brother is not hurting. I don't think anything could hurt him right now."

Matt's grin left him quickly. "Why is Dane buying him drinks?"

"They've become pals. Your brother arrived with Greg Hess, but Greg only dances with Jenny Lemay."

"I don't know who Greg is. Do you know everyone and everything that happens here?"

Gaylon shook his head. "No. I know the regular customers, but I've had my eye on Dane all night. I think he overheard Steven tell Bella he was your brother, Dane's been buying him dance tickets and drinks since. Bella took a shine to your brother right off."

"And Sherry?"

"She caught his eye, and he hasn't shown any interest in anyone else. You know Sherry, married or not, she's got her eyes on him." Gaylon said, watching the ballroom.

Across the room, Dane Dielschneider sat at a table with a wide grin while staring at Matt. He waved his left hand to get Matt's attention. Matt ignored him, stepped inside the ballroom, and stood against the wall near the bar. He watched his brother begin to jump up and down like a monkey while shouting out monkey sounds. Matt chuckled as Sherry tried to copy him in her elegant dress. They both looked ridiculous.

Bella approached Matt and laid a hand on his chest as she laughed. "Matt, you have to bring Steven back! I love him! I haven't laughed so hard in years. I think Sherry loves him, too."

"She can keep looking for someone else. He's married." Matt said with a fading grin. "Why did you let Dane back in here?"

"Lighten up, Matt. He's fine." Bella said with a pat on his chest. Her humor faded as she explained, "It's your fault. Dane assumed he could kiss the dancers because he saw you and Christine kiss, which is why I made the rule against showing affection on the dance floor to begin with. It would never have happened if you and Christine had obeyed the rules. So, I decided to give him another chance."

Matt waved a thumb towards the entrance, where the rules and expectations were clearly visible on two large pieces of wood. "Gaylon makes sure everyone reads the rules before they come in here. He tried to kiss Christine intentionally to get to me."

"Not everybody can read, Matt." Bella reasoned. "He agreed to pay for the damages his friend caused, which saves me money. I agreed to give him a chance, and he's been just fine. I need to tell you, married or not, that I invited Steven to stay after closing."

Matt spoke frankly, "No. I'll be taking him back to his wife. We have a funeral to attend tomorrow, and Steven doesn't drink. I'm surprised he's here at all. Tomorrow he won't be so funny when he's hungover, and his wife is furious with him too."

Bella snickered. "Well, he's enjoying himself tonight, so you just let him be."

Dane was suddenly at Matt's side, staring at him from a foot away. "Hi, Matt. I met your brother." His friendly grin remained, but it felt uncanny, like a permanent fixture that didn't belong, like a drape guarding a much darker secret that was unspoken and unknown to anyone except him.

Matt's left hand gently pushed Dane back a foot or so. "Did you? You don't need to be so close to me." There was no friendliness in his words.

Dane's grin widened just a touch. "He's your brother."

Matt's countenance hardened. "Stay away from him, Dane. I'm warning you."

Bella laughed uneasily. "All he is saying is he met your brother, Matt. Dane's a good customer. Leave him be. Here comes Steven." she laughed loudly.

Matt watched Steven running towards him like

a monkey scratching its ribs while swaying his upper body from side to side and making monkey sounds. The joy on Sherry's face could be seen from a greater distance than a shooting star. Steven suddenly stood up straight and put a mock-serious expression on his face. He put a burly arm over Sherry's shoulders and spoke sternly, "Attention! Matthew Bannister is in the room. No more horse-play or buffoonery! Sherry, straighten up and lose that smirk! This is not a place for fun. Stop that laughter, Bella. Matt is here!"

"Steven, what are you doing here?" Matt asked.

"I told you!" he exclaimed with a stern glare at Sherry. She laughed. Steven continued, "Someone get my brother a drink or a dozen shots of whiskey so he can get caught up with me. We're on different plains." He laughed and put his other burly arm around Dane's shoulders. "Good for you to join us, Matt. Have you met my buddy, Dane? I was going to dance with Christine, but I was sidetracked like a sucker fish to a fat juicy worm with blonde hair. Have you met Sherry? We decided if we had a child, we couldn't name it an S name, or we'd sound drunk no matter how sober we were with all the SSSS sounds we'd be saying. It would sound like we were always slurring. Ssssteven and Ssssherry sssittin besidesss a creek kissssen up a ssstorm. Oh, hell, I'm okay with that because I'd just drool and let the spit run down my mouth until people figured I had an excuse." He let a mouthful of spit run down his chin and drip on the floor. "But Ssssherry wouldn't be ssso pretty doing that, sssso they'd think sshe was just a drunk. Bartender," he shouted, "get my brother a drink. You have to drink with me, Matt!"

"I think you drank enough for both of us. Where is Nora?" Matt grimaced. "A better question is, where is your wedding ring?"

Steven looked at his ring finger. The ring's impression was there, but his silver wedding band was gone. He grinned. "I ain't exactly sure. Did I take it off?" he asked Sherry. His head weaved from side to side as he focused on her.

She nodded affirmingly. "When you were trying to persuade me to marry you. It's on the table."

Matt spoke. "Sherry, will you go get that ring for me? I don't want him forgetting it."

Dane volunteered, "I have it. I didn't want it getting knocked on the floor and him losing it." He reached into his shirt pocket and pulled out the silver ring. He handed it to Matt.

"Nora?" Steven questioned with a scowl. "I'm not branded, and rings can be removed. Have you met Sherry? Well, she's the one I'm with tonight. Nora's staying at her friend's house, and I have the room at the hotel to myself. I should have married Sherry. When we have a kid, he won't be named Matt, either! He will be named... Ssspike." A pool of saved spit ran freely down his chin. He continued with slurred words. "I'd kisss Sssherry, but *ssshe*," he pointed at Bella with his right arm, which jerked Dane forward. "won't let me!"

Matt was not humored. "I think it's time to go, Steven. I'll take you home."

"Home?" he shouted. "I live in Willow Falls.

That's too late to go tonight. I'll stay here."

"I'd take you home." Sherry said flirtatiously.

Steven shouted, "Well, let's go! I got a hotel room, and my wife ain't there. We'll get started on creating Ssspike or Ssss Ss Ssuzie."

"Okay," Sherry said. "I'm off work in fifteen minutes."

"Steven, let's go," Matt said firmly. "You're going to hate yourself in the morning." He made eye contact with Christine, who was standing nearby. "I came by to see you, but I have to take him home before he gets himself in trouble."

Christine nodded understandably. "I'll see you tomorrow."

Steven laughed. "Wait. We have to wait for Sssherry. Ssssherry's coming with me. Aren't you, doll? She's my mon-kaay!"

"I can't leave for another fifteen minutes." Her flirtatious eyes and seductive smile encouraged him.

"We'll wait!"

"No, we're not waiting." Matt said abruptly.

Steven laughed. "I'm in room number eight at the Monarch Hotel. Just come on in. I'll leave the door unlocked."

Matt was quickly getting irritated. "Sherry, I'm taking him to my house. Don't bother. Christine, I'll pick you up before the funeral. Steven, let's go! Now!"

Dane, hearing there would be an empty room at the Monarch Hotel, followed Matt as he escorted Steven across town. He watched Steven stumble and pause to put a finger down his throat to vomit up the remaining alcohol in his stomach a few blocks from the dance hall. Once Matt led Steven across Main Street and showed no interest in going to the Monarch Hotel, Dane darted to the hotel and watched through the door for the young man at the front counter to leave the front desk. It took thirty minutes, but the young man finally closed his book and put a small sign on the desk before yawning and walking towards the back of the hotel.

Dane opened the two sets of doors to enter quietly. The sign said for anyone needing help to ring the bell. Dane went behind the curved counter and opened the guest book to scan the names of the registered guests. Steven and Nora were written in for room eight. Annie Lenning signed into room number ten. Dane had learned a lot talking with Steven the more he drank. For instance, Dane knew Tiffany was staying in the Monarch Hotel, sharing a room with Annie. He knew the funeral was the following afternoon at two. A reception at the community hall would follow it then there was a family reunion tomorrow night in the hotel. There would be plenty of opportunities to find Tiffany alone if he was in the hotel.

Dane wrote the name Dick and Lyla Jones in one of the empty room spaces, number fourteen, and scheduled the couple for two nights before closing the book. The cabinet where the room keys were kept was locked, but a quick shimmy with a thin jackknife blade specifically ground down for such locks opened it without any scarring of the wood around the lock. He took a key for room fourteen and thought about taking the spare key for room number ten, where Tiffany was staying, but it would leave an empty hook among other keys and raise questions. He could always come to get it if needed. He closed the cabinet door and quickly ran up the stairs to find room fourteen before he was discovered.

Chapter 20

Audrey tossed and turned in her bed. It wasn't as comfortable as it seemed the night before, and she couldn't get her pillow in a comfortable position. The bedroom was too hot, and there was no window to open for fresh air. She had no idea what time it was as the room was pitch black except for a faint light under the door and a slight glow of the wick of her lantern.

Thirsty and frustrated by a lack of sleep, she turned her lantern up just enough to see and grabbed her robe to cover her night dress. She carried her lantern into the kitchen to get a drink from the bucket of water on the counter. She was startled to see Morton sitting alone in the family room in a lantern's light, lost in his thoughts. He turned his head to see who had entered the kitchen.

"Can't sleep?" he asked softly.

"No. That room is too hot and stuffy. I came out here for a drink." She used the ladle hooked on the bucket of water to dip in and fill a coffee cup with water. "You can't sleep either?"

He shook his head slightly. "No. You can have a seat if you want." he invited, hoping she would. Though he would never say so, she was the reason he couldn't sleep. He had hoped she might come out of her room and join him, but now that she had, he didn't know what to say.

"I might as well. It's much cooler out here." She sat on the davenport with her second cup of water. "How come you're not sleeping?"

He shrugged. "Same as you, I suppose. This house retains the heat in the summer, but the opposite is true in winter. It's always cold. Where are you from, Audrey?"

"California most recently."

"Do you have family?"

"Yes. My folks and sisters live in Colorado. We don't have a big family like yours, though."

He nodded slowly while biting his bottom lip. "You're probably lucky you don't. How do you like this family?"

She leaned forward with a grin and covered her face with her hands, hesitating to answer. Her eyes raised to meet his. "I like everyone fine. It isn't exactly like Alan explained his family in his letters, but that's just my first impression. I'm sure once I get to know everyone, I'll see them the way he does."

"What was your first impression of me?" Morton asked.

She snickered quietly. "You looked mean."

"Mean? Like how mean?"

"Forgive me for saying so, but you looked like," she hesitated. "Well, if I saw you on the street, I'd think you might be a killer."

Morton's eyes lowered as a slightly hurt frown overtook his features. "I suppose that looks mean, alright. And now?"

Slowly a warm half smile formed. "I think as awkward as it is to suddenly be in this family, you, Daisy, and Travis are the only ones that make me feel somewhat comfortable."

"I suppose that's a good thing?"

"A very good thing. It's not easy to begin your life over in a house that belongs to strangers. It would be different if Alan had his own house, but he sleeps in the barn." Her forehead wrinkled with distaste as she finished.

"I can understand that. Alan doesn't make you feel comfortable?" Morton questioned.

She took a deep breath before answering. "Can I trust you to keep it between us, or will you tell everyone what I say?"

Morton smiled daringly. "You'll have to answer that question for yourself. Do you think you can trust me?"

For an uncomfortable moment, she stared at him thoughtfully. "I'll trust you. I don't know why, but I will."

He nodded once. "Good choice. I won't tell anyone what you say. Let's talk freely. What do you think about Alan? Is he all you thought he would be?"

She wrinkled her nose unintentionally. "No. He's very odd. He seemed confident, self-assured, and talkative in his letters and never spoke of..." She paused uncomfortably. "You know, um... well, you know, fornication. Now that I'm here, sharing a bed is all that he seems to think about. He never mentions the Lord, prays, or talks about the Bible. I don't understand how a Christian can love the Lord and not shine with his love or want to talk about Jesus. I'm not suggesting he needs to sound like a reverend, but he hasn't said a word about the Lord and tries to change the subject when I do. Is he even a Christian?" she asked.

Morton's lips turned downward. "I think you should ask him that."

"I will. He scared me today when he got angry. Short tempers are unpredictable, and I don't like that. Does he have a short temper, Morton? I'd like to know before I agree to marry him."

"You've already agreed to marry him."

"Yes, but... I can change my mind and leave before I do."

He shifted in his chair. "Are you changing your mind?" he asked with interest.

"No, but I don't want to make another mistake. I choose to believe today was nothing more than a bad day for him and a rare occurrence. That's what your mother told me. I know I didn't make a mistake coming here. I firmly believe that the Lord led me here for a reason, and that is to marry Alan. I trust the Lord and his providence even when it seems... weird." she added after a moment of searching for the right word.

"Hmm." Morton grunted. "How did you like the Reverend Cass today?" His sarcasm wasn't hidden.

She grimaced. "I know no two reverends are cut out of the same cloth. But yours seems a bit rougher than any others I have known. He didn't appear to be very educated about the Bible. I suppose in towns like this, you aren't going to get to many highly trained Bible scholars, but I thought your reverend might know the difference between Baptist and Catholic beliefs. It seems strange to me that he couldn't answer any of my questions."

"It just seemed strange?" Morton thought it was a ridiculous idea to have Cass Travers pretend to be a reverend. He would have bet his last dollar on Audrey seeing through the deception and leaving town. He was surprised she hadn't.

"Hmm mm." She took a drink of water. "What about you, Morton? You told me you don't pray. Does that mean you are not a believer?"

"A believer in what? Marriage?"

She lowered her brow with a quick chuckle. "No. Do you believe Jesus died on the cross for our sins so we can be with him in heaven?"

"I'm afraid I don't know too much about that."

She wrinkled her nose. "Maybe you've heard about ancient people sacrificing lambs and animals on the altar to God in the Old Testament? They did that to cover their sins and be right with God. But it didn't forgive their sins."

"What is your definition of sin?" Morton asked. "Because mine might differ."

"It's not my definition that matters or yours. What matters is what the Bible says because God is the creator of this world, the creator of us, and he makes the rules. We don't have to like his rules, and you're free to break them, but that's where sin comes in. Doesn't it? Our will over his. The Bible defines sin in 1 John pretty simply; *sin is the transgression of the law.* What law, you might wonder? The Old Testament law found in the first five books of the Bible. To simplify, the book of Romans says, *No sinner is in the divine image. All have sinned, and to have the divine likeness restored, need to have their sins blotted out. Until this is done, they come short of the glory of God.* Sacrificing the animals did not blot out the sins, but it covered them."

"You don't sacrifice animals, do you?"

"No." she laughed lightly. "Let me explain it like this. You can say those people were buying their groceries on credit to be paid at the end of the month in full. There are over three hundred prophecies in the Old Testament foretelling of a future Savior, the Messiah, who would become the sacrificial lamb for all mankind, to forgive those sins once and for all. To wipe them away, past, present, and future sins of all who humbly ask. Only one person could fulfill every one of those prophecies to prove to us who he is. He is the Son of God or God in a human body. God humbled himself to become a man and live among us. His purpose wasn't to get rich, marry, or be a political leader; Jesus was born to live a life without sin and die for our sins. He was crucified on a cross, God poured our sins upon that man, and he paid that grocery bill for us once and for all with his blood. The ultimate sacrifice; the blood of God's perfect lamb. Jesus is the lamb that bore our sins upon the cross and paid the debt, so we don't have to pay the consequences of our sins, which is death. Spiritual death, hell.

"We all have the debt of sin, but Jesus lived and died for one reason: to pay that bill for us, but he needs our permission to do it. In other words, I can go down and pay your credit account at the store, but if you refuse to let me, then you end up paying it. It's the same thing with eternity. If we accept Jesus as our Lord and Savior, we are promised to be with him in heaven when we die. But even greater than that, we are promised to be able to approach him at any time in prayer. We no longer need a priest or a temple to be in God's presence because he lives within us and is always willing to lean his ear down to hear our quietest whisper of a prayer to him. He loves us that much. Jesus promises to work for our good in this life right now, so it isn't just about heaven. It's about living a life of constant assurance of hope, comfort, forgiveness, and a more fulfilled life today. Morton, if you've never accepted Jesus as your savior, you can do so right now."

Morton offered a hopeless attempt at a smile. "Miss Audrey, I doubt God has much interest in me."

She leaned forward. "Of course, he does. You're alive, aren't you? God loves all of us just the same, whether we believe in him or not. The difference is that those who do accept his grace become a child of his. It is very personal, Morton. You become a child of God, and he becomes your loving father. Remember, Jesus paid the tab for all those groceries, and that's a lot of food. It just so happens there is a large wedding banquet waiting in heaven, and you are invited. Everyone alive right now is invited to sit at God's table and celebrate Jesus' paying for us to be there. It doesn't matter what sins you have done, how big, awful, or mean they may have been. Jesus is faithful to forgive our sins if we sincerely seek to know him. Saying the prayer doesn't mean anything if it doesn't change your life. Jesus changes lives from the inside out. Jesus paid your tab for eternity. All you have to do is accept his gift of salvation and those past sins are paid for, blotted out, and nowhere to be found. A clean slate and worthy of the Glory of God."

"And if I don't?"

She spoke thoughtfully, "I can invite you to dinner, Morton, but if you refuse to come, that is your choice. You won't get the dessert, and that is what heaven is like. I don't like to scare people into accepting Jesus as their savior. I want people to know how good the Lord is and choose him for how comforting, loving, and secure life is with Jesus. But the fact is, if I died right now, say the roof collapsed and I was killed, I would go to heaven. Not because I'm that good or perfect, I'm certainly not, but Jesus is. In him alone am I saved. If you can't say that, then you need to really think about where your eternal destination is. It's a very sobering thought. You appear to be a very tough man, but I assure you there are no tough men in hell. They'll be just as terrified as everyone else. You're invited to sit at God's table as a child of God's and enjoy the greatest meal ever known to mankind. You, Morton Sperry, are invited; do not think for a moment that you're not. It is up to you to decide to accept or decline God's invitation to have a life with Him. You think it over, and if you're courageous enough, go get on your knees, pray to Jesus, and ask him to prove himself to you. Pour your heart out to him, Morton. I dare you."

He rubbed the goatee around his mouth thoughtfully. "Do my sinful ways show that much?"

"We all sin. The difference is Jesus forgives mine. He'll forgive yours too. No matter what you have done in the past, Jesus can make you a new man and change your life. Go pray." She stood from her seat and yawned.

Morton watched her admiringly. "You dare me, huh?"

"I do. I think you are a good person, Morton, but that isn't enough. God is inviting you to become his child. To be born again. I dare you to go somewhere quiet, get down on your knees, and pray to Jesus. Don't worry about what to say, just talk to him. Ask him to open your ears and your eyes to the truth. Goodnight."

"Goodnight." Morton said and watched her walk back towards her room. When he heard her bedroom door close, he said quietly, "If you knew anything about me. You'd know God wants nothing to do with me. I'm already condemned."

Chapter 21

"Steven, you might want to wake up. I'm sure Nora will be looking for you soon." Matt said while shaking his brother awake.

"Huh?" Steven grumbled as he opened his eyes into a squinted glare at Matt. "What?" He was sleeping on the davenport at Matt's house, covered with a light blanket.

"I said; I'm sure Nora will be searching for you pretty soon. It's after eight in the morning. There's some coffee made if you want some, and Truet was nice enough to pick up some muffins from the bakery for breakfast. Where is your wedding ring?"

"Huh?" Steven looked at his ring finger and grimaced. "Where's my ring?" He sat up quickly and paused as the night before returned to his memory. His eyes widened in alarm. He stood and searched his pockets. "Where is my ring? Oh, no! Did I lose it?"

"Did you take it off?" Matt asked.

"I don't… I must have. Ohh, no," he groaned. "Do

you think Bella's is open? I need to find it."

"No. They don't get out of bed until noon there. Why would you take your ring off to begin with?" Matt asked curiously.

"I don't know. I was drunk." His forehead began to bead with sweat, and his heart pumped quicker as his anxiety grew. He dreaded the idea of facing Nora and explaining why his wedding ring was missing. "What am I going to tell Nora?"

Matt sat in the smaller davenport facing Steven with a cup of coffee. "The truth might be good."

"It might be good, but I don't think saying I was drunk will explain my ring missing." Steven said with a raised voice. He sat heavily onto the davenport and buried his head in his hands. "I messed up bad. I never should've been there to begin with."

"Mon-kaay," Matt mimicked his brother's actions from the night before. "Do you remember that?"

Truet Davis laughed from the kitchen table, where he dipped his muffin into a cup of coffee. "It sounds like Steven unleashed the beast, huh?"

Matt answered, "Well, the mon-kaay at least. He was the highlight of the party."

Steven shook his head shamefully. "I remember. I did my monkey dance, didn't I?"

Truet laughed heartedly. "That stupid dance you did at Annie's?" he asked and then continued to laugh. "How'd Christine like that?"

Matt answered, "By her expression, I'd say she didn't. Sherry did, though."

Truet almost choked as he bit his muffin. "Don't say that too loud because Nora and some woman are crossing the yard." he said, watching the window. He left the table to answer the door.

A wave of terror ran up Steven's spine. "Oh, no!"

Matt tossed the wedding ring to Steven. "Your friend Dane was stealing it." He pointed warningly at his little brother. "Stay away from Dane and Sherry. You're lucky I stopped by there last night, or you may not have gotten home alive, and if you had, you would have lost your wife today. Sherry was ready to go to your hotel room, and Bella was going to let her." He kept his voice low but forceful as he said, "Do not go back there again, Steven!" he stood as Nora knocked on the door.

Truet opened the door. "Nora, are you looking for Steven?"

"I am." Her fierce eyes bypassed Truet to her husband as he sat on the davenport, looking like a guilty child about to be scolded. Nora entered the home and pointed at Matt, "How dare you take my husband to that pit of sin! Your fiancé may live there, but that doesn't mean you can invite my husband to dance with other women and get drunk! That is not acceptable, and I am very disappointed in you, Matt! I expected more out of you. Steven, get up, let's go!"

"Whoa, Nora," Matt said, raising defensive hands. "What are you talking about? I had nothing to do with him being there. I brought him home because he was too drunk to walk straight." Matt didn't need to tell Nora he intended to stop Steven from making a vast mistake by taking Sherry to the hotel.

"Then who did?" Nora's burning eyes tore into

Matt heatedly. "Greg said he took Steven to the Monarch Lounge for a drink and you took him to the dance hall. Steven didn't have any money, so who bought him drinks to the point of not being able to walk straight? Huh? You obviously!"

"I took him?" Matt questioned.

Nora's eyes filled with moisture as she vented heatedly, "Greg saw him fawning over some floozy and you encouraging him! I know you don't like me, Matt, but we are married and are a family! How dare you?" Her bottom lip trembled emotionally.

Matt hesitated as he watched her. "Nora, first of all, I like you very much. I don't know why you think I wouldn't. I think the story you heard is a little twisted, and I will have a personal conversation with your friend Greg," Matt said irritably. He explained, "I went there before the dance hall closed at midnight to talk to Christine, and Steven was already there. Very drunk, I might add. I don't know Greg or your friend standing behind you, but I know Greg was buying him drinks. Ask Steven; he was there. I wasn't. I would never take Steven anywhere that could compromise your marriage."

Steven rubbed his temples as an indication of getting a headache. He spoke softly and slowly, "Matt had nothing to do with it. Greg and I didn't go to the Monarch Lounge; we went to Bella's Dance Hall. Greg bought me drinks, as did a man I met. It started with one drink, and I don't know how many drinks I had, but I got drunk. I don't know what happened to Greg, but Matt brought me here. I wasn't fawning over anyone, by the way. Greg is a liar."

"Greg wouldn't lie to me." Sue Hess argued.

Steven rubbed his eyes. "Well, I don't know him, but if Greg said Matt took me there and not him. That's a lie. That's all I know. That, and I don't feel good." He yawned.

"Good!" Nora snapped. "You shouldn't feel good about going there. You're married, Steven, and that's no place for a married man to go. Don't you remember what happened to Kyle Lenning? That was just about a year ago, coincidently. He left your sister as a widow because he got tied up with those wicked dancers. I am so disappointed in you! Go take a bath at the hotel and get cleaned up. We have a busy day, and you have no excuse not to be a part of it, no matter how hungover you are. I'll be at Sue's house until noon. I want you there by ten at the latest, Steven!"

"I'm going to visit my family today. If you have plans with your friend, fine. But I'm visiting my family."

"Fine," she snapped. "Maybe Sue and I will find some men we can pay to dance with us."

Steven rolled his head back to look at her tiredly. He winked at her with a slight affectionate smile. "You could, but they won't know the monkey dance."

Her glare softened, and her eyebrows rose in a type of jest. "Oh, I can show them!"

The corners of Matt's lips lifted just a touch. "Nora, will you show me real me quick so I can teach Christine."

Nora rolled her eyes and reached for the door. "Thank you for getting Steven here safely. But...

goodbye."

Once Sue and Nora had left, Matt asked Steven, "Does Nora know it was Christine that Kyle was with that night?"

He nodded. "She doesn't really like Christine, Matt."

Truet chuckled. "I don't think she likes Matt either."

Matt nodded in agreement, "She's disappointed in me anyway."

"Well, you should not have taken your brother to that wicked place last night." Truet scolded him while finishing the last bite of a second muffin.

Matt said seriously, "Steven, if you ever see Dane again, don't be friendly with him. William and I killed his brothers and most of his friends in Prairieville and he's here to take Tiffany back with him. Stay away from him because he could be dangerous."

Steven squinted his eyes into a tight grimace. "I need some coffee. I'll never understand how you and William can talk about killing people like it's just another day on the farm." He stood to get a cup of coffee.

Matt frowned curiously. "Do you want me to say it with more sensitivity? Let me try; they were trying to kill us, so we killed them." he finished with a shrug of his shoulders. "The point is, if Dane wants revenge, you were the perfect piggy for him to poke with his knife in an alley last night. Unsuspecting, unprepared, and unknowing. If you see him around anyone in our family, you let me know immediately. Understood?"

Steven grabbed a muffin and poured a cup of coffee. "He's looking for Tiffany?"

"Yes. Dane thinks he has the right to marry her."

Steven hesitated. "I wish I had known that beforehand. I told him where we were all staying, and I don't even know what else he asked about."

Matt exhaled with a sigh. "I was afraid of that. If Tiffany is surrounded by family, she will be fine. Just beware of him."

There was an unexpected knock on the door. Truet answered it. "Christine? Isn't it a little early for you to be up? Come on in."

"Not really." She paused when she saw Steven. "Steven... ah..." She shook her head, deciding not to finish, and looked at Matt. "Someone robbed all the girls last night while we were dancing. They left all the rooms facing Rose Street, like mine, alone, but every other room was robbed of jewelry and money. Poor Jenny lost over seven hundred dollars. Whoever did it tied sheets together and went out Susan's window to the alley behind the building. Bella wanted to get a hold of you last night, but I knew you were taking care of Steven. Sheriff Tim Wright came over and took a report. No one knows who did it or saw a thing."

Matt grabbed her hand gently. "I'll walk you back over and talk with Gaylon and the others."

Chapter 22

Bill Cooney sat on the top bunk inside of the Branson Sheriff's Office jail. He swallowed nervously when Sheriff Tim Wright said, "Cooney, this is U.S. Marshal Matt Bannister. He wants to talk to you. My deputies and I will be waiting outside. Matt, he's all yours." Tim unlocked the cell door and opened it for Matt to enter.

Matt had gone to the dance hall and searched for any evidence, but all that he could learn was that the only time Gaylon left the front was when Bill started a fight at the bar. Matt had a pretty fair idea of who stole the money and jewelry and spoke to Tim Wright, who had also investigated the robbery and left with no evidence to solve the crime. Speaking with Tim, Matt learned Bill Cooney was quite a respectful, quiet, and unthreatening man with a gentle nature.

Matt could see the nervousness and guilt forming in Bill's eyes as he lowered his head like a puppy in trouble as Matt carried a chair into the cell to sit on. "I understand you were Dallen Foster's good friend."

Bill's head lifted with a perplexed expression. "He was my only true friend. How do you know that?"

"Tiffany told me."

"Tiffany? You saw Tiffany?"

Matt nodded. "Yes. I'm curious, Bill. If Dallen was your only friend, why are you helping Dane Dielschneider try to see Tiffany? You know he wants to take her back to Prairieville and force her to marry him."

"Danetta asked me to come with him to keep him safe. He's one-handed, you know."

"I know why too. Do you?"

"He got shot."

"Hmm, mm, by my deputy. I have no empathy for the weasel. Do you think Dallen would want his daughter marrying Dane?"

Bill's head lowered. "No, Sir."

"Then why are you here to help Dane find her? You must know Tiffany would not leave here willingly. Right?"

"No, Sir. Danetta said Tiffany did not want to come here with you. Now that she is fifteen, she is of marrying age and was supposed to marry Dane. That's what Tiffany told Dane, but Danetta just wants her to come home to be a family."

"You're courting Danetta?"

"Yes, Sir. We are engaged to marry."

"You do know she conspired with her brothers to have Dallen killed, right? Danetta was terribly abusive to Tiffany, and when Dallen found out, he wanted a divorce."

"No. She wouldn't do that."

"She did; I think deep down, you know it is true. I think you know me bringing Tiffany here was the best thing for her. I didn't force Tiffany to come with me. That's a lie. You're already being lied to by Danetta and manipulated to do things you probably would never do if Dallen were alive. Tiffany is part of my family now. She's not going back to Prairieville, ever."

Bill watched Matt thoughtfully. "She's happy?"

"I'll let you ask her that yourself when you are released. But first, tell me why you threw a young man over the bar and started a fight in Bella's Dance Hall. Before you answer, think about it. I may already know the truth, and if you lie, I won't help you when you face Judge Jacoby. This is where you earn my trust or not."

He took a deep breath and closed his eyes as he exhaled. "Dane asked me to." he answered shamefully. "I didn't mean to hurt that kid. I didn't want to hurt anyone."

"Why did Dane ask you to start a fight?"

"So he could go upstairs."

"Thank you. Those ladies work hard, and Dane stole a lot of money. He didn't care much about you being arrested. Did he?"

Bill shrugged halfheartedly. "I don't know. He said he'd bail me out if I was arrested."

"He hasn't inquired about doing so yet, has he? My guess is he won't. He'll let you sit in here, see the judge, and be sentenced to a month or two in jail and pay for that young man's stitches. In the meantime, he'll go back to Prairieville with a pocketful of money. Bill, there is no honor among thieves."

"Sir, I'm not a thief. I work for a living."

"You support Danetta and her girls, don't you?"

He nodded.

"May I speak frankly? I could search for Dane, but I have too many things going on, and I'm leaving town tomorrow. The sheriff and his deputies will be looking for him here shortly. I talked to Sheriff Wright, and he agreed that I could make you a deal. Listen carefully; if you agree to pay for the young man's medical bill and agree to bring Dane here to be arrested, the sheriff will drop the charges against you. And you'll be free to go. Dane won't come here by choice, so you'll have to bring him by force. You just tossed a man Dane's size over a bar and successfully fought five or six men. I'm sure you can handle Dane. Just watch out for his knife. Can you agree to that?"

"Danetta would be mad if I did that."

"The choice is yours. Dane has over a thousand dollars in his pocket and a bunch of jewelry. Do you think he's going to risk going to jail for you? I don't. I think he's going home and leaving you here."

"Then I'll stay here, but I can't go home without him. Danetta would be mad."

***

"Little one stub tied sheets together and repelled down the side of the building? With one hand? Now that's impressive. I'm impressed." William Fasana said quite sincerely. He and Matt walked up the stairs to the second floor of the Monarch Hotel to Annie's room. William continued, "I doubt he's playing cards with all that money. It's hard to play poker and count money with a stub." He chuckled. "I swear he is as dumb as a sheep. He'd be better off just standing on a corner with a finger up his nose wearing a sign stating, *Inbred. Please help*. He'd make a fortune because no one would question if he's faking it." He knocked on Annie's room door. William asked, "Do you think Dane was planning on knifing Steven last night to get even with us for our decimating his family?"

"It was my original inclination."

Annie opened the door and groaned. "What brings both of you here? I'm trying to enjoy some peace and quiet in the only luxury I get. So, are you leaving?"

"No," William said and walked into the hotel room, followed by Matt. "I came to take you and Tiffany down to meet my soul brother, the wild man, David. I don't know why Matt is here. He's saying something about a little red stain on my boot heel or something." He picked a chocolate candy from a dish and tossed it into his mouth. "I like these."

"I do too. Stay out of them." Annie said with a harsh scowl. Every hotel room was given a dozen chocolate candies in a small bowl. There were only a few left when William took one.

William grabbed another. "I'll have some more sent up here to you. You must come meet David."

Annie had almost been asleep when they

knocked on the door. "I wanted to take an hour-long nap. I never get to lounge like a lazy gambler or marshal. I work."

"Yeah, but David brushed his facial hair expecting to meet two beautiful ladies. One of which is around his age. And *that,*" he emphasized, "is making the mad dog nervous." William slowly grinned. "Come meet him."

"Fine. Tiffany, let's go meet David."

"Okay," Tiffany said from her hotel bedroom. She had been lying on the bed, reading a book. "I'm not going to scream when I see him, am I?" she asked William with concern.

"Probably. Most people do. No, you're not going to scream. Heck, he's groomed himself as every dog does before meeting a lady."

They went downstairs, and William spoke as he entered David's room near the reception desk, "I brought the women. Have you got the booze for the party?"

"No," David replied. "Pamela wouldn't let me leave the hotel to pick it up. She takes that whole healing thing seriously." he replied with quick wit.

William rolled his eyes with playful irritation. "Darn it, David, I can't count on you for nothing. This is my cousin Annie; she's Matt's baby sister. And the blonde is Tiffany; she's Annie's daughter." He leaned down and whispered loud enough to be heard, "She's your age and loves dogs." He clicked his tongue a couple of times approvingly. "Give her a bark."

David chuckled awkwardly. His white teeth

showed under the trimmed hair of his upper lip. Though he wasn't ashamed of his appearance, it was still embarrassing to be put in an awkward position while meeting a pretty girl.

Annie put out a hand to shake. "Hello, David. It's nice to meet you."

"Miss, it's nice to meet you too." Annie was a very pretty lady herself. Her thick dark hair was in a ponytail, but she had friendly brown eyes and a nice smile. Her hands were dry and rough, though.

"Call me Annie. The word *Miss* makes me sound old, and I'm not. Wow. Your hair is soft, isn't it?" she asked while shaking her right hand and rubbing his forearm with her left. The three to four-inch-long hair that covered his body was thick, leaving no skin to be seen, but it was as soft as silk.

David had heard it many times by nearly all who touched him. "It is."

Tiffany stared at David's face in awe. She had never seen a person with such long and thick hair where there was usually skin, so a person could not tell what race he may have been.

David's attention left Annie as she let his hand go. He looked at the attractive blonde-haired girl in a blue dress named Tiffany. She appeared uneasy. It wasn't the first time David had witnessed the same reaction or expression of those who gazed upon him as a freak of nature. Over the years, it humored him to see how people reacted at the first glimpse of him. Tiffany apparently couldn't take her eyes off him but didn't know what to say.

David's lips twitched and then twisted into a

scowl that revealed his teeth like a snarling dog. He growled at Tiffany as he slowly reached his hand out towards her. Her eyes lifted in alarm as she took a slow step back. David laughed good-naturedly. "I promise I won't bite. I'm just playing. I'm David."

Tiffany hesitantly took his hand in hers. "My name's Tiffany. How are you?"

"I've been a little better before I was stabbed, but I'm healing."

William motioned toward David. "Tiffany, he's not going anywhere right away, so if you get bored while in town. You're welcome to visit him. You'd like that, wouldn't you, David?"

"Sure. I'm always here."

Chapter 23

Dane Dielschneider had left his room on the third floor and loitered near the staggering stairway to watch who was going up and down the stairs in hopes of catching Tiffany alone. He heard Matt Bannister's voice before he saw him and stepped back to remain out of sight. William Fasana walked up the stairs with Matt to the second story. William made fun of Dane having one hand and referred to him as Little One Stub. The comment about wearing a sign stating he was inbred irritated Dane to the point that he almost punctured his bottom lip while biting it. He watched as the two cousins went to Tiffany's room, and before too long, they returned and descended the stairs with Matt's sister and Tiffany to meet someone named David. Dane caught a glimpse of Tiffany wearing a blue dress, and it upset him to see William Fasana put an arm around Tiffany's shoulders and jerk her close while pretending to drive a fist into her face. The sound of her laughter flowed up the stairs like the sweet scent of jasmine on an easy breeze.

Dane was catapulted into a simmering rage as his beloved fiancé laughed with the man responsible for Dane losing his hand. Worse, seeing her enjoy the presence of the two men that murdered his brothers and several friends was a slap across the face. It was a betrayal that nagged at him like a woodpecker pounding on a tree's bark, weakening the wall of resistance that stopped him from running down the stairs and stabbing William in the back. Matt Bannister's gun, clearly seen on his hip, was the only deterrent that stopped him.

Dane hurried down the stairs to the second story and went to room number ten. The door was unlocked and he went inside, carefully verifying the room was empty. It was a standard room for the Monarch Hotel with two bedrooms and a central sitting room with comfortable chairs and davenport facing each other. A table with a basket of fruit and a blue bowl with a single candy was at one side of the room with four chairs tucked under it. He hurried into one bedroom, which was Matt's sister's room. He crossed the sitting room and entered the other bedroom, knowing it had to be Tiffany's.

The bed was made but had been slept in. Dane sat on the bed and picked up the pillow, seeking her scent. It proved to be disappointing to any aroma that smelled like Tiffany. Across the room was a green vanity with rolled edges and a curved mirror with the padded seat moved back. Tiffany's hairbrush, toothbrush, and other items were set next to a water bowl. Dane stood in front of the mirror and looked at himself for a moment.

His clothes were a bit shabby. The brown cotton pants were a bit too big and held up with black suspenders over a tan striped shirt that once belonged to his brother Devin. The shirt was too big for him and saggy around the shoulders. He wasn't wearing a hat to protect his bright red hair or fair skin from the sun. He had lost his hat in a river on the way to Branson. His hat disappeared down the rapids after Bill had playfully pushed him into the river. All Dane could do was watch his hat float away and curse at Bill.

Freckles covered Dane's skin, varying in size but consistent over his face and arms. He looked at his thin face with dark brown eyes, neck-length bright red hair, and smooth skin that hadn't grown a single whisker. Dane opened his mouth and spread his lips to look at the yellow plaque that colored his teeth over the past few weeks since he last brushed his teeth. A few black cavities pockmarked his teeth but had not affected his front ones.

He grabbed Tiffany's toothbrush and poured some toothpowder on it. He wasn't used to using the powder and poured too much, leaving the extra to pile on the green vanity top. He put the toothbrush in his mouth and began brushing his teeth. It didn't disgust him to use Tiffany's toothbrush. It was nice to share the toothbrush with the love of his life like they would when they were married, but they would be sharing a lot more than a toothbrush once they were married, though. He used water in a small pitcher and glass to rinse his mouth and spat into the bowl. He wiped his mouth with a hand towel and smiled into the mirror again. His teeth were still yellow, but the plaque was mostly removed. He lifted her hairbrush, pulled out the yellow blondish hair caught within it, and held it in his hands. He sniffed it and closed his eyes like a sailor lost at sea, hanging on to the last possession of his beloved bride. Unlike the sailor, he was intent on taking his bride home where she belonged.

The door opened as Annie and Tiffany came back into their hotel room. Dane set the brush down, nimbly dropped to the floor, and crawled under Tiffany's bed. He could hear them talking plainly in the sitting room about someone named David. Jealousy stirred within his chest as he listened to Annie tease Tiffany about another man.

"He's much cuter than a puppy. I wonder if he has puppy breath?" Annie asked Tiffany in a suggestive jest.

"Stop it." Tiffany laughed.

"I'm sure you'll tell me later."

"I'm not kissing him." Tiffany exclaimed with a raised voice.

"You know William is going to set up a nice romantic dinner table for you two. I think it's sweet. It's like a real courtship's beginning, except I won't be supervising you." Annie teased.

"You know I like Gabriel." Tiffany protested.

"He's your cousin, Tiff! You can't court Gabriel."

Tiffany laughed. "He's not my cousin! Not by blood anyway. He's only related because I moved in with you. I think Gabriel is coming to the funeral today."

"Oh? That would be a nice surprise for Matt. But don't you go running off to see David at the reunion tonight. I want you there to meet everyone first. My aunt Eleanor is here, and I haven't seen her in years."

"She's the one that lives on the coast. Right?"

"Yes. I hoped Aunt Eleanor was staying here at the hotel, but she's staying at Uncle Joel's house with most of his family. I can't wait to see her. Anyway, we better get dressed for the funeral. It's getting close to the time to leave for the church."

***

Dane could peek from under the bed into the vanity's mirror and see Tiffany's reflection as she entered the room and pulled a black dress from the closet where it hung. He watched with growing enthusiasm as she reached behind her back, unzipped her dress, and pulled it off, exposing her white undershirt and pantaloons that reached below her knees. He had in the past spied on her as she changed her clothes and once while she bathed, but she was younger then. His breathing quickened as his excitement grew to see her in her night clothing.

Suddenly, his empty stomach growled, betraying him like an internal Judas, angry at not being fed in a timely manner.

A strange sound and a slight movement in the mirror caught the corner of her eye. Tiffany peered into the mirror and saw the familiar face of Dane lying under the bed, watching her with an obscure grin. She covered her breasts with her arms and screamed with all the terror of finding a man in her room. Her terrified scream echoed throughout the room, reaching to the first floor and beyond to the street.

Dane hoped she would be more welcoming, perhaps even thankful for coming to bring her home. The volume of her shrieking and the fearful expression surprised him. He slid out from under the bed and got to his feet quickly. "Shh! Hey, it's me. I'm here to save you." He tried to reach for her shoulders affectionately to calm her, but she stepped back against the wall, clinching her arms against her chest, wailing with sobs while tears rolled down her cheeks. "Tiffany, shh, it's me. We're going to be married."

"Annie!" Tiffany screamed between her sobs as she squatted into a ball, terrified.

"Tiff!" Annie hollered with concern as she came quickly towards the bedroom door.

Dane, beginning to panic at the sound of Annie's voice, whispered, "I'll be back! Be ready to leave." He dashed towards the bedroom door and pushed Annie down as he barreled over her in a desperate sprint towards the entry door.

Dressed only in her nightshirt and pantaloons, Annie landed forcefully on her back but quickly got up and chased Dane into the hotel hallway. "Get back here!" she yelled as Dane reached the stairs and ran down.

William Fasana came out of his room wearing only a black pair of pants while holding his revolver. "What's going on?" he asked hurriedly.

"He was in Tiffany's room!" Annie yelled furiously.

William ran down the stairs knowing it had to be Dane. A sharp pain from the stitches across his abdomen tearing through his flesh nearly stopped him, but he gritted his teeth and ran through the lobby, outside onto the street. He caught sight of Dane running down Main Street, and William tried to follow but came to a stop when his ankle twisted slightly on the uneven ground of a wagon wheel rut. Shoeless and shirtless, standing in the middle of Main Street. William raised his revolver and, for a quick second, had Dane in his line of fire, but the second was gone when a pair of women walked between them. Dane turned a corner, and William lowered his gun. He cursed loudly.

"Language, sir!" A lady walking with her young boy condemned him.

He glanced at her. "My apologies." He removed his left hand off his stitches and saw the blood smeared across his hand. He cursed again lightly before entering the hotel. His knife wound from the week before had separated with the torn stitches.

Annie wore a robe around her night clothes and met him in the lobby as he entered. "Did you catch him? Are you okay? You're bleeding."

William grimaced with the throbbing of the torn stitches. "No. The slippery little eel got away. I'll be fine." He looked at Pamela behind the curved courtesy desk. "Pam, I want Annie to switch rooms with me. Don't write it down; we'll just switch rooms. If he comes back, I want to be there."

"Who?" Pam questioned.

"That little red-headed devil that just ran by here!" he snapped. "The same little one-handed fool who was here yesterday. Dane Dielschneider. When did he come in, and why was he allowed upstairs?" William demanded to know. He held his bleeding side and grimaced in pain.

Pamela shook her head unknowingly. "I've been here all morning and haven't seen him until now."

"Well, he came in at some time!" William exclaimed in a rare moment of anger.

Annie explained to Pamela in a calm voice, "He was under Tiffany's bed, watching her change."

"Oh, no!" Pamela said with concern. "I've been here all morning like I said, and he did not come in while I was here, not that I know of. Let's definitely switch your rooms."

"Did he sign in?" William asked, taking a look at the guest registry. Dane could afford to rent a room with the money he stole from the dance hall.

Pamela replied honestly, "The name isn't familiar. But I need to speak with Josh because he assigned a room last night to a couple staying in room fourteen, it doesn't say funeral to indicate it's a free stay, and the registry says paid for a two-night stay, but there isn't any money in the till to account for them paying."

"I'll see Josh at the funeral and ask him about that." He turned his attention to Annie. "How is

Tiffany?"

"Frightened. How in the world did he know which room was Tiffany's?"

William's lips sneered and he took a deep breath from the stinging of his wound. "You can thank your brother Steven for that. Matt told me Steven got drunk last night at the dance hall, buddied up with Dane, and told him about everything. I'll bet Dane stayed in Steven's room since it was empty. Let's change rooms, Annie. If little one stub returns, I want to be the one that greets him."

Chapter 24

Audrey had woken up much later than expected after a night of little sleep. She had tried to sleep, she even read selected chapters of the Book of Numbers about numbers to fall asleep, but the room was too hot and uncomfortable. The sun was undoubtedly beginning to rise by the time her exhaustion overrode the heat, allowing her to sleep. She had no idea what time it was when she sat on her bedside and stared at the white wedding dress that hung on a nail against the plank wall. It was a white cotton dress with an adorning lace neckline across the breast. It wasn't the most expensive wedding dress she could buy, but it was affordable. It was the dress she had bought when she traveled to California to marry her first husband, Grant White.

If there were ever two words that struck a chord in a lady, it was the phrase, *true love*. Every woman dreams of marrying a wonderful man and living a life with true love. She felt drawn by the spirit to accept Alan's proposal when she came to Natoma, but now, she felt a hesitance in her soul. There was an uneasiness that stirred within her.

Audrey had planned on having the wedding on Saturday if she was still in mind to do so after spending a few days with Alan. Nothing was going quite as she planned, and she felt hurried, pushed, and perhaps manipulated into agreeing to marry Alan today. It was Thursday, and they had not nearly enough time in conversation to get to know each other. It was hard to tell if Alan had a short temper and lacked the ability to communicate or if his apparent flaws were merely from the anxiety of her being there, as his mother claimed. Apostle Paul admitted in 2 Corinthians that he could write a bold letter and speak forcefully, but he was quiet and meek in person. Perhaps Alan was the same way where he expressed himself better in writing than he did with the spoken word. All Audrey really knew was she was expecting more from Alan than she was seeing, and at the moment, she was reluctant to commit her life to him.

There was a knock on her door.

"Yes." she replied and then yawned.

"Can I come in?" It was the voice of Alan.

"Give me a minute. I need to get dressed." She stood from the edge of her bed.

The door opened immediately as Alan entered with a broad grin to see her undressed. He closed the door behind him while his gaze slowly roamed over her body, covered only by her night dress.

She covered her breast quickly with a stunned

expression. "Get out!" she ordered.

Alan reasoned, "In about six hours, we're going to be married and getting naked anyway. So, what's a little peek at the goods going to hurt, huh?"

Audrey's eyes burned into him with a fierceness from deep within. There was no longer any gentleness within her. "Get out!" She yelled. She was humiliated by his lack of respect.

Alan was surprised but also offended by her reaction. His excitement faded. "What's it matter? Seriously, Audrey. We'll be naked every night from now on anyway. What do you have to hide? I'm going to be your husband in a few hours. Let me have a peek at the goods."

"Get out of my room!" she yelled.

Alan was unphased by her angry words. He leaned against the door and let his eyes roam over her with a lustful smirk on his lips. "Sweetheart, this isn't your room. I'm going to finish *our* room and get the bed made and some candles. When the wedding is over, we're going straight to the barn. I'm glad you slept in late because you'll be up late tonight. Ma and Jannie are making a wedding cake, but no matter how good it is, you are my dessert."

She screamed, "Get out of my room, or there will be no wedding!"

Alan chuckled. "I love angry women. They give a little fight before the taming. I'll get our room done and get everything set up nice for tonight." He left, closing the door behind him.

Audrey sat on the edge of the bed and exhaled to calm her rattled nerves and slow her heartbeat.

There was something in Alan's green eyes that she couldn't quite describe, but it scared her. She knew men could be impulsive and reacted differently than women regarding matters of more intimate desire. Audrey wanted to get to know the man she came to marry through conversation, laughter, and growing their friendship before the wedding. Alan hadn't shown an interest in conversation or trying to win her heart, but he was mighty anxious for one thing, and it was approached without honor, dignity, or respect for her. His actions moments before stirred the mixed emotions already fluttering in her stomach.

She dressed in a light blue dress and pulled her hair back into a bun. After making herself presentable, she went out into the family room. "Good morning." she said to the ladies who busied themselves in the kitchen.

"Morning?" Mattie snapped with disgust. "It's more like noon. We haven't got time for laziness around here. I'm glad you're moving out to the barn with Alan if you're going to sleep all day. We have a lot of cooking to do around this hot stove for your wedding, and it's hot enough already. So grab that big bowl and start mixing dough for the bread." She sounded very cranky.

Jannie slowly sliced potatoes while Bernice measured a cup of flour for a pie crust.

Mattie shouted, "For crying out loud, Daisy! Get those kids outside, or shut them up. I can't think with all that racket."

Daisy glanced up from blowing on the tummy

of her year-old daughter, Alisha. The little girl squealed with laughter every time Daisy did it. "We're just playing."

"Get outside and play if you're not going to help. We're working in here."

"Tad's outside. He likes to tease the babies until they cry." Daisy explained.

"Tell him I'll grab my switch and beat him senseless again if he does. Just go, Daisy. Get that screaming kid out of here!" Mattie turned her attention to the stove where she was boiling some meat. She mumbled to herself irritably.

Audrey stood near a counter, watching. It was easy to feel the tension in the kitchen between the three women cooking and the disheartened expression on Daisy's face as she glanced down at her waiting child for her mother to blow on her belly again. "I apologize for sleeping in so late. I never do that, but I don't think I fell asleep until nearly sunrise. It was so hot in my room."

Mattie turned her head and glared heatedly at Audrey. "Everyone has a spilled piss story. Clean it up and move on."

"Huh?" Audrey asked, not understanding what was meant by the words.

Bernice nudged Audrey's elbow to get her attention. On the counter where flour was spread out for the dough of the pie crusts was the word *Shhh* written in the flour. She wiped it away as Mattie slammed a large metal spoon down on the stovetop.

Mattie shouted, "We've all spilled our piss pots, yeah? What do you do? You clean it up and continue your day. You don't apologize to anyone; you just wipe it up and go your way. I don't care if you slept half of the day away. It's your wedding day, not mine."

"Yeah," Audrey said hesitantly. Her heart pounded, and her voice cracked as she said, "I decided I don't want to marry Alan today. I think it's best to get married on Saturday like I originally planned."

Mattie turned around with tightened lips and fierce eyes. "Why? Because he took a sneak peek at his bride today?"

Audrey was expecting Mattie to be upset, but she was startled by Mattie's sour expression. The tension in the room expanded in volume and pressure as Audrey saw the fury behind Mattie's eyes. She swallowed nervously as her mouth suddenly grew dry. "Because it's the day we originally planned." She swallowed nervously. "It's only a couple of days away, and I want to get to know Alan better."

Mattie set her hands on her hips with frustration. "Well, that's fine. We'll just throw this food we can't afford to waste away and do it again on Saturday when you are ready to get married! Or will you change your mind then to maybe Sunday? No, Monday? We're working over a hot stove in ninety-degree weather for you! The least you could do is marry my damn son!" she shouted.

"I don't think it's ninety degrees yet, Ma." Daisy commented from the family room where she was removing the cloth diaper of the youngest to take her outside. There was no need to waste a dry diaper while they were outside.

Mattie grabbed the spoon from the stove and threw it at Daisy. The spoon hit her in the side of the leg.

"Ouch!"

"You shut up and get that brat out of here!" Mattie pointed at Audrey. "And you! You tell Alan that you want to wait. That poor boy has been excited all day about marrying you, so now you tell him he's not getting married today. And you're paying for the food on Saturday because we've already spent all we had on the meal we're making. It's garbage now! Alan and Vince are in the barn finishing your new room. You won't be so hot out there, so maybe you can crawl out of bed before noon. Let him know you changed your mind again!" She walked away towards her room and slammed the door behind her.

Jannie laid the knife down. "Well, we can have fried potatoes for dinner instead of mashed. It saves me work. Audrey, what difference does it make if you marry Alan today or Saturday? Just marry him and get it over with."

Bernice Sperry had never spoken of any extent to Audrey. She did not now either, but she did reply to Jannie. "A few days can make all the difference in the world." She nodded at Audrey. "I think it's a good idea to wait."

"Thank you. I'll talk to Alan. Where is Morton?" Audrey asked.

"Working. He and Henry have jobs." Bernice said with a condescending sigh.

"Don't Alan and Vince?"

Jannie commented, "You're supposed to be asking about Alan, not Morton. Alan's the one you're engaged to, you know."

"Jannie, shut up." Bernice said as she turned to finish her pie crust.

Jannie raised her eyebrows. "If they still burned witches, Bernice, I'd turn you in for the price of a stale biscuit. With all that ugly red hair, you'd be charred in no time."

Audrey offered, "Bernice has beautiful hair. It shines because it's clean." she said as she walked out of the house.

Bernice smiled quietly at the compliment.

***

Alan was on the hayloft floor, reaching down for Vince to hand him a sawn board. He grabbed the end and pulled the board up to nail it across two vertical posts to create a wall. He saw Audrey walk into the barn. "It's just my opinion, but I think you looked nicer in your night clothes. Did you come out to see our room? Come on up."

"No." The hay loft was eight feet above the dirt floor, but their room was above the pig pen, where three good-sized hogs lounged in the cool dirt. The barn smelled like any other barn that kept pigs, straw and hay, a goat or two, cows, and horses. She wrinkled her nose, but the distaste wasn't the scent of a farm. It was the tiny room Alan was making with a mattress on the loft floor near the dwindling haystack.

"I will build the wall up to the roof to give us privacy. You're probably wondering how we will stay warm in the winter, huh?" Alan chuckled. "That's why we have a small bed."

She ignored the comment. "Alan, I came to tell you I want to postpone the wedding until Saturday, as I originally planned."

Alan answered, "Well, sweetheart, the church won't be rebuilt by then. So, we might as well get married today. We'll have this wall built in an hour. It won't take long."

Audrey explained, "It isn't the wall or the church I'm concerned about. I just think it… I want to wait until Saturday. It's only a couple of days away."

Alan's excitement dwindled. "I thought you said we could get married today? That's what you said yesterday."

"I know," Audrey explained gently. "I felt pressured yesterday, and I don't want to be pressured into getting married before I'm ready."

Vince Sperry was standing by two sawhorses with a handsaw and measuring line. He wore black cotton pants with suspenders over his bare chest and was sweating in the day's heat. He spat onto the ground. "I thought you were ready to marry him when you agreed to come here?"

"I am. I haven't changed my mind, but I want to wait until Saturday."

"Ma and the women are making food." Alan protested as he leaned on a barn support post that reached the roof. "They spent money on that food, and Cass is bringing our cousins over. It's a little late to delay it now, don't you think?" His irritation was clear to hear in his voice.

She shook her head. "No. It's noon. There is time to postpone the wedding. It's only for two days. That may not seem important to you, but it's important to me."

He gasped. "I'm building our room. Don't you think it's important to me? You were supposed to be my dessert tonight. What do you think I'm out here working for?"

Vince chuckled as his eyes enviously roamed over her.

A wave of disgust turned her stomach. "First of all, I'm not dessert, and I don't like to be referred to as that. I want to wait until Saturday, and that's what I'm doing. I can pack my things and return to California if you don't like it. I didn't have a great life there, but I wasn't making the worst mistake of my life either."

Alan jumped eight feet from the loft, landing on his feet with bent knees. His face was stone cold. He leaned against the post and knocked over a pitchfork set against it. He gazed at Audrey as his lips rubbed against each other irritably for a moment. His voice was plain, simple, and direct, "You came here to marry me, and you will. If you want to wait until Saturday, fine. On Saturday, you will marry me, climb that ladder up to our room, and be my wife. There won't be any more waiting. And sweetheart, I'm afraid you're stuck here and will be my wife whether you're ready or not. You don't have much of a choice anymore. You have no more money. Now, how about you make me happy and give me a real kiss?" He stepped forward. "You want to keep me happy, don't you?"

"What?" she gasped.

"A kiss. You know, for making me wait. It's the least you could do."

"You took my money?"

"It's our money. We're going to be married."

Vince offered with a slight snicker, "You and Mort wiped up some of your money when Jannie puked the other night."

"You had no right." she said in disbelief. "Excuse me." she turned and hurriedly walked towards the house.

"No kiss?" Alan asked with a growing grin as he watched her briskly walking away. He looked at his brother. "She'll learn after I show her who the boss is."

Vince grabbed the pitchfork off the ground and leaned it against the pig pen. "Ma will put her in her place."

Chapter 25

Audrey searched her smaller travel case for her money and discovered it was gone. The money she earned from months of washing dishes, cooking, sweeping, mopping, washing sheets and blankets, making beds, and being at every beckoned call to make the boarding house a pleasant stay for others was stolen by the man she had come nearly nine hundred miles to marry. She was infuriated.

She sat on the edge of the bed and began to weep. There were only seventy-four dollars to her name after paying for her food and stay on the SS Columbia train and stage routes from California. Alan invaded her personal belongings, took what wasn't his, and left her with nothing, just like the thieves who stole her broach had done.

She wiped her tears and walked into the kitchen with a fiery glow in her eyes. "Alan stole my money from my carrying case! I had seventy-four dollars in there, and it's gone!"

Mattie slowly turned from the counter where she was cutting an onion. Her eyes glistened from the onion's mist. "Alan didn't take it, Sweetheart. I did. I meant to tell you, but you were sleeping so soundly this morning."

"What? Why would you get into my personal things? You had no right to take my money. I want it back!"

Mattie raised her eyebrows, wrinkling her forehead. Her voice was as hard as an oak chopping block, "Maybe you haven't figured it out yet, but we're not exactly rich. In fact, we are quite poor. I spent everything I had to pay for your passage up here, and forgive me; you were supposed to get married today! We have many mouths to feed and many more coming to your wedding. While you were getting your beauty sleep, I quietly checked your cases for any money to help pay for your wedding reception. I didn't steal it; it was for your wedding gift and reception! I didn't want to wake you up because you were sleeping like a log. But I did not expect you to come out here and accuse my son of robbing you! We're family now. I didn't think you'd mind donating some to pay for your wedding reception." She paused for just a second while giving Audrey a sour scowl. "The girls and I have been sweating like rain to make today special for you. This is the thanks we get. You postpone the wedding, and the food goes to the pigs! We can't afford it!"

The fire in Audrey's expression cooled towards guilt with an added touch of shame. "I'm sorry," she said weakly. "I didn't want to be any trouble."

"Trouble?" Mattie huffed. "If you don't want to be any trouble, the best thing you could do is marry that boy today and pretend it's Saturday. I haven't seen him so excited about anything since he was a child. We're already cooking!" She tossed her hands into the air irately.

"Yeah," Jannie added. She was still seated at the counter where she was slicing potatoes. "The sooner we're sisters, the better. I'll be your maid of honor." she offered.

Audrey had always given in to more dominant personalities like Mattie's. It was something she was trying to correct and stand up for what she wanted, but at the same time, she could not help but feel the guilt of causing more work for the women in the hot kitchen. Mattie's frustration was understandable. However, by the same measure of understanding, the pressure they put on her to marry Alan that afternoon was as thick as molasses in the dead of winter. Audrey hoped Mattie would understand that it was a woman's prerogative to decide who she would marry and when the wedding would take place. She may have been a mail bride who accepted a proposal, but there was no contract stating she had to marry Alan if she found him unfit to marry. A lady had a choice, and it was hers to make.

Mattie did not give her a moment to respond, "We'll wait to Saturday if you must, but what a pain in the butt it will be to cook this all over again. And I promise you, we won't have the excitement that we do today! It's very disappointing. I'm disappointed. I don't see why you can't get married today like you agreed to yesterday."

"Me either," Jannie volunteered. "I say just get it done and over with."

Bernice listened to her mother-in-law's rant but didn't agree with any of what was said. Bernice offered her opinion, "Audrey, I think you should wait until Saturday if that's what you want to do. It's *your* wedding and if you don't want to rush it, don't. I could make a much nicer cake by Saturday anyway."

Mattie snapped at Bernice, "You can make a cake today just fine! She doesn't want to be any trouble, Bernice! Hush."

Bernice shrugged her shoulders unconcerned. "I think Saturday would be better because Henry and Morton would be able to clean up and dress appropriately instead of just getting off work and smelling like the tannery. They'd like to see their brother get married while looking nice."

The reasoning couldn't be argued with. They never knew what Morton and Henry would come home looking or smelling like after working at the tannery. The two brothers did whatever needed to be done, from driving wagon loads of bark to un-plugging pipes, skinning dead and bloated animals to save the hide or anything in between to fill in where needed.

Mattie forced a fake smile on her bitter face and gently put her hands on Audrey's shoulders to have her full attention while she spoke gently, "Honey, I know it's sudden, but you came all this way. Alan gets jittery around beautiful women and isn't quite himself, but he will be after the wedding. You read his letters; you know what a kind and loving man he is. You have to give him a chance and not pass up a good thing because of a rough start. Instead of wasting all this food, how about we just go ahead with our plans and you marry him today? I hate to use our poverty as an excuse, but honey, we can't afford to throw all this food to the pigs. It's up to you, Sweetheart. How about we get you two married today?"

Audrey's stomach felt like a knot in the center of a rope being pulled at both ends, making the knot tighter and more uncomfortable. On one end, there was an obligation to keep her word and not become a burden to the Sperry family and marry Alan. The other end of the rope was internal, where a heavy sense of hesitation was like a concrete pillar unmoving and uncompromising. The inner voice screamed that she should wait.

"What's it going to be, Sweetheart?" Mattie pressed while holding Audrey's shoulders, refusing to let her go until she had an answer.

"I… I need to think about it." Audrey answered uneasily.

Mattie's arms fell to her sides, and her fake smile faded as quickly as it had arrived as her harsh natural expression took over like a dark cloud covering the sun. "Well, you better think quick! For crying out loud, girl, there's food cooking, but we need to know if we need to make more or not!" She turned from Audrey and swung her arm at a housefly buzzing by in the air. "Go think it over and let us know! The sooner, the better."

Audrey walked to her room, returned carrying her Bible, and walked out the back door with her eyes clouding with tears.

***

Audrey walked down to where Heather Creek cut through the Sperry property and sat on the cool grass under an apple tree. The sound of the running waters spilling over rocks as it flowed from the mountain brought a calming peace that she found pleasant. One of the Sperry cows was nearby, eating the grass under a tree.

She felt like she was being squeezed in an apple press. She had agreed to marry Alan at five o'clock that afternoon, it was now about just after noon, and she was hesitant to marry him. There was something about Alan that struck her as odd. He did not seem like the man that wrote the letters that won her heart with their kind words. She had the letters tucked inside of her Bible and reread them in the cool shade to help her come to a decision. The words written on paper that she had read a thousand times still sounded sweet, but something felt wrong. Letters often didn't leave room for the whole story, and perhaps she was being overly critical now that she was angry, hurt, and confused. Mattie had taken her money without asking and turned it around to make Audrey feel guilty about getting angry. Yet, she was now stuck in their home with no money to purchase a stagecoach ticket back home or to the nearest town if she wanted to leave. Audrey already knew she wasn't getting her money back.

She lowered her head to pray. "Lord Jesus, I am confused, and you are not the lord of confusion. I need your help. I don't know if I am supposed to marry Alan anymore or not. I felt led here, but he's not what I expected. Jesus, will you please reveal to me somehow what I am supposed to do? I thought he had fallen in love with me too, but he doesn't act like it. All he acts is lustful. What am I supposed to do, Lord? I can't leave because I don't have anymore money. Jesus, help me. Speak to me through your word." She closed her eyes, flipped the Bible open randomly, and put her finger on the page before opening her eyes. Her finger set on the Gospel of Matthew, Chapter 13, the parable of the wheat and tare.

She read out loud:

"Another parable put he forth unto them, saying, The Kingdom of heaven is likened unto a man which sowed good seed in his field: But while men slept, his enemy came and sowed tares among the wheat, and went his way. But when the blade had sprung up and brought forth fruit, then appeared tares also.

So the servants of the householder came and said to him, Sir, didst not thou sow good seed in thy field? From whence then hath it tares?

He said unto them, an enemy hath done this. The servants said unto him, Wilt thou then that we go and gather them up?

But he said, Nay; lest while ye gather up the tares, ye root up also the wheat with them. Let both grow together until the harvest, and in the time of harvest, I will say to the reapers, gather ye together first the tares and bind them in bundles to burn them, but gather the wheat into my barn."

Audrey lowered her brow with a disappointed exhaling of breath. "That's not exactly what I was looking for, Lord. I hoped you would be more clear on what I was supposed to do."

Morton Sperry's voice interrupted her, "I don't mean to bother you," he said. He stood about ten feet behind her and slowly descended the hill. "But that sounds like darnel ryegrass, called darnel for short, also known as cockle. I apologize for interrupting, but I figured you'd rather know I was here. I heard you reading. I would think you were reading the farmer's almanac if I didn't know it was your Bible. I thought the Bible was a bunch of thee do's and thou don'ts, not farming."

"I thought you were at work." Audrey replied, not happy to see him. She wiped the moisture from her eyes.

"Lunch time. I was at the house, and Ma sent me

down here to tell you she needs an answer. I don't know what the question is, but that's what she said. You look sad. Did something happen?"

She ran a hand over her hair and took a deep breath. "They want me to marry Alan today."

"You don't want to?"

"I wanted to wait until Saturday, but they're already cooking a big meal to celebrate."

Morton waved his hand dismissingly. "Trust me. If they wanted to celebrate that much, they'd butcher a pig. Mind if I sit for a moment?"

She desired to be alone to pray, read the Bible, and sit in silence uninterrupted, but unexpectedly, she shook her head, inviting him to sit a few feet from her.

Morton gazed uphill towards the house before speaking. "This isn't a bad spot to sit and think, but for future reference, there is a nicer spot about a hundred and fifty yards upstream. A bit more private too, without the cow peeing." he said with a scowl as the cow let a thick stream of urine loose.

She chuckled. "That is distracting. I was just reading the parable of the wheat and tares in the Gospel of Matthew. The Bible is infinitely more than do's and don'ts. The Bible is like a red rose that you might offer the woman you love. It has length like a stem, with some thorns along the way to keep us on the path to a Godly life. You know, like a barbed wire fence for your cow, let's say. You don't want the cow wandering off and getting stolen or hurt because it's valuable, right? The Bible isn't meant to hurt us or others but to protect us from hurting ourselves.

"The Bible has very green leaves like a rose. Sixty-six of them, in fact, each leaf is a book in the Bible. Amazingly, those books were written in three languages by over forty-six authors on three continents from all walks of life, from Kings to lowly sheepherders, over a span of one thousand and five hundred years. You'd think all those leaves would be jumbled and override each other with contradictions, but they don't, not one time. A long stem rose with its stem, thorns, and leaves is gorgeous.

"But what makes it beautiful is the red rose. *That* is the life and sacrifice of Jesus on the cross for our sins. When we understand that God became a man to be tortured and die for our sins just so we can be with him in heaven, that is beautiful. The scent of forgiveness, freedom from sin, and for me, the comfort, hope, and security that Jesus is a part of me and active in my life right now to help me is all I need to know that I'll be okay. I trust him. Roses aren't just beautiful; they have a wonderful scent, and so does the Bible when you know the Lord Jesus. It's not just a book; it is a living book, written by our creator through forty-six men and women over fifteen hundred years to give us his promises and an invitation to know and love him. He loves you, Morton, just as much as he loves me. See? It's so much more than do's and don'ts. It's more like a love letter from God in the shape and context of a long-stemmed rose. Jesus loves us, Morton. That's what the Bible is all about."

"I never read it. But I do know about what you were reading when I came down. The Crawford's grow tons of wheat, and darnel gets mixed in there. That might be what your reading called tares. It's a mimicking weed that looks a lot like wheat. In fact, it's hard to tell them apart until the grains mature. Wheat's brown, darnel is black. It's also a poison. Have you ever seen the difference side by side?"

"No." Audrey answered with interest.

"I'll talk to Jimmy Crawford and see if he still has his example. He's the apprentice reverend down at the church. I don't go to church, of course, but Jimmy is a friend, and he once showed me a head of wheat next to a head of a tare that he had coated with lacquer to preserve them in a little box for a sermon he was doing about that very subject. I remember that."

"I would like to see that. Do you know what that parable means?" she asked.

He shrugged. "A way to get even with your enemies?" he guessed.

She grinned with a short chuckle. "No! Jesus explains it himself a little bit later. The wheat are the Godly people on earth, the church, believers, people like me. The tares are people who act godly but are not. Their hearts are not true, and they may even be very involved in the community or church, but it's an act to appear Godly without truly knowing the Lord. Compromising the Word of God and living a sinful life with a Christian brand does not get you into heaven. What it will get you is plucked like a tare and thrown into hell. Not because the Lord didn't love you, but because you didn't love him and rejected his gift of salvation. The harvest is judgment day, which we will all face. If you ever decide to become a Christian, Morton, do it for real and not as some half-hearted prayer where the words are said, but there is no commitment or sincerity of heart. God loves us enough to be tortured and die most painfully. And believe it or not, Jesus would do that all over again just for you. He loves you and wants you to be with him that much."

Morton was silent as he listened thoughtfully. "Huh." he grunted lightly.

Mattie Sperry shouted from the top of the hill, "Mort, I didn't send you down there for conversation! I need an answer."

Audrey groaned loudly. "They're waiting for me to decide, and I don't know what to do."

Morton tossed a pebble into the creek. "Why do you want to wait?" he asked softly.

She held up her Bible. "Marriage is a sacred commitment to God that I don't take lightly. Am I wrong to want to take my time and make sure it's what I want to do before I commit my life to someone?"

"I sure don't think so. Listen, if you don't want to marry Alan today, then I support you on that. So would Henry and Bernice. The rest of them don't matter much if you ask me. You do what you want to do, and don't let them talk you into something you're not comfortable with. They'll try but say no." He gazed at the letters his mother wrote to her on the grass. "You should take a pencil and paper to the barn and ask Alan to write you a love letter real quick or at least list his reasons for marrying today. You might find he is quite a poet." he said with annoyance.

Audrey groaned with frustration. "It seems the only way we can communicate is through writing. He hasn't had a real conversation with me since I arrived. I've had more meaningful conversations with you."

Morton pointed at the letters. "Have him write something; you'll see what I mean. Trust me." He took a deep breath and exhaled. "I want you to know..." he paused, debating. "I think you're all right."

She gave a slight chuckle. "You're okay too."

His expression grew solemn, and he turned his head downstream to avoid her eyes. "I don't know about that. I'm a..." He bit his bottom lip hesitantly. "I'm sorry they're pressuring you." He turned his head to look into her eyes. "Don't let them force you into marrying Alan. You're stronger than that. You have to be. I must go back to work, but before I go, promise me you'll wait," he paused uncomfortably. "Like you want to."

Her brow narrowed questionably. "Okay. I promise."

He nodded. "I'll see you after work. Do you want me to tell my ma while I'm here?"

She shook her head. "No. I'll be along shortly and tell her I want to wait. I'm strong enough." She finished with an appreciative half smile.

"I'm glad to hear it." He stood. "Maybe we could talk later?"

She nodded. "Anytime."

***

Morton walked up the hill towards the house and noticed Alan leaning against the barn door, watching him. Alan called Morton over to where he and Vince were.

"I have to get back to work. What do you want?" Morton asked plainly.

Alan's chest puffed outwards. "I want you to leave my fiancé alone. Ma found her for me, not you. I think you're sweet on her, and you need to pull the reins back a bit. Ma will find you a woman, but Audrey's mine. You hear me?" Alan ran one side of his bottom lip against his top teeth while his eyes held coldly on his brother.

Morton looked towards the thick briars and trees of the mountain towards the cabin on the hill. "Are you going to treat her better than you did, Racheal?"

"How I treat my bride is up to me. I guess it depends if she minds me or not."

Morton spoke plainly, "I was younger and dumber then. I shouldn't have allowed anything like what you did to her to happen. I won't let you lay a hand on Audrey if she does marry you, which

I doubt she will. I think she can see through you, Alan."

Alan chuckled. "How are you going to stop me? I could whip you on any day before I went to prison, and I've only gotten meaner since. I killed men tougher than you with my bare hands. You aren't going to stop me from doing anything. I could go down there right now and do whatever I wanted to her, and who's going to stop me?" He laughed. "The only reason I don't is the headache I'd get from Henry's wife yipping like the dog she is! Don't tell me what you won't allow because, quite frankly, you don't matter."

"If that's what it comes to, so be it. But I won't mind my own business and listen to her scream and cry this time. That lady down there deserves far more than you or I can give her. We need to send her back home. Did you take her money?"

"I took a little money the other night when we went to the saloon, but Ma took all her money. Audrey's staying here whether she likes it or not. She's my woman, and she'll be a good wife, willingly or by force, I don't care which. I only care about one thing, and that's what happens up there." He pointed towards the room he was building.

Morton's voice revealed his disgust, "I liked you better when you were in prison, Alan."

Alan chuckled slightly. "You're getting weak, Mort. I'm back, taking the gang over, and have a bride. You, little brother, better get back to work. That's what you'll be doing for the rest of your life. Clock in, clock out, day after day. Welcome to your own prison, Mort. I'm telling you now that you're no longer a part of the Sperry-Helms Gang."

Morton chuckled softly. "I already quit the gang because I want no part of it. But while you're either in the grave or back in prison, I will be working to pay for my own way. But I will have absolutely no fear of the law. That is a freedom that you will never know."

"You're scared of the marshal. Cass is right; you're a coward."

"I'm not scared of Matt. On the contrary, I respect him. I like him. I'd much rather be his friend than his enemy."

"Being friends with the law might make us enemies," Alan warned. "I won't be able to trust you."

Morton waved towards the creek, where Audrey remained seated in prayer. "If you don't send her back home, we'll become enemies anyway. As I said, I won't stand back and let you hurt her."

Alan nodded with tightened lips. "Your choice. But remember the Sperry Rule, brother. If I whip you, it's settled."

Chapter 26

Matt wore a black suit over a white shirt with the top button left undone to Hannie's graveside funeral. In his hands, he held his newest brown Stetson hat that Christine insisted on buying him if he was ever to wear a hat while with her in public. Christine did not like his sweat-stained and filthy old Stetson that was misshaped and floppy from use and abuse that he had worn for over ten years all over the country. Matt preferred to wear his old hat as it was much more comfortable and shaped perfectly for riding in the sun or rain to fit his desired needs. But for today, he was thankful that he had a new hat to wear with his suit as it was more appropriate for the funeral. Matt bowed his head in prayer and sniffled repeatedly.

Reverend Painter led the prayer, "Lord Jesus, our hearts were broken when Hannie's young life was taken from her. There is no such thing as fairness in this world, and some questions of why can never be fully answered in this lifetime. Everyone here loved this young lady and mourns for the loss we will know for years to come. Jesus, the sadness can be overwhelming, but I know that as we commence her body into the ground, Hannie is right now more alive in heaven than she ever was on earth. As young as she was, and as much as she loved her family and friends, I know she would not trade heaven to come back to us even if she could. As you said to the thief on the cross, today she is in paradise with you. Let us take comfort in knowing she is not buried in the ground as we leave here, but she is alive and well with you. For those of us who are committed to you, we will see her again. Lord, help us to remember that this is not a goodbye; it is merely until we meet Hannie again. And what a glorious day that will be when we enter your house forever and ever. And Hannie will be there waiting for us."

"Amen." Matt said softly as the prayer ended. He lifted his head to look around at the many family members and friends that came from near and far to mourn at Hannie's service and support her family. Solomon Fasana, the owner of the county's only funeral parlor and Great Uncle of Hannie, had not charged the Longo family a single penny for the service. Still, he had given Hannie the prettiest and most expensive cherrywood casket in his showroom. She was family, and the tragedy was hard enough for her parents without another financial burden.

Reverend Painter added softly, "That completes our service. There will be a memorial dinner at the community hall, and you are all invited by the family to join them for a time of visiting and sharing a meal. I assure you there is plenty of food."

To leave the casket behind to be buried was difficult for Hannie's mother. Matt watched with a knot forming in his throat and watering eyes as Karen Longo was escorted from the graveside by her husband, Jim, and her father, Joel Fasana. She wore a black dress with a matching cap and veil covering her face. Karen wailed loudly, "Hannie... Oh Lord, Hannie." while sobbing uncontrollably as she was forced to leave her firstborn baby behind. Matt bit his bottom lip tightly while fighting the tears that threatened to fall.

He felt the comforting hand of Christine rub his back lovingly as he put the Stetson on his head to shadow his face from the sun. He watched a long line of people wearing black follow the grieving parents towards Main Street. Matt wasn't in a hurry to leave the cemetery.

Matt escorted Christine into the Branson Community Hall, where the memorial dinner was being held. As they entered the front door, they saw rows of tables with chairs to eat. A potluck of food was set up on two tables, along with multiple pitchers of drinks. The food smelled appetizing and the noise level of people talking and children running around was pleasing.

Mary Ziegler approached them with a well-dressed robust lady in her mid to late fifties on her arm. "Matt, you remember your aunt Eleanor?"

Eleanor Archer's face curled into an emotional ball as she raised her arms to hug him while stepping forward. "Matthew." she wrapped her arms around him tightly and wept. Her body convulsed as she held him. She pulled back to look at him as tears flowed down her cheek. "I haven't seen you since you were just a little boy. My, how you've grown. You look so much like your mother. I can't believe how much all you kids do." She stared at him with a trembling lip in a tight emotional smile while a tear rolled down her cheek.

"Aunt Eleanor, it's good to see you again," Matt said. "It has been a long time."

She wiped her tears. "Too long. I heard you and your fiancé were coming to the coast for your honeymoon. Please, come to Astoria and visit me when you do. This young lady must be her?"

"Yes. This is Christine. This is my Aunt Eleanor."

Christine reached a hand outwards to shake. "It's nice to meet you."

"Family doesn't shake hands, dear. Give me a hug, girl." Eleanor hugged Christine firmly. "Oh my," she sniffled as she let go and wiped under her nose. "I think I may have lost five pounds in tears alone today. Are you planning on coming to Astoria?"

"We are." Christine confirmed.

"Wonderful. If it's okay with you, I'll arrange where you will stay while on your honeymoon. I've lived there for a long time, and you'll get nothing but the best. We'll talk a bit later about it. I have so much catching up to do."

Billy Jo Fasana approached them and stomped her foot playfully, exposing her profile while spreading her arms out low to high as if finishing a dance and awaiting applause. "I'm back!"

"Ohh, great." Matt moaned unenthusiastically before chuckling and reaching out to hug her. She playfully slapped his arm away before hugging him.

"Are you back for good or just visiting?" Matt asked.

"I'm back for good. The coast is too cold for me. It's summertime; it's not supposed to be sixty degrees and cloudy. All those gray skies, rain, and wind don't compare to the sunshine and blue skies over here."

Annie Lenning walked behind Billy Jo without her noticing. Annie spoke frankly, "I'm surprised you didn't bring some fisherman with bad luck back to add to the chaos with Joe Thorn and that other nut you were courting. What was his name, Wes?"

Billy Jo turned around and hugged Annie with a laugh. "I would have, but I didn't meet any. Aunt Eleanor and Uncle Bob don't associate with the fishermen. He's the head engineer at a ship-building company, so they're like Lee and Regina and live high on the hog over there. But I am done with Wes and Joe. Joe is sitting over there with our boys. They were sure glad to see their daddy. Joe and

I are going to talk later. But I'm not rushing into anything with him."

"Good," Annie said approvingly. She warned Matt with a severe scowl, "You better find that little red-headed bandit before I do because I'm going to shoot him if I see him again. He was hiding under Tiffany's bed in the hotel room. He used her toothbrush! Thankfully we could tell by the crap caught in the bristles and bowl he spat in." Her repulsion was evident on her face.

Christine shivered with disgust.

"Do you have your little gun?" Matt asked.

Annie pulled a Smith & Wesson silver plated two-shot .38 caliber Derringer from a hidden pocket on her dress. "I didn't have it on me when he was in our room, but I do now. William chased him outside but tore open a couple of the stitches on his belly."

Matt could feel his frustration growing. "I would be looking for him, but we had the funeral, now this, and more family stuff tonight. And I have to ride to Natoma tomorrow because the stage was robbed. Of course, I heard that from William and then the stage depot, not the sheriff over there. I want to know why he didn't wire me. I swear Sheriff Jones is as useless as a dead horse."

Annie tilted her head. "It's Natoma. A dead horse is good money. The tannery, remember?"

Matt chuckled. "Use your gun if you must, but you keep Dane away from her." He nodded towards Tiffany, who was chatting with other teenagers there.

Mary Ziegler touched Matt's arm. "You and Christine better go get something to eat."

"We had better." he agreed. Matt gazed around the community hall at the familiar faces of little Hannie Longo's family and friends. They had come together to show their love for Hannie and support the Longo family.

Chapter 27

Daisy Sperry poured a small cup of whiskey and set the bottle down on the counter. She put her finger into the cup and rubbed it on her daughter Alisha's gums, where three teeth were trying to break through her bulging gums. Daisy held her crying child and asked Jannie, "Is it normal for three teeth to want to come in at once? I don't remember Elliot or Walter's teeth doing that."

Jannie poured a glass of whisky for herself. "Tad and Travis had several teeth come in at once, but their teeth are all straight. Louise's teeth came in slower but came in crooked, and that one is higher up in the gum. Eve's never had more than two come in at once, but she has that gap in front. So, maybe that means Alisha's teeth will be straight like yours. Rubbing that on her gums isn't going to do anything. You should make her drink an ounce or two of that whiskey to cure her pain."

Daisy shook her head slowly. "A baby's stomach

can't be made for that."

"It didn't hurt my kids any." Jannie took a drink of the whiskey. "You hold her too much. She'll never start walking if you're always holding her. She's not a baby anymore, Daisy. She's one and almost ready to start walking."

"She's still a baby, and she's not feeling good today. I'm pretty sure her teeth are hurting her. Can you hold her for a moment? I need to use the privy."

"Yeah, give her to me." Jannie took her little niece into her arms. "Let me see those gums, Alisha." She squeezed the side of Alisha's cheeks to peek inside. The little girl began crying as Jannie peered at the white edge of a small tooth that was cutting through the swollen flesh.

Mattie watched out the window as Daisy entered the privy. "Give that baby some whiskey so she'll shut up and fall asleep. I'm tired of listening to her cry."

Jannie took a drink of her glass of whiskey before putting it against Alisha's lips and pouring a bit into her mouth. Alisha winced as her face scrounged, and her tongue reached out with a gag. The back of her hands touched her face with a scream. The whiskey burned her mouth and throat.

Jannie chuckled lightly. She spoke to Alisha, "The first drink burns a little, but it gets better, believe me." She poured more from the glass into the baby's mouth and leaned her back so the fluid would be swallowed. Jannie took a drink herself and then forced another drink into Alisha's mouth despite the little girl's screams.

Bernice walked out of her bedroom, curious why Alisha was screaming. "Give her to me!" she hollered irritably, seeing what Jannie was doing. She had been lying down with her youngest to take a nap.

Mattie, already in a bad mood, pushed Bernice forcefully backward. "Leave it be! That baby's been screaming all day. Now she'll go to sleep. You're already on my bad side Bernice. You'd better watch yourself!" Her right hand was balled into a fist.

Bernice trembled with rage. "I'm talking to Henry when he gets home."

"I'd hope so; he's your husband." She lowered her voice and hissed, "How dare you encourage Audrey to wait until Saturday to marry Alan! I had them this close to marrying today." She pinched her thumb and index together. "Get out of my sight."

Alisha screamed and then choked on the mouthful of whiskey that Jannie poured into her mouth. "Oops, that was too much." Jannie laughed.

"What are you doing?" Audrey shouted as she entered the front door, holding little Eve's hand. They had been picking flowers and Eve had a yellow buttercup in her hair. Audrey's eyes filled with angry tears as she yanked Alisha off Jannie's lap, pulled the screaming child close to her breast, and went to the water bucket on the kitchen counter to rinse Alisha's mouth out.

"Excuse me..." Jannie said. "She's crying because she's teething."

Audrey tried to get Alisha to drink some water, but she was fighting it as she wailed. Audrey turned to face Jannie with tight lips and a harsh glare. "She's screaming because that burns her! What's wrong with you?" she shouted. "She's a baby!" A frustrated tear fell from Audrey's eyes. She filled a cup with water. "I'm taking her to the creek to play in the water. It might be the only way she'll wash out her mouth and drink something good for her. I cannot believe you would give her that. Or that you two would stand by and let her!" Audrey snapped at Mattie and Bernice.

Mattie's upper lip twitched with anger. "Before you go, I saw you and Morton sitting by the creek talking all nice and close-like. That's more than I've seen you and Alan doing."

Audrey looked at her with a careless expression. "I suppose if Alan wanted to talk to me, he could. Couldn't he?"

The venom in Audrey's eyes took Mattie by surprise. It sent a wave of concern through her that Alan was losing the lady's interest. Mattie sputtered, "If I were you, I'd be wary of my son Morton. He is one of the rapists I told you about when you arrived and has a bad case of syphilis. I suppose he forced himself upon the wrong woman and will force himself upon you if you're not careful. Stay away from him for your own protection. And whatever you do, don't tell Alan you were alone with Morton. They already have bad relations because they are opposites. Alan is a gentleman; Morton is a mess. A shame to my name. Isn't that right, Jannie?"

Jannie scratched her greasy brown hair near her ear as she finished the glass of whiskey. "Right.

I tried to warn you about Morton." She filled the glass again.

Mattie warned, "Morton is trouble. I'd be done with him long ago if he wasn't my son. For your protection, do not put yourself in a position of being alone with him. He will hurt you. Understood?"

Bernice had walked quickly to her room while Mattie had spoken. Though the words were a warning that needed to be heeded, they were surprising. Morton had seemed a rougher man than she had known in the past, but he also appeared to be an honest gentleman. But the fact was, she was holding a child that needed to drink some water. "I need to get Alisha to the creek. She doesn't trust me to give her a drink of water now." Her glare darted to Jannie accusingly.

"What's wrong?" Daisy asked, returning.

***

"It's only two days, Alan. Certainly, you can keep your suspenders hitched up for forty-eight hours!" Mattie Sperry snapped at her son. Her tone and the harsh glare warned him to stop his whining and control his temper. She wasn't pleased to hear Audrey say she wanted to delay the wedding until Saturday either, but it was a choice that their guest had made.

Alan slammed his fist into the barn wall. "I have done everything to make her feel comfortable! What more can I do? I tried being nice to her this morning and she kicked me out of her room. I think she needs to be thrown down and shown who the boss is. Do you know what it's like to have her walk around here and know she's my wife, but she doesn't do anything? I can't even get a kiss." he took a deep breath and released it with a slight snarl of his upper lip. "We were supposed to get married today." He had to control the sudden urge to scream.

Mattie snapped, "Knock it off! She has the right to want to wait. A bigger concern is your brother Morton. I think she might be growing more interested in him, and I know my son, I can see that fluttering heart of his taking root on her. We need to end that today. I may have already ended her interest in him, but we'll see."

"I've already had words with Mort. Next time, it won't be words I speak with."

The coldness of his voice startled Mattie. "I don't want any fighting between you two. I can handle any infatuation Morton may have for her. What I can't handle is you sitting out here like a spoiled child feeling sorry for yourself. You need to spend more time in the house talking to Audrey and show her you're part of this family like a family man would."

Alan's jaw tightened. "All those screaming kids aggravate me."

"I don't care. Put on a gentleman's cloak and play the part she wants to see for the next two days, or I'm thinking she may not marry you. I fear I may have misjudged her desperation to be married; showing up wasn't enough. She's looking for love, Alan. So, you need to start acting like a soft-hearted weakling and pretend that you like flowers and children, and want to know more about how she feels. Go read part of the Bible and talk to her about it. You already won her heart with my letters; now you just have to keep from blowing it. You have two days. Even a ninety-pound weakling could hold up an appearance for that long. I suppose you can too."

"I'll try. I'll put on a happy face, wander down to the creek, and talk to her. Maybe go wading in the water with the baby." he said, looking out of the barn to the creek where Audrey played in the water with Daisy, Alisha, and Eve. Three other older children played in the water with them. Audrey's laughter occasionally reached the barn.

"Now you're thinking, go do that. I'll go to town and have a few words with Morton."

***

Alan walked down the hill to the creek with a gleeful smile. "Who is afraid of crawdads?" he asked loudly.

"I am." Four-year-old Elliot answered. He stood knee-deep in the creek, throwing pebbles into the water.

"Are you, Mandy?" Alan asked. Mandy was Henry and Bernice's oldest child. She was a quiet seven-year-old girl with a lighter shade of red hair than Bernice that appeared orange in the sunlight.

Mandy didn't seem to like her Uncle Alan too much as she shrugged her shoulders and went back to playing with her small fabric doll. She had stacked rocks into lines to create a house for the doll.

Audrey stood at the water's edge, holding Alisha's hand as she bent down and splashed in the water. "Did you come down to play?"

He nodded with a wide grin as he untied his boots and removed them. "Oh yeah. I love playing in the creek with the kids."

Elliot's voice questioned, "You do?"

"Of course," he chuckled with a glance and a slight shrug towards Audrey. "Watch this, Elliot." He dove into the deeper part of the creek and stayed underwater for longer than expected. He surfaced with a large reddish-brown crawdad in his hand. He shouted with exuberance as the refreshing water revived his youthful spirit. "Look what I found. They're all over the place, Elliot. I'm surprised one hasn't pinched you yet." He cast a glance at Audrey. "Do you want to hold this one, Elliot?"

"No." Elliot answered with a concerned expression. He was afraid of being pinched by the large claws.

"I'll teach you to hold it so you don't get pinched." He moved across the water towards Elliot.

"I don't want to." Elliot walked out of the water and began to run as Alan chased him out of the water with it.

"Arrgh! It's going to pinch you!" Alan shouted as he chased the little boy and pressed the crawdad's belly against Elliot's bare back. The boy screamed in a panic and ran sobbing to his mother.

"Alan," Daisy yelled, "stop teasing my son! He's

scared."

Alan stammered, "Well, if the little pansy ass is going to play in the creek, he needs to get over that fear, doesn't he? I was just playing. I wasn't going to let it pinch him. Your boy is a sissy! You need to toughen him up while you can."

Daisy scowled. "He's four. He has plenty of time to learn how to catch a crawdad without you chasing him with one. We're here having fun with the kids."

"I know. So am I." He lowered the crawdad to scare Mandy while she played alone.

She lurched away from the crustacean and waved a hand, annoyed. "Stop it."

Daisy said with annoyance, "Leave her be. I swear, Alan. Can't you just play without teasing the children? I think Tad learned it from you."

He was slightly embarrassed by being chastised by his baby sister. Audrey wasn't looking at him, she had all her attention on Alisha.

"Fine. I'll be nice." Alan said and walked behind where Daisy sat on the ground holding her son Elliot. Daisy wore a plain gray homemade dress with short sleeves she had crafted for hot days. Alan smirked as he lowered the crawdad and set its opened pincher against the skin on the back of her upper arm. The powerful pincher clamped down with a viscousness that only an angry crawdad could muster. He let it go as Daisy stood abruptly with a cry of pain, dropping Elliot to the ground. She jumped up and down painfully as the crawdad hung on tightly until she could swipe it off.

Alan laughed.

Tears gathered in her eyes from the pain, anger, and humiliation. Daisy glared at Alan. "Go away! I hate you sometimes. Get away from me and my children, Alan! You're such a jackass!"

"It was just a joke." He looked at Audrey, but she appeared uncomfortable and not at all humored. His ill-fated smile faded. "I wanted to talk with Audrey."

"Too bad!" Daisy shouted. "We're playing with the kids, and you're not welcome anymore. You're just lucky I don't say what I want to say. Get away from me before I do."

He put up a hand in surrender. "Audrey, do you want to come to the barn and talk?"

Audrey shook her head. "No. Right now, I'm having a good time with the children. We can talk later."

He nodded as his lips tightened. He grabbed his boots and walked up the hill in his socks to the barn. Once inside, he hit the barn wall abruptly with his fist and cursed.

***

Mattie walked sternly into town and made a direct path towards the tannery, where she found her two sons, Morton and Henry, on ladders putting a new coat of white paint on the front of the tannery.

"Mort, get down here!" Mattie shouted as she approached the boys.

"Ma?" Morton questioned. He was surprised

to have his mother and sister visit him at work. He descended the ladder leaving his can of white paint wired to a ladder rung twelve feet above him. "What are you doing here?" he asked. The furious expression on his mother's face made him curious.

Mattie restrained her voice to keep it from carrying across town, but there was no denying the fury behind it, "Morton, if you want a wife, I'll get you one, but you leave that woman alone! She's not your property. She's Alan's!"

Henry stepped off his ladder to join his brother. He chuckled. "Ma, Alan doesn't own a thing of his own."

"No one's talking to you, Henry! You stay out of this." Mattie snapped. "This is between Morton and me."

Morton was taken aback by the abruptness of the conversation. He narrowed his eyes with a shake of his head. "I'm not going to stop talking to Audrey because you want me to."

Mattie's right hand swung through the air and slapped Morton's face with a loud crack. "Don't you ever speak to me like that again! All I have to do is tell your friend Matt Bannister that it was you that put a bullet in the back of Sheriff Walt Coburn's head that day along the creek and you'll end up in prison or being hung, and if you say a word to Audrey to stop this wedding, I will! If you think I won't tell him, try me! You stay away from Audrey and let sleeping dogs lie, and I will too!" Her eyes bore into Morton, daring him to him respond. When he remained quiet, she knew the conversation was finished and turned away, feeling a victory.

Henry couldn't believe his ears. "Ma, why is it so important to you that she marries Alan? He's terrible."

She spun around. "I don't care about that! I care about making your brother happy. The happier he is, the less likely he'll go back to prison. Audrey will make him happy. And I will do whatever it takes to keep my son at home! I don't want him going back to prison."

Morton spoke plainly, "Sorry, Ma, but I won't let her marry Alan. I'll go to prison or be hung, but not before I tell her the truth about the letters. I've ruined my life already. I won't let you ruin hers."

Mattie seethed with grit teeth. "The family comes first, Morton, not the women that marry into it. Don't ruin this for him. I'll find you a prettier wife. I promise."

"I don't want a prettier wife!" Morton snapped.

Mattie spoke pointedly to both of her sons, "Leave it be! One word and neither of you will ever step foot on my property again. You'll be hung. I'll make sure of it." she said to Morton.

Henry watched their mother walk away. "Don't worry. I'll testify in court that Pick Lawson or Charlie Walker killed Sheriff Coburn."

Three months after Alan and their cousin Barry Helms were convicted and sent to prison, the Natoma Sheriff Walt Coburn was fishing along Heather Creek when someone fired a single shot into the back of his head. There had never been a suspect beyond the Sperry or Helms families, but to narrow the murder down to who pulled the trigger was never determined, and the murder remained unsolved.

Morton said, "Maybe it's just best to let sleeping dogs lie, as she said. Killing a lawman is a hanging offense." Morton scratched an itch on his leg. "I don't know how Racheal got away from here, but I might have to do the same for Audrey."

Henry took a deep breath. "You like Audrey, don't you?"

Morton nodded. "More than I should. I find myself thinking about her an awful lot."

Chapter 28

Dane Dielschneider had watched the funeral from a distance and noticed one of Matt's deputy marshals with blonde hair waiting at the far corner of the cemetery, leaning against a tree. A sheriff's deputy was at the cemetery's other end, sitting on a wooden bench in front of a family plot. It didn't take a dull muleskinner's brain to figure out they were there to watch for him.

Dane figured Bill Cooney had confessed and told them who had stolen from the ladies at the dance hall. Dane was grateful that he didn't try to bail Bill out of jail, or he would have been arrested too. Dane's brothers would have shot Bill for stooling on them like a six-year-old tattletale. Dane might've shot Bill too, but he didn't carry a gun.

The two deputies posted at both ends of the cemetery made him nervous, and the extra adrenaline helped him to be more cautious. There were other deputies in town that he wouldn't recognize if he didn't see their badges first. Dane knew he was the most recognizable man in the city, which put him at a significant disadvantage if he didn't do something to disguise himself. His red hair and missing hand stood out like a camel between the pews of a crowded church.

He followed the funeral procession at a careful distance towards the community hall. Suddenly spotting the two deputies talking together at the corner, Dane entered the closest store, the Barton's Pottery Shop.

"Hello, welcome to our shop. Please look around and let me know if there's anything you like." Lucille Barton said with a warm greeting. She was a lovely young lady with long curly black hair and was quite attractive. She was five months pregnant and showing it with a protruding belly.

Dane glanced out the window to ensure he wasn't seen. The pottery shop was filled with practical stoneware such as table settings and cooking bowls, but the more decorative pieces were pretty and caught his attention. He gazed with interest at the display tables and the shelves built along the walls that went from the floor ten feet up to the ceiling. "You got tons of stuff. Do you make all this?"

"My husband, our employee Jinhai and I do, yes." Lucille answered.

He snickered awkwardly. "Where are they then?" Dane asked. The shop was empty, except for her.

The blank expression in his dark eyes made Lucille feel uneasy. "Jinhai already went home, and my husband is in the house, just inside there." She motioned towards a door.

Dane gazed at her shoulders and height with interest. "My fiancé is about your size. I want to buy her a dress. Would you want to sell me yours?"

Lucille felt a chill run down her spine. She had been asked many odd things in her lifetime, but no one had ever asked to buy one of her dresses. "No. I suggest going to Lesko's clothing shop downtown or the mercantile. Fanny's sells dresses, and so does the hardware store. I suggest you look there."

Dane grinned wider than the conversation allowed for. "I don't know what size she wears. What if I get her one that is too big, and she thinks I think she's fat?"

"You should be able to tell if it's too big or not if she's your fiancé."

Dane's grin disappeared quickly. "I said she was, didn't I?" he snapped with a raised voice. He didn't like people doubting Tiffany was his fiancé. He blinked numerous times before adding softly, "We're going to get married."

"Congratulations," Lucille said with concern. The way he snapped was alarming, and she did not feel comfortable being alone with him. "I'll be right back. I need to speak with my husband."

"Before you go, can I see that plate with the elk on it, way up there? Elk are her favorite animals. I'd try to get it myself with your ladder, but I'd want to use two hands so I don't break it." He revealed his missing hand.

Ten feet up, on the top shelf just below the ceiling, was a collection of white plates with black drawings, which appeared similar to the art of scrimshaw, of various local forest animals such as deer, elk, bear, mountain lion, wolves, and smaller game like raccoons and beaver in their natural habitats. The collection was called Barton's Pacific Northwest Collection, which Jinhai Zhang had drawn with perfect details. They were not intended for eating on but to display as artwork. The Monarch Restaurant had already bought a complete set to decorate the restaurant.

"Can I look at it, please?" he pressed. "Tiffany loves elk."

"Those plates are very expensive. They are ten dollars per plate." Lucille advised, looking at how poorly Dane was dressed and not wanting to go to any great effort if he couldn't afford the plate.

Dane pulled a handful of paper money out of his pocket to show her. "I have plenty of money. I'd like to see that plate now."

Lucille was hesitant to climb the ladder. Jinhai insisted she stay off the ladder, but he wasn't there, and Lawrence couldn't keep his balance with one leg to climb that high either. She would have let Dane climb up the ladder to grab it, but he was missing a hand. Lucille grabbed the wooden six-foot stepladder, carried it over, and set it up in front of the plate he wanted to see. She climbed the ladder rungs until her feet were four feet off the ground, putting her head over nine feet. Lucille was not comfortable with heights and shook noticeably as her protruding belly set against the top rung as she reached for the plate and removed it from the display stand.

Dane stepped behind the ladder to watch her climb up and glanced at the bay windows to ensure no one was looking inside. Dane bent over slightly and ran forward, shouting a curse right before driving his shoulder into the back of Lucille's knees, forcing her bodyweight to fall onto his shoulders and upper back. Dane lifted her legs as she fell and threw her legs over his head as she flipped in the air and fell head first.

Lucille cried out as she fell and reached her arms out to break the fall. Her arms collapsed upon impact, and her upper forehead hit the floor with a jarring force. Like a falling tree leaving the stump, her body slammed against the timbers of the floor with all her body weight centered around her pregnant belly. The sound of the plate shattering near her was the only sound as she turned to her side while grabbing her stomach and wincing in pain while trying to breathe.

Her lungs longed for a breath, but she couldn't breathe. A pain-filled grimace twisted her facial features as she slowly pulled her legs into a fetal position and wrapped her arms tighter around her stomach. She made a choking sound as her breath started coming back to her. Blood ran down her face onto the floor from a sizeable gash near her hairline. Lucille began to groan, then sob quietly in pain.

Dane stood over her, unmoving, watching in a pleasurable daze. His words lacked emotion, "Are you okay? I stumbled. I'm sorry." Dane tried to sound concerned, "I'll get some help." He went to the house door and banged on it loudly. He opened it and saw Lawrence using his crutch, hurrying towards the shop after hearing his wife cry out. "Your wife fell. Take her to the doctor."

"Oh Lord," Lawrence prayed with an unspoken urgency as he quickly hobbled past Dane towards Lucille. "What were you doing on the ladder?" he asked with a weakening voice. "Oh, no! Lucille!" He dropped to a knee beside her. She was also bleeding from her nose and having severe cramps in her stomach. She sobbed uncontrollably, harder and louder with each given minute. Lawrence could see she was in great pain and bleeding severely from the gash on her head. It scared him. "Get some help!" he shouted to Dane. "Get some help!" Lawrence repeated as he moved to lovingly cradle her head on his lap while he covered the gash with his hand. Lawrence's heavy tears burned his eyes. He wept while holding his wife in a loving embrace. "It's going to be okay. Lord Jesus, please let her and the baby be okay." Lawrence prayed with a quivering voice.

Dane stood like a statue, watching as blood appeared to pool from under her dress. He pointed at her legs. "She's bleeding down there too."

Lawrence pulled her dress up and gasped when he saw the blood on her pantaloons. He glanced at Dane desperately, only to see the stranger peering at Lucille like a predator admiring their kill. Lawrence shouted, "Are you deaf? Get some help!"

The Bartons' five-year-old son, Michael, and his younger brother Ray came into the shop and were frightened to see their mother sobbing in pain, along with their father crying and all of the blood. "Daddy?" Michael asked with a shaking voice. Tears already welled in his eyes.

Dane walked out the shop's door and quietly waved two men passing by into the store to help. One of the men, recognizing it was an emergency, went outside and yelled for more help and for a wagon passing by to stop to take her a few blocks to the doctor's office.

While everyone's attention was on Lucille, Dane maneuvered quietly to the back of the shop and slipped into the house when no one was looking. He found Lucille's bedroom and searched for a dress that buttoned up the front that would fit over his baggy clothes. He couldn't find a dress that would fit over the baggy sleeves of his shirt, which once belonged to his much larger brother Devin. Frustrated, he pulled the shirt off and grabbed a plain V-neck shirt out of a drawer belonging to Lawrence. He pulled a pink and yellow flower-design dress over his legs and put it on before buttoning it up to his neck. It was tight but would cover his pants once he rolled up the cuff another turn. He found a white bonnet with which he covered his hair and tied it under his chin. Looking in a mirror, he knew his brothers would have laughed and teased him relentlessly for dressing up as a woman. He had to chuckle about it himself. He stuffed his shirt in a handbag belonging to Lucille and left the house.

He had to cut a small hole in the seam of the dress to be able to reach his knife in a hurry. He hoped the hole wouldn't be too noticeable as the dress had no pockets, and the seam would expose the white shirt underneath. He was pleased that the two deputies had left their spot on the corner to help get the pretty pregnant lady to the doctor. Dane walked along Main Street until a brown wig in the window of the Lamb's Barber Shop and Beauty Salon caught his attention.

He went inside and grinned at Gail Lamb. "Miss, I need a wig for a costume party I'm going to. I'm dressed as a woman."

Gail Lamb wrinkled her nose. "You make an ugly woman."

"That could be because I'm not a woman." he answered shortly.

"Of course not. I have several wigs that might give you a womanlier appearance, but I doubt you'll win any prizes for the best costume. Where is this party at anyway? I haven't heard of any such parties."

Dane's first thought was the only place where he had spent some of the money. "Madam Collet's Brothel."

"Oh. That figures. Since you have red hair naturally, do you want to wear a red wig? I have this fine curly long-haired wig which is a lighter shade of red but very attractive. I will sell it to you for three dollars. It is of fine quality and will look natural once pinned to your hair."

Dane nodded as he licked his lips. "Yes. How do I wear it?"

Gail answered, "You leave that to me. If you want, I can lighten up your freckles and make you look far more feminine with some powder and makeup. You might even pass as one of those harlots over there by the time I am done with you, but I can't transform you into a woman for free."

"I can pay. I have plenty of money if you can make me look different."

Gail smiled slowly. "When I'm done, you'll have to tell those men seeking a woman that you're a man." she teased.

Dane grinned widely. "I have a knife to make them look more like a woman than me if they insist." He chuckled. "Yes, I want the men to think I am a woman. That's exactly what I want. I have money to pay, so do me up right. Whore-a-fie me!" He giggled.

Chapter 29

Dane stopped along the boardwalk of Main Street to look at his reflection in a closed store window. He felt like he could float on air by the attention he was drawing in his womanly costume. His new friend, Gail Lamb, who helped him prepare for the costume party at Madame Collet's Brothel, was convinced Dane would win. He had looked in the mirror, and he was unrecognizable. Dane couldn't take his eyes off his reflection in the window. If he weren't himself, he'd be attracted to the lady in the pink and yellow dress he admired in the window. Gail had done him up right, and it was worth every cent he had paid.

The curly red-haired wig fell to his shoulders while the long bangs fell over the sides of his face. His face had been heavily coated with a bright white lead-based paste to cover the freckles. The white base gave Gail Lamb a blank canvas to work her cosmetic artistry for Dane to beat the competition in the brothel. A touch of pink rouge layered gently over his cheeks added some color. She was most proud of the bright red carmine dye mixture she applied to his thin lips to give them a fuller and more radiant appearance. To add some depth to his eyes, Gail applied some bee wax to his eyelashes and rubbed fine ash dust from the barber shop's ashtray on them for thicker and deceivingly longer lashes. A mixture of bee wax, a drop of oil, and a blue talc powder created a paste that she applied thinly over his eyelids: coal powder and beeswax shaped and colored Dane's eyebrows black.

Not quite finished with her masterpiece of transforming Dane into a woman, Gail reached for her small brass mouche box. Mouche is the French word for the common house fly. In the 17th Century, France popularized the use of gluing fake moles made of velvet or satin onto faces to cover blemishes and scars. However, it soon became fashionable, and beauty patches became a trend that still had its uses for enhancing a lady's appearance. Gail licked the adhesive on the back of a beauty patch and pressed it an inch over from the corner of Dane's mouth. She added another fake mole half an inch from the corner of his eye to enhance the other side of his face.

To mask his appearance a bit more, she had Dane strip naked under the dress for a better fit. Gail sent her husband to the mercantile to buy a roll of gauze and two medium-sized, firm tomatoes, which Gail wrapped over his shoulders and under his arms to portray breasts. Gail tied a sling made from a white towel around his neck to conceal his missing right hand.

Dane stared at his reflection in the window and couldn't be more pleased. He would not be recognized by anyone, not even his friend Bill Cooney. He stared at the sheriff's office for a moment, debating. He knew Bill Cooney was inside, and an idea came to him of how to get rid of Bill for good. The fact was that there was only one person who could testify that he had stolen the money from the dance hall. No one could prove he stole the dancer's money without Bill as a witness. However, Dane could prove that he was not with Bill that night simply by asking the dance hall owners. They could testify that Dane said he and Bill had argued earlier that day and were not together.

Dane began breathing fast and hard to mimic being out of breath and yanked the door open. He spoke urgently in a feminine voice, "The marshal's been stabbed behind Madame Collet's and needs help now! Hurry!"

"Matt?" Deputy Mark Thiessen asked with concern.

"Yes! Go! He needs help now, and no one is in the marshal's office. I checked."

"Where?" Mark asked while grabbing his gun belt and hurrying towards the door.

"Behind Madame Collet's Brothel in the alley." Dane watched the deputy go and then turned towards the jail cells, where Bill lay on the bottom bunk staring at him. Dane grinned slowly. "I suppose you are wondering if I was going to get you out of here, huh?"

"Dane?" Bill asked in disbelief. "Why are you dressed like that?" He stood from his bunk and approached the cell door.

"It's the only way I can get close to Tiffany without being noticed. Thank you for causing the scene for me to get upstairs. I got enough money for you to buy a new wedding ring and dresses for Danetta and the girls, just as I said."

"Matt tried to tell me that Danetta had Dallen killed by your brothers. That's not true, is it?" Bill asked.

"No. Come hold this door, and I'll open the lock." He set his handbag down and pulled the dress over his left leg to reveal his hunting knife was tied securely just below his knee with gauze. He pulled the knife out of the sheath. "I'll have to wedge it open, which I can do with your help. But I need you to stand over here, stick your right arm outside the bars, grab the door right here, and pull it towards you as hard as possible. Lean your shoulder against the bars to use as a fulcrum point." He grinned at his friend. "You taught me that word. Remember when we were lifting the corner of the wagon with that bar and wood block?"

"Yeah. Dane, wouldn't pushing from the other side of the door give me more power?" Bill asked curiously.

Dane shook his head. "Na. Usually, it would, but

not with this lock. Lean into the bars like so." He helped adjust Bill's body the way he wanted it. With Bill's attention on pulling the door, Dane's lips twisted, and he plunged the six-inch blade through the four-inch bars into Bill's right side into his liver. While still inside Bill, Dane turned the blade sideways and yanked the knife out. He struck the knife with an upward thrust under the rib cage, piercing a lung. By that time, Bill reacted by pulling his large arm free from the bars.

Bill was perplexed as he covered the blood that flowed quickly from the wound on his abdomen. "You stabbed me. You had me hold that door to stab me?" he asked in disbelief that his friend had stabbed him.

His white face and red lips grinned with a soft chuckle. "You're never going to see Danetta again. With you gone, I can walk away free."

Both of Bill's large and strong hands shot forward in a desperate attempt to grab Dane by the throat, but Dane backed up against the wall as Bill hit the bars with his chest and grimaced. Bill looked at Dane bewildered and slowly shook his head as he bent over, growing weaker. He crept to his bottom bunk and sat down as he stared at a large pool of blood around the cell door that dripped across the floor to him. His chest ached, and it hurt to breathe. Tiny droplets of blood came out of his mouth as he spoke in a mere whisper, "You were my friend."

Dane watched the blood flowing from Bill's side onto the mattress and dripping to the floor with a gleaming in his eye while a strange half-grin grew. He replaced the knife in the sheath. "Friends don't tattletale, Bill. I'll tell Danetta you left her for another redhead." He snickered as Bill laid down to finish bleeding to his last breath.

***

Butterflies swarmed in Dane's belly as he opened the door to the Monarch Hotel's entry. The restaurant window drapes were closed for privacy, but he could hear talking and laughter from inside. He paused inside the lobby to look through the opened restaurant door at the people inside. He did not see Matt or his fiancé, but there was a whole other side of the restaurant that he could not see.

Pamela Collins, the hotel's Assistant Manager, lowered her brow as she addressed the strange-looking woman that had entered the hotel. Her immediate impression was it was a prostitute hiding her sores from syphilis under the white paint. She was not the type of clientele the Monarch Hotel was accustomed to having. "Miss, may I help you?"

Dane lifted his lips. "Yes. My husband and I have a room." he said in an intentionally higher-pitched feminine voice.

"Oh? Can I get your name to check my registry?" Pam questioned.

He nodded. "Lyla Jones. My husband Dick is not feeling well."

"Oh. Yes. I was wondering about you folks. It

says you paid your two-night bill, but we never received a payment."

He blinked slowly to show his blue eyelids. He pointed towards the restaurant. "We're cousins. There is no cost, correct?" Steven Bannister had been the most helpful when it came to offering information. Dane would have never known he could get a free room if he were part of the family mourning Hannie.

"Oh. You must be related on the Longo side?" Pamela asked. William Fasana had already told Pam that Dick and Lyla Jones were unrelated to his family.

"Yes."

"Okay," Pamela said with a relieved expression. "That explains the misunderstanding. When you signed in, the night clerk should have written the word funeral instead of paid. As you know, there is a private family party inside the restaurant. I hope your husband feels better. Is there anything we can do for him?"

Dane nodded. "If you see Tiffany come out here, tell her Uncle Steven needs to talk to her in room fourteen."

"I thought your husband's name was Dick?" Pamela looked at the registry quickly to double-check.

"Richard Steven is his name. I call him Dick; everyone else calls him Steven or Uncle Steven. If you could tell her, I'd appreciate it."

Pamela furrowed her brow as she wrote it down on a notepad so she wouldn't forget. "I'll do that. Out of curiosity, how is Steven related to Tiffany if you're relatives on the Longo side?"

Dane stared at her blankly for a moment without blinking. "It's a small world and smaller yet in a small town. Her father is my brother-in-law."

"Oh. I'll give her the message."

"Thank you." Dane said and stood at the restaurant door. He was surprised to see Tiffany sitting at a table at the far end of the restaurant with a group of other teenagers. The beautiful and heartwarming smile he had longed to see for so long was being offered to a handsome teenage boy with short dark hair. Tiffany pushed the boy playfully as she laughed. The sound of her laughter and the flirtatious push lit a fuse of jealousy within Dane that quickly sparked his anger. He gritted his teeth as he stared at the young man's face to memorize it. The other teens with them were of no concern.

"Gabriel, I am shocked!" Tiffany shouted.

"Well, it's the truth!" Gabriel Smith grinned as the others laughed. "Okay, solve this one. It's a phrase." He pointed towards his eye.

"Eye."

He nodded approvingly and hugged his chest tightly.

"Hug?" one of the other boys guessed.

He shook his head.

"Love?" One of the girls asked.

He pointed at her and nodded. He raised four fingers and pointed at his leg.

"You love four-legged women!" Jerimiah Bannister exclaimed. He was Adam Bannister's oldest son. He was fourteen, almost fifteen.

Gabriel was exasperated. He shook his head with a disturbed expression. He put his hand about three feet high and moved his fingers back and forth as if scratching.

"Dogs?" Katy Stevenson guessed. She was related to the Longo side of the family.

"Four legs scratching. Um, ear mites?" Jerimiah guessed. "Scours?"

"Scours don't itch!" Katy's brother Carl laughed.

"I'm guessing." Jerimiah stated defensively.

Gabriel sighed as he shook his head. He lifted his leg, untied his boot, and removed it to expose his wool socks.

"I would say scratching between his toes, but he doesn't have four feet. Wait! Feet! You love feet!" Katy exclaimed.

He pointed at the sock again, put his hand out at the three-foot level, and repeatedly used both hands to push down about two inches.

"Socks, four feet, three feet high, and what... soft?" Tiffany questioned.

Gabriel nodded.

"Sheep! You love sheep!" Tiffany answered.

He closed his thumb and index finger nearly together to indicate she was close.

"Goats?" Jerimiah guessed quickly. "They're close to a sheep."

"Pigs aren't soft like socks," Carl reasoned to himself. "I would say a donkey, but they're taller, usually."

"I hear llamas are soft," Jerimiah said to Carl. "I don't know how tall they are, though."

"I know the answer. You hug sheep?" Tiffany asked as a joke.

"You better watch that!" Carl laughed.

Gabriel gave up. "Ewe! I love you. Come on. I told you at the beginning it was a phrase. A Four-legged woman, Jerimiah?" Gabriel asked his cousin.

Adam Bannister turned around from the table beside theirs and said, "I thought it was a good answer, Jerimiah." He chuckled at his oldest son's answer.

***

An older, robust lady with graying hair approached Dane with a drink in her hand. She had been sitting at the first table, in front of him, with two older men and a woman. "Are you one of my nieces I haven't met yet?" she asked.

Dane shook his head uneasily. "No. The other side of the family." He couldn't get the answer wrong either way.

"Longo's side of the family?" she asked.

Dane kept his focus on Tiffany. "Sure."

Eleanor Archer waved a hand, "Well, come in and join us. We're all family, after all. I'm Hannie's Great-Aunt Eleanor, on her mother's side. What is your name?"

Dane could feel his heart pound when he saw Steven Bannister stand up to get another plate of food on a table in the conference room. "Dan... Lyla Jones. My husband is Dick."

"Lyla, come join us."

"No. I must get back to my room. My husband is sick."

An old man with a long gray beard sitting at a table beside Eleanor's chair stared at Dane with a disturbed expression. "Does your husband own a paint company, or did you get burned?"

"Luther, stop it!" Eleanor said with a slight chuckle. She explained to Dane, "He's had too much to drink."

Luther raised his hands questioningly. "I'm just saying that's more gallons of paint used there than it would take to paint the entire quarry pit. Turn around, let's see the name of the paint store. There must be a promotional sign on her somewhere." He looked at Charlie Ziegler. "Am I wrong?"

Charlie chuckled. "Probably just for saying it."

Luther continued, "That much paint means you're hiding something. If she's ugly, that's one thing, but she can't look worse than she does now. And I'm drunk!" he emphasized to the laughter of Charlie and Mary Ziegler, and Eleanor. He turned around in his seat and hollered, "Adam! Hey, Adam, look at this woman. Is that a whore, clown, or Halloween costume?" he laughed. His sudden shouting for Adam Bannister across the restaurant got everyone's attention on Dane.

Adam raised his voice in answer, "Uncle Luther, you better slow down on that bourbon before she's looking pretty and you wake up with smeared paint on your face."

Luther laughed loudly as he gave an appreciative glance at his nephew. "I don't normally drink, but

I could finish a full bottle, and she'd still look like Queen Elizabeth from the Tudor age." He turned his head and spoke to Dane, "Listen, lady, they didn't think the Queen was pretty during the Golden Age of the Fifteenth Century. What in the world makes you think all that paint would be considered pretty now? I always wondered, but now I know why Elizabeth was known as the Virgin Queen."

Eleanor covered her mouth, trying to hide her embarrassed grin while she tried not to laugh. "Lyla, I apologize for my brother. He's normally not like this. I'm afraid your side of the family will hate ours by the time this night is over. Let me give you a hug because we're all family here."

"No! I don't like hugs." Dane said in his usual soft voice. He was furious about the insulting words of the old man and being laughed at. He wanted to leave, but his attention kept going back to Tiffany. Dane burned with anger to see the dark-haired boy touching her hand affectionately.

"Bull," Eleanor said. "Everyone likes to be hugged." She wrapped her arms around him without warning and pulled him against her firmly in a warm hug. She whispered in his ear, "You ought to wipe that stuff off your face. It looks silly. I bet you are a beautiful lady."

Dane was frozen like an icicle hanging from a gutter, unable to move. He could not remember the last time anyone hugged him. His mother, to his memory, had never hugged him. It was a strange sensation to be hugged by a woman he had never met. A scowl overcame his face. He stepped back to break the hug. The horrified expression on his face startled Eleanor. He stammered, "Why did you do that?"

"Because we're family. And in this family, we hug."

He stepped further back. Dane wanted to write a note to the boy talking to Tiffany to meet him outside in the alley, where he planned to kill him for stealing Tiffany's affection. Dane was too perplexed to do so now. He was torn between the horror of being touched and the hug's uneasy warmth to his soul. He quickly walked away, throwing his finger towards Pamela at the desk. "Tell Tiffany what I said!" He quickly ran up the stairs to room number fourteen.

He closed the door behind him and sat heavily on the davenport. He breathed deeply as his mind wondered why the stranger had forced a hug upon him. It made no sense. Yet, there was something about it he longed to feel again. He pushed the thought away and focused on Tiffany's flirtatious shove and laughter with the teenage boy.

He opened a window to let the cool evening breeze blow into the sitting room. The third-story window faced an alley four feet from the neighboring building. It was only a two-story building, and its roof was four or five feet below the window. A fellow could jump across the alley and escape across the neighboring roof quickly enough if need be. Or, if a fellow wanted to, he could carry a ladder onto the adjacent roof and pry a window open to get into the Monarch Hotel without anyone noticing him. Dane leaned out the window to look where Tiffany's room was along the neighboring roofline. It would be easier to place a ladder in the alley to reach her room's window. He knew where a ladder was. The pottery shop had a ladder he could borrow, and he could pick the lock to get inside quickly enough. Tiffany would have her hotel room window open as warm out as it was. He'd bet his left hand that he could slip right into her room tonight, unnoticed, and take her home.

Dane sat on the windowsill and enjoyed the breeze and the quiet of a nice room. Holding a blue stoneware bowl filled with chocolate candies, he ate one piece at a time until the bowl was empty. He held the bowl out the window and watched it fall thirty-five feet to shatter on the brick walkway below. "Oops." He swallowed the last of the chocolates and stared at the second-story window that belonged to Tiffany's bedroom.

Chapter 30

Morton Sperry sat at the bar having a drink in Avery's Saloon. He sat alone and didn't want to be bothered by anyone, especially his brother, Vince, and sister, Jannie. They were at a table playing cards with gang member Elliot Zook and a local man who worked for Crawford Farms named Joe Higgs.

Natoma didn't have a wide variety of places to go in the evening hours except for Avery's. Not long ago, Morton enjoyed going there with his family and friends to drink, get rowdy and laugh. Over the past months, something had changed within him, and Avery's Saloon wasn't as much fun as it used to be. At the end of the bar sat the town sheriff, Zeke Jones, sipping on his drink. Zeke was an old man, never married, and perhaps the saddest fellow in the town. He smoked another rolled-up cigarette and sat lost in his thoughts without his badge pinned to his shirt. He stopped wearing his badge after office hours when he was harassed by a couple of troublemakers passing through town. The two troublemakers never made it back home and were buried up in the woods outside of town. The horses they rode made some good meals for the Sperry and Helms families, while the hides earned them some money at the tannery. Those men just disappeared as people sometimes did in Natoma. No trace of them was left.

Zeke had watched Morton and his cousin Jesse Helms kill the two men and knew all the details, but he'd never say a word. They had saved Zeke from being hurt or possibly killed by the two mean-spirited men. To avoid any further trouble after that, the old man left his badge in his desk drawer when he went home from work. In truth, there was no law in Natoma except for poetic justice by those wronged. Zeke was merely a symbol of what was supposed to be.

Morton watched Zeke and wondered if that was a photograph of his future; sitting at the bar night after night, drinking alone. His eyes shifted from Zeke to the mirror to look at his sorrowful face as it reflected back at him. Smiles didn't come easily anymore, not that they ever did. Even alcohol couldn't bring the laughter it once did; in truth, that was the only time he laughed.

Audrey Butler didn't make him laugh like the kangaroo at the circus did, but he felt a mysterious joy in her presence that he couldn't identify. Smiling came easy when he was near her; if he could, he'd like to spend all day sitting beside the creek talking to her.

The excitement he felt to talk with Audrey again and to see her smile plagued his thoughts throughout his working hours. It filled him with an urgency to get back home, clean up, and hope to find her alone somewhere where they could talk again. The opportunity came sure enough, but she made it known, not with words but by intentionally avoiding, that she didn't want to talk to him. She seemed uncomfortable, and it bothered him. He had not done or said anything that could have offended her; he didn't think. It made him wonder if his mother had threatened Audrey to stay away from him like Mattie had threatened him to stay away from Audrey. It would explain why Audrey was acting the way she was. Morton thought they were becoming friends, but now her welcoming smile appeared to fear him.

Zeke Jones finished his drink and moved down the bar to sit next to Morton. "Mort, you seem under the weather."

Morton rubbed his forehead, uninterested in talking. "I can't afford to buy you a drink, Zeke," Morton said plainly. "If that's what you want, you might as well move along."

"No. I just thought I'd see how you are." He sat beside Morton.

"Zeke, how come you never married?" Morton asked quietly.

Zeke shrugged his shoulders and took a deep breath. "Pride, foolishness, and stupidity. I had my chances when I was your age and younger. My first love was the love of my life. I was in my early twenties. We had a misunderstanding, I could have gone after her, patched things up, and married her, but I was too prideful to say I was wrong. I could have made that right, but I was too prideful, foolish, and stupid to do it. She married another man. I suppose my other loves weren't quite as hurtful or haunt me as much. Well, that was over forty years ago, and I don't even know if she's still alive. But during that time, Morton, that brief moment of my life, I swear they were the happiest days I've ever known. I've kicked myself in the ass ever since." He looked into Morton's eyes with intent. "If you ever love someone, and I mean really love someone to the point that you want to marry that woman, don't let her go. You go after her and fight for her with everything you got, or you'll end up like me, spending your life wishing you had. I don't have much of a legacy to pass on to anyone, but if I did, that's it. Just the knowledge that pride can make you foolishly stupid."

"What if she's engaged to someone else?" Morton asked quietly.

Zeke nodded knowingly. "If you're talking about your brother, then that's a hell of a fight that I would not want to be in the middle of. The question you need to ask is; is she worth it? If you can answer that question, then you have your answer. I'll see you tomorrow, Mort."

"Thank you, Zeke." Morton carried his drink to the table where his brother and sister were sitting. "Jannie, can I talk to you outside?"

"Do you want to play, Morton?" Joe Higgs asked as he shuffled the cards.

"No. Jannie, let's go outside."

"I'm playing cards." she whined.

"Now." he said with an authoritative tone that revealed no patience for her whining.

"What do you want?" she asked, annoyed as they stepped onto the front porch.

"Our mother threatened me today to leave Audrey alone. Did she threaten Audrey too?"

Jannie snickered. "Wouldn't you like to know?"

Morton's eyes hardened. "Yes, I would. I'm in no mood to play, Jannie. What did she say?"

***

Morton walked up the dark road to their homestead, furious. The lies his mother told Audrey about him were not just a personal insult; they tarnished his already bad reputation to the level of a lowly rapist, which was as low as a criminal could go. Morton had robbed, stolen, intimidated, and murdered people; all of that was true. But he had never forced himself upon a woman nor allowed a member of his gang to do so. Not to say they hadn't, the Sperry-Helms Gang had that reputation under Alan's reign, but Morton never approved of doing so. His mother had transferred Alan's crimes to Morton's name, which infuriated him. He understood now why Audrey had avoided him. She probably thought he was gaining her trust until the opportunity came for him to attack her.

His mother knew too well that Morton had no patience or tolerance for a man that raped a woman. Daisy's oldest child, Elliot, was the product of her being raped by an acquaintance of the Sperry-Helms Gang. That man wasn't worth burying after Morton and his gang killed him. They stripped him down and left his body to be eaten by animals six miles out into the mountains. The Sperry and Helms were rough families that attracted other rough men to join their gang. The Sperry sisters were often available in a town where available women were sparse. Those who were available belonged to more respectable families and didn't consort with rough men like them. Three former gang members had ended up in the ground at different times over the years, and a traveler who got rough with Jannie. It didn't pay to lay a hand on a Sperry sister or a Helms wife because those who did, paid with their lives. Morton's mother knew all that; she knew Morton never had and would never force himself upon a woman. It disgusted him to no end that she would tell Audrey he was a rapist and had syphilis to top it off. He was furious.

Morton walked briskly towards the house with every intention to barge into his mother's room and confront her. Duke, the large dog, barked as it approached him in the dark. "Shut up, Duke, before you get shot! You stupid dog!" he barked with a harsh tone.

"He's just trying to protect the home." Audrey's voice said from the darkness. It startled him.

"I didn't see you there." Morton said. Audrey

was sitting on a swing tied to a thick oak tree limb across the lawn at the edge of a ravine where the creek ran below.

"My room is too hot again. It's such a warm and beautiful night. I thought I'd come out here since everyone is asleep."

Morton walked closer. He put his hands up defensively in the available moonlight. "Jannie told me what my mother said to you. I'll let you know right now that I'm not a rapist. I may be a lot of things, but I have never forced myself on any woman. And I don't have syphilis either. She lied to you because she thinks I'm trying to steal you away from Alan. I was warned about that today by her and Alan both. I'm just telling you right now, that ain't the case."

She held the ropes to the swing. "I didn't know what to think at first. She told me those things to keep me away from you. I can't pretend to understand why she would lie, but it didn't add up. Henry and Bernice both told me it wasn't true."

He sighed noticeably with relief. "At least I feel better about that."

"Morton, why would your mother lie to me like that?" she asked.

He knelt in the grass. "For the same reason she threatened me. Ma's afraid I was stealing you away from Alan."

Audrey tilted her head with concern. "What is going on? Alan wrote such open letters that touched my heart, but now he's different. The difference is as vast as listening to a Biblical scholar who has studied the Bible in the original languages give a sermon and your Reverend Cass give one. I tend to think your Reverend Cass probably thinks the word *Protestant* is a southerner's term for a prostitute. No disrespect intended."

Morton chuckled. "You're funny. But you're more right about that than you might know."

Audrey dropped her hands onto her lap and asked, "Why is Alan so different than the man I came here to marry? You and I have had a more meaningful conversation in the last five minutes than any I've had with Alan. I don't know if I can communicate with him. He is so guarded and changes the subject of everything back to wanting a kiss, or you can imagine what. He gives me a bad feeling. I didn't come here to make a mistake, and the more I talk with Alan and see how he is, the less I want to marry him. I don't have anyone to count on, Morton. I thought Bernice might become a Christian friend I could talk to, but she never says anything to me. I'm kind of stuck here, and the closer Saturday comes, the more afraid I become."

Morton frowned helplessly. He wanted to tell her the truth about the letters. He longed to tell Audrey the whole courtship through the mail was a deception intended by their mother to keep Alan from returning to prison. He wanted to share with her that Alan was a felon, an evil man, and she'd be a fool to marry him. He was tempted to tell her the truth, but he resisted. If she knew the truth and reacted unwisely, Morton knew she would end up beaten, whipped, or worse when he wasn't there to protect her.

Morton may have been tempted to tell Audrey the truth, but for her own good, he refused to tell her. He wasn't sure how he would do it, but he was going to help her escape the hell of marrying his brother. He hesitated to answer. "Give it until Saturday morning, and if you don't want to marry Alan, let me know. I like to think we're friends, Audrey."

She smiled joyfully as she leaned back in the swing and kicked her legs up momentarily. "I'd like to think so too. If you want to know the truth, I was sitting out here waiting for you. I wanted to apologize for treating you rudely earlier. I didn't know the truth yet."

He stood and walked behind the swing and pulled the swing back gently.

"Are you giving me a push?" She questioned brightly. "I haven't been pushed on a swing since I was a kid."

"Hang on tight." he said and ran forward to lift the swing over his head as he ran under it.

She laughed as she swung back about seven feet high and came forward towards him. She could not help but feel the exuberance of swinging in the middle of the night like a child under the bright stars. The joy in Morton's smile as he watched her swing warmed her heart. She screamed with laughter as he ran under her again to make her go even higher.

Chapter 31

The hour was getting late, and the family members were slowly leaving the restaurant to go to their rooms or across town to home. Pamela Collins had worked late so Joshua Bannister could visit with his family, but the night clerk, Wendell Jacobson, was starting soon, and then she could go home and get some sleep.

Matt Bannister and Christine had left earlier to go to the doctor's office. Their friend Lucille Barton had fallen off a ladder, which caused her to miscarry the baby at five months. It was a devastating experience for Lucille and Lawrence both. Matt learned by the description of the man that it was Dane Dielschneider who pulled her off the ladder. Lucille was convinced that he had intentionally pulled her off the ladder intending for her to fall, even though he claimed it was an accident. Lawrence could find no evidence of any missing money or anything else that was of any value. Nothing had been taken or moved that he could tell. Matt was left with no evidence to prove it wasn't an accidental stumble into the ladder, as Dane had claimed.

It was then discovered that Bill Cooney was stabbed to death while in his jail cell. The sheriff, Tim Wright, notified Matt because his name was involved. Deputy Mark Thiessen explained a woman with a painted white face had burst into the office, claiming Matt was stabbed and needed help behind the brothel. Mark assumed the woman was a prostitute employed there. He left to help Matt and found absolutely nothing. He returned to the jail about forty minutes later and found the jail cell covered in blood and the lifeless body of Bill Cooney lying on his bunk. There was no explanation other than the puddle of blood spread across the floor from the cell door to the bunk. Matt suspected that Dane hired a prostitute to alarm the deputy to get him out of the office, leaving Dane free to go inside and kill the only witness to his crime of robbing the dance hall girls. It made the hunt for Dane Dielschneider much more urgent to find him, now that he had killed a man.

Matt had missed most of the evening with his family. When Matt was called to the sheriff's office, Christine returned to the dance hall. Matt had returned to the restaurant late and discovered his son, Gabriel Smith, had ridden the sixteen miles from Willow Falls to be with the family. Gabriel missed the funeral and reception but wanted to be at the reunion.

Truet Davis had been struggling recently with

the first anniversary of his wife Jenny Mae's death quickly approaching. Several men had attacked her, and the result caused her to miscarry their baby. Jenny Mae hemorrhaged and bled to death on a doctor's table while in Truet's arms. The memory was painful, but then the news came of Lucille falling. Truet went to the doctor's office with Matt to see their friends, but the sound of Lucille screaming in pain, crying, and Lawrence's tears and words to his beautiful wife brought Truet's experience with Jenny Mae back to life. It was too much for Truet's emotions to handle. He had said good night to Annie and left so he could be alone. Truet had not returned, and Matt did not expect him to. Sometimes, a man must be alone to mourn and talk to his God. It had been a sad night, and Matt was in no mood to celebrate.

The restaurant was emptying, and the last to leave were Matt, Annie, Tiffany, Steven, his wife, Nora, William Fasana, and Aunt Eleanor as they slowly moved out into the lobby.

Eleanor spoke to the one nephew she had heard about years before but had never met, Gabriel Smith. It was stunning how all her late sister Ruth Bannister's children and grandchildren seemed to look like Ruth. "If you're going to Portland to visit your grandfather, why not hop on the train and come to Astoria and visit me?" Eleanor asked Gabriel. "My husband and I could show you the Pacific Ocean and take you out on our boat to catch some salmon or crabs or shoot a sea lion. It would be fun, and we'd love to have you."

William interrupted with a serious expression, "Aunt Eleanor, we have a good supply of crabs right here in town if he wants to catch some. Madame Collet's has an abundance of them." He and Steven were the only two that laughed.

"Crabs?" Nora asked Steven, not understanding the joke. "The closest we have is crawdads around here, isn't it?"

Steven nodded. "Yes, dear, that's what's so funny. We have crawdads." He rolled his eyes at William.

"Hmm." She didn't see the humor.

Gabriel gave William an odd look and shrugged his shoulders, unknowingly. He was now finished with school and moving into the world of adulthood. To celebrate, he and his adopted brother Evan Gray were taking a trip to Portland to spend a week with his grandfather, Floyd Bannister. His parents were taking Evan and him to Natoma the following week to put them on a stage to Walla Walla, and then they could take the train. Gabriel was excited about the trip because he had never been outside Jessup County. "I would love to see the ocean, Aunt Eleanor. I'll talk to my parents about it."

"Good. Even if you don't come this time, the invitation is always open. We have plenty of room for family. And we don't get enough visitors."

Matt hadn't had the opportunity to talk to Gabriel yet and hadn't heard that Gabriel would visit his grandfather, Floyd Bannister. The idea made him feel uneasy. "Gabriel, that's a long way from home. I don't know if I like that idea."

Annie scoffed intentionally. "You went a lot

farther than that at his age, remember? He's only going for a week; you went for fifteen years! He'll be fine. You sound like his mother."

Gabriel added, "Yeah, Mother isn't too fond of the idea either. We'll be staying at Grandpa's, so it will be fine. He's going to show us around."

Matt had invited his son to stay the night at his house so they could talk for a while. He had missed the boy's entire life, and it was relatively recent, the past November, when Gabriel learned that Matt was his biological father and not Tom Smith, who had raised him. It was then, near Thanksgiving, when Gabriel met his grandfather, and the two bonded immediately. "Gabriel, let's get going. We have a lot to talk about. Aunt Eleanor, I'll see you..." He paused. "I was leaving town in the morning, but I have more important and immediate things to do now. I'll see you tomorrow."

After hugs and saying goodnight, Annie and Tiffany started for the stairway to go to their room for the night. Pam picked up the note she wrote herself and said, "Oh, Tiffany, your Uncle Steven wanted you to come by his room before you called it a night. He's in room fourteen on the third floor."

Steven Bannister wrinkled his brow curiously. "I'm her only Uncle Steven, and that's not my room."

Tiffany was confused. "I don't have an Uncle Steven except for him." She waved towards Steven.

William opened the registry. "It says Dick and Lyla Jones. What did he look like, Pamela?"

"I spoke with Lyla. The lady with the white face and bad makeup that Luther was making fun of?

Her." Pamela said.

William slowly grinned as he watched Pamela. "And you wondered where I got my sense of humor from? Steven, stop Matt. Tell him to come back here and we'll go upstairs and talk to this mysterious Uncle Steven. As a professional gambler, my money says Dane is Uncle Steven."

Matt returned to the hotel with Steven and Gabriel a moment later. "You think Dane is here?" he asked William. He spoke to Tiffany after William explained about the note, "Tiffany, I need you to come with us in case he asks who's knocking."

"I don't want to see him!" Tiffany objected with a show of anxiety.

"You have nothing to worry about," Matt reassured her. "Once you say your name and he opens the door, you can walk away with Gabriel."

"He killed someone tonight." Tiffany said anxiously.

William couldn't resist answering, "If the one-handed Leprechaun can manhandle Matt, Steven, and me at the same time, then you better call a whole brigade of the 7th Calvary to come running because this world just doesn't have a chance against a fumbling gnome. Let's go. Pamela, give me a key to that room just in case we need it."

They went to the third floor, followed by Annie and Gabriel. They had Tiffany knock on the door. "Uncle Steven, it's me."

The door opened, and seeing Matt standing there, Dane tried to slam the door, but Matt kicked the door open fiercely as Dane stumbled back. Matt pulled his revolver, but he held it downwards as he focused on the heavy coated white makeup with pink rouge on the cheeks, red lipstick, and thick eye lashes with blue brows under black eyebrows. He wore a red wig and a pink and yellow dress. Dane's arm was no longer in the sling around his neck. Dane was alarmed and stepped backward.

Matt was speechless as he stared at him with a dumbfounded grin. He chuckled. "You're… you're taking that friendship with Steven last night a little too far, aren't you?"

Steven's mouth dropped open as he stepped into the room. "Dane? Oh, my word, look at that!" he laughed. "It's Dane!"

William grinned. "Say, were you applying for Bella's Dance Hall, Dane?" he laughed.

"Did Bella hire you?" Steven questioned through his laughter while wiping the sudden moisture from his eyes. He bent over, laughing loudly.

Hearing the laughter, Annie stepped through the door and immediately burst out in laughter.

Dane grinned awkwardly. "It's funny, yeah?" he nodded awkwardly while his eyes moved from Matt to the others laughing at him.

Matt shook his head as his humor faded. "Disturbing is more like it. That's Lucille's dress. She had a miscarriage, Dane."

Dane turned his hands upwards with a non-caring shrug. "Was it yours?" Dane asked as if he hoped it was.

Matt's eyes narrowed with hostility. "No. You're under arrest for the murder of Bill Cooney, among other things, but that's the one that's going to leave you swinging on the gallows. I wish I could say I feel bad about that, but I don't."

"You can't prove I did anything." He grinned.

"Dane, proving it isn't any harder than seeing Bill's blood on your pretty dress." Matt pointed out the several irregular blood splatter stains on the dress.

Dane pulled the fabric outwards to look at the material and saw several blood droplets staining the material. He grinned widely. "Oh." Knowing he was caught and there was no way past the three men, a plan was formulated in his mind. While opening the window earlier, he noted that the neighboring building's roof was only four or five feet below his window and a four-foot jump to reach it over the separation between buildings. He could easily dive across the four feet and land on the roof. Run to the front, which wasn't too far, scale down the awning posts, and disappear down the street before Matt and his family could run down the three flights of stairs and reach Main Street. He could get away, but he needed to be fast.

"Yeah, oh!" Matt said bluntly. "Put your hands on your head and turn around. I know you have a knife somewhere." Matt stepped forward to arrest him.

Dane widened his eyes in terror and raised his hands defensively. "Don't shoot me!" he yelled at William. Matt looked back quickly at William with concern.

Dane snickered with glee as it was the fleeting

second or two that he needed to turn towards the window and run four steps before lowering his body to make the dive out the opened lower half of the window to the neighboring roof. Bending over to make the desperate dive lowered the front hem of the dress to the floor and his left boot stepped on the hem, stopping his momentum as the top half of his body flew out of the window. His left thigh hit the windowsill as he fell out. His boots flew upwards and hit the opened window frame as he fell head first straight down to the brick-layered alley below. The sound of him yelling in terror ended with the gut-wrenching sound of a heavy thud, like a watermelon being dropped from a barn loft.

"Ohh, my…" William said, losing his laughter as he heard the fall. He met Matt at the window to look down.

William cringed. "That's the craziest thing I've ever seen. It's bizarre! He looks like a demented clown. Steven, Annie, come check this out."

"Is he dead?" Steven asked.

Matt nodded affirmingly. "I'd say so. Have a peek. I don't think you'll ever see anything like this again."

Steven approached the window cautiously to look down. His body shook involuntarily with chills as he quickly turned away from the window.

Dane was lying thirty-five feet below. He had landed on his head and snapped his neck upon impact. It was easy to tell as his body was face down with his buttocks exposed by the raised dress, but his painted white face was fixed at an unnatural angle, parallel to his shoulder, twisted backward like an owl staring up at the window. In the moon's haunting light, the white paste of his makeup glowed in the alley like a lantern in a dark cellar, revealing Dane's tongue dangling by a thread of flesh on his cheek. A stream of blood had pooled and glistened in the moonlight. His dark eyes were opened wider than usual and appeared black and haunting as they stared upwards at the window as if sending a witch's curse. The raised dress exposed the knife wrapped around his leg with gauze.

Annie came forward to peek down. She turned around and covered her face with her hands. "Oh my! Oh my! I should never have looked!" She walked away with her face covered by her hands and shivered. She sat down, disturbed.

"Well," William said to no one in particular. "I would have won my bet. But he didn't rent a whore; he just dressed like one."

Annie ignored him. "I'd say he's dead, Steven."

"No kidding." Steven agreed. He was disturbed by what he had seen as well.

William put his hands on the windowsill and leaned out to get a better look. "Well, if anyone is dumb enough to accidentally kill themselves while dressed like a woman, it's Dane." He chuckled.

Annie was not amused. "I just watched someone die. I don't think it's funny."

Matt peeked out the window and frowned with the heaviness that filled his soul. He spoke slowly, "The dress explains why he pulled Lucille off the ladder. It won't help her to understand why any better, but she'll know she was right about it being intentional. Lucille won't want the dress back, so I say we send Dane back home to his sister just like that."

William chuckled. "She'd never believe you didn't dress him up like a female clown out of spite. The next thing you'd know, Danetta will be coming here to get even for dressing her brother up like that."

"After what he did to Lucille so he could wear that dress, I'll assume he must like it a lot. William, I want you to tell Uncle Solomon not to change a thing. I want the makeup and everything left on Dane just the way it is, including the wig. Tell him to embalm Dane without touching the makeup and send him back to Prairieville." Matt yawned. "I'm heading home to talk with Gabriel for a while. Truet and I are leaving early for Natoma. You are taking care of getting Dane back to Danetta for me."

A high-pitched shriek sounded from the alley, causing Matt to peer out the window. Tiffany was running away sobbing. Gabriel stood near Dane's body. Matt glanced at Annie. "It's Tiffany."

Annie's eyes widened and she hurriedly left the room without a word. She ran down the three flights of stairs as quickly as possible and saw Tiffany burst into the hotel lobby with her arms open wide. She was sobbing uncontrollably and ran into Annie's arms. Annie wrapped her arms around her and held tight as Tiffany wailed.

Gabriel quickly followed and stopped short

when he saw his father and the others come down the stairs. He explained, "We heard a scream and went to see if he needed help. We didn't know it was him until we got there. We were just walking around the block until you arrested him." he explained innocently.

Annie closed her eyes as a tear tumbled down her cheek. She rubbed Tiffany's hair affectionately. "It's a horrible sight, I know. He's gone now, and there is nothing to be afraid of anymore. You're my daughter now, and we have a whole lifetime of living left to do. I love you, Tiffany. Don't ever think I don't."

Tiffany squeezed Annie tighter. "I love you." She pulled her face out of Annie's shoulder with a disturbed look. "His head was backwards..."

Annie said empathetically, "I know. Let's get you upstairs." Annie gave William and Matt a severe glare. "Get him out of the alley or covered until Uncle Solomon gets here."

"I'll get it taken care of right now." William said somberly.

Chapter 32

Alan Sperry had just finished the final wall of his and Audrey's room. It wasn't a big room because, like most small barns, the loft only had limited space for hay and straw. The six by eight-foot room contained a simple mattress on the unfinished planks of the loft. The bed left about three feet on the end and side for storing clothes and personal belongings. A wool blanket nailed over the doorway served as the door. Alan was proud of his room and sat on the bed to admire it. It was a luxury compared to his prison cell.

"Knock, knock." Daisy said as she climbed the vertical ladder to the door. She had to grab the edges of the doorframe to keep her balance as she climbed the last three rungs to reach the six inches of decking between the blanket and the loft edge. She pulled the blanket back to look at her brother's room. "You owe me an apology for letting that crawdad pinch me. That was mean, and you knew it would hurt. Do you want me to put a crawdad on your lip while you're sleeping?"

A slight lifting of his lips revealed a hint of a smile. It wasn't humor from his actions earlier that day but a touch of pride in his baby sister's countenance. "You're right. I do owe you an apology. It was mean of me, and I apologize."

"You also owe my son an apology. He's afraid of crawdads because he's been pinched by one, and it hurt him. He doesn't need his uncle making it worse. Tad does enough to terrorize these kids. Uncles are supposed to protect and watch over him, not make him cry and laugh about it."

"I was trying to have some fun. I'm sorry if I scared your son. I'll try not to make him cry again. What did Audrey think?"

"She didn't think you were funny. She didn't say anything, but I'm guessing she thought you were a jackass like I did. Between you acting like that and Jannie feeding whiskey to Alisha, I'm surprised she doesn't leave now. She was furious at Jannie for doing that and Ma and Bernice for letting her."

Alan lowered his head between his knees melancholically. "I was just trying to have fun with the children. I'm obviously not good at it." He slammed the side of his fist against the wall with frustration.

Daisy squinted curiously. "What's the point of that? Are you going to beat up the barn? I've been talking to Bernice and Henry about the Bible and reading it myself. I'm more inspired now that Audrey is here because she knows so much about it. But you should read it too. Bernice told me one day that there was a whole other world beyond ours, and it is best to learn about it now while we can. I'll loan my Bible to you. It might make you in a better mood. It does me."

Alan lifted his head to look at her. "What do you think of my room?" he asked to change the subject.

She looked around the room. "I like it. I think you did good."

Alan leaned back across his mattress and placed his hands behind his head. "The question is, do you think Audrey will like it?"

"I don't see why not. She's always complaining that the house is too hot at night so she goes outside. I saw Morton last night pushing her on the swing. It sounded like they were having fun."

"Could you hear what they were saying?" Alan's tone grew more concerned.

"No. I went outside to grab a clean diaper off the clothesline and heard some laughing, so I looked around the corner and saw them."

Alan's eyes hardened to stone as the sinister beast of jealousy began to rise within him. "You didn't hear what they were saying?"

"No. Alisha was crying, so I went back inside and changed her butt. I think Audrey will like sleeping out here where it's cooler. My room has a small window, so I don't get too hot, but hers doesn't. Are you going to ask Morton to be your best man tomorrow?"

Alan's teeth clenched together. He was sick of Morton talking to Audrey every chance he had. A spark of jealousy days before had become an artery of venom being pumped into his soul that quickly turned to wrath. Morton was becoming a threat, and threats needed to be eliminated before any harm could be done. "No. Vince is my best man."

Daisy leaned against the door frame. "It's too bad Jack won't be here. I know he'd love to be, but no one has tried to get a hold of him because he's staying at Mark's."

Alan sat up. "Mark wouldn't come anyway. Does Audrey ever talk about me?"

Daisy lowered her brow in thought and looked up at the roof. A bit of light was shining through a crack. "You better get that hole fixed, or you'll get wet when it rains."

He glanced up. "I plan to. So, what has Audrey said about me? Have you heard her say I'm handsome, at least?"

"I think so. She talks more about Morton. Don't worry though, Audrey's engaged to you."

It wasn't hidden to Alan that his younger brothers, Morton and Vince, were both attracted to Audrey, but it was becoming clear that Morton was trying to sabotage Alan's engagement. "Morton seems to…" He changed the course of the question. "What does she say about Morton?"

Daisy shrugged. "You'd have to ask her or Ma. Audrey talks to me about having children, being a mother, and the Bible. She loves children, though. In fact, Audrey is watching Alisha and the other kids out front right now. It's nice to have a few minutes to myself. Alan, she'll be a really good mother to your children. I think you're lucky. I really like her."

His brow lowered, and he sat up quickly. He spoke sternly, "Daisy, you know all those screaming brats drive me insane. I don't want kids. I never wanted kids to begin with, but they popped out anyway. I tried beating them out Racheal when I learned she was pregnant, but she has like an iron-clad fortress inside there or something that kept those things nice and tucked in no matter what I did. I'll tell you right now that if Audrey ever gets pregnant, I'll cut that thing out of her if it doesn't come out by itself. I hate children!"

Daisy's mouth dropped. She was barely a teen-ager when her brother went to prison, and since his return, she was learning that Alan was not the man she remembered. "I have three. And I love my children very much, thank you."

Alan's eyebrows rose questioningly. "Yeah, I heard about how those things came about. I'm sorry I wasn't here to protect you. I would've killed those men as soon as they took an interest in you."

Daisy ignored his statement. "If you want to protect someone, don't let Tad join the Sperry-Helms Gang. Tad's mean enough without becoming an outlaw. You should quit the gang, too, before you go back to prison. I don't think Audrey would agree to being an outlaw's wife."

Alan answered heatedly, "First of all, I don't care what Audrey thinks, feels, or believes. Once we're married, she's my property and will do what I say or pay the price. Secondly, Tad's old enough to decide what he wants to do, but I will teach him how to do it right. And Sis, I'll never go back to prison. I'll draw an empty revolver on a dozen lawmen to ensure I'm dead before I'm taken alive."

Mattie had walked into the barn five minutes before and overheard a good part of their conversation. She was appalled. "Alan!" she shouted.

He immediately popped his head out of the blanket to look down at his mother. He could see the anger burning in her cold eyes. "Yes, Ma?"

She lowered her voice, but the tone was commanding, "You better learn to keep your mouth shut! If it were Audrey coming in here, she would overhear everything you're saying. I didn't go through all that trouble to get you a wife for you to screw it up the day before your wedding! Here." She held up a piece of purple paper that she wrote on. "Give that to Audrey and tell her you wrote it this morning. I warned Morton about trying to steal her away from you yesterday, and Daisy saw them together last night having a romantic midnight rendezvous at the swing. Boy, you better get your head out of dreamland and start winning her heart or start kissing that paper because that's the nearest thing you'll have for a wife! Talk to Audrey like a lady and quit trying to consummate the marriage before you even have one. Don't be stupid, Alan!"

He gave a wry smile. "It doesn't hurt to try. She's human too."

Mattie's expression hardened. "She's not one of your fifty-cent whores for a five-minute romp. You're acting like that stupid dog Vince brought home, Duke, when Bernice's worthless mutt is in

308

heat. Don't ruin my investment in your future like some simple-minded fool. Talk to her like a gentleman. Better yet, talk to her like Morton does. He seems to have caught her attention right under your nose. How is that possible? I don't know because she came here to marry you! How on God's green earth can you let that happen, Alan?"

"I don't know." he said softly.

"Understand this; I'm afraid you have lost so much ground to Morton that I don't know if I can save your relationship with a letter. You give that note to her and talk like a gentleman, and if that doesn't work…" She paused to exhale in frustration. "Then I guess you and Morton will be fighting it out with the Sperry Rule. If that's what it takes to get Morton to leave her alone, then so be it. I warned them both yesterday, and it did no good. Those midnight rendezvous are still happening. You get out of your little hideaway and talk to her right now!"

***

Audrey was lying on the grass while watching little Alisha sitting up, trying to bite on her rattle. She was a grumpy baby because three of her upper teeth were trying to break through her gums at once. The innocence of a child is one of the most beautiful miracles common to man and most definitely worth dying to protect. Audrey couldn't care less what anyone thought of her when she stopped Jannie from feeding the baby alcohol. She had been with Alisha and the children consistently since then. Audrey had run Tad off from teasing his sisters and enjoyed the day spent with the children as they played, and even Eve offered a rare affectionate hug and joy-filled smile. Audrey wondered what kind of a person Alisha would become and what she would do with her life. Audrey decided that if she did marry into the Sperry family, she'd be the best aunt she could be to help raise Alisha, her siblings, and their cousins in a loving and warm environment. Silently, she prayed for Alisha and all the children on the Sperry farm one at a time, that the Lord would watch over them, protect them, and draw them to the Lord Almighty.

A shadow crossing the grass raised her eyes to see Alan approaching. He held a purple paper in his hand. She had no interest in talking to him and put her attention back on Alisha.

Alan stood wordlessly for a moment before speaking anxiously, "I'm done building the room. You should come see it."

"Right now, I'm watching Alisha and the other children." Audrey did not sound interested in talking to him.

"I know. I wrote this letter this morning. You might want to read it." He dropped the note down in front of her.

"Oh? Okay, I will."

He knelt and rubbed Alisha's chin with his finger. "Hi, Alisha. You're such a cute baby." He grinned uneasily. "Are you going to read that?"

"Do you want me to read it now?"

"Yeah. I thought we could talk about what it says."

She unfolded the paper and began reading silently:

My dearest Audrey,

I couldn't sleep last night and decided to go for a walk and do some praying to our Lord above. It was then that I saw you and Morton at the swing, talking. I saw him pushing you in the moonlight and heard your laughter. And I wished it was me. It was then that I realized what a fool I have been. I have been withdrawn, private, and not forthcoming with who I am. I tend to write better than I talk, but it is made worse by how nervous you make me. With all your beauty and upstanding character, I cannot believe that you would come here to marry me. I am struggling with accepting that you want to marry me. How blessed am I? It scares me, and I don't know how to relax and be myself when I'm around you. But I promise if you marry me, I'll learn to relax quickly, and all those bad qualities you have seen will fade away to reveal the real me. I want to be true, honest, and forthcoming with you. I know I have been overly aggressive with wanting to kiss and more inappropriate things before we are married. That is just my way of dealing with my fear of losing you. As I told you when I proposed, I love you for who you are, just the way you are.

I love my brother Morton, but this is not the first time he has tried stealing a potential courtship. He has always tried to swoon the ladies away from me. Mark has nothing to do with this family anymore because of Morton. And most recently, Jack moved away from here to keep Morton away from his lady. My mother warned you about Morton and his violent side. If I seem jealous, it is because I love you and worry for your protection while sneaking out to meet Morton in the middle of the night. He can be a bad man. Be careful of him. With all my heart and devotion, I am committed to living my life with you, serving our God.

Love
Alan

She read the letter twice before laying it down.

"Well, what did you think?" Alan asked anxiously.

"You're scared of me?"

"Huh? No!" he scoffed at the idea of being afraid of a woman. "Why would you say that?"

"That's what it says right here. You don't know how to relax because of my beauty and character. You can't believe I'd want to marry you."

"Right. Yes." He nodded.

Her tone turned sour, "I don't sneak out to meet Morton, and I'm irritated that you assume I did. Of all the people here, Morton is the only one that seems to want to be my friend, and he seems pretty sincere to me."

Alan nodded with a wrinkled brow. He had not read the letter before giving it to her and quickly regretted it. He expected it to be a romantic love letter that would have her swooning over him, perhaps even giving him a loving kiss. The letter his mother wrote was beginning to sound like a more in-depth note than he expected, and unfortunately, Audrey wanted to talk about it.

Audrey continued defensively, "Morton didn't even see me on the swing until I spoke to him, and he was a perfect gentleman. Morton told me he's never been in a long courtship, and you told me you've never been in love. So, who were you courting that he tried to steal away?"

Alan was dumbstruck and stuttered as he searched for an answer to a question that he didn't understand the content of. "Um... Racheal." The name just slipped out of his mouth without thinking about it.

"I'll ask Morton about her. If he lied to me, I'll know I can't trust him, but the same goes for you."

"He lies a lot. You trust me, don't you?"

She answered honestly, "Alan, I did when I came here. But since I've been here, you only seem interested in one thing, and it's not conversation. Morton is not a Christian, but he told me so. I know what he is. It's you who baffles me. You stated that you are a Christian in your letters; even this note refers to you being one. But I don't see it in your actions or conversation. I don't see, hear, or sense any relationship between you and Jesus. That concerns me because a tare is poison, and I don't want to start a family in a mixed field. Do you understand?"

"No." He shook his head.

"Maybe that's the problem. You can't just say the Lord's prayer and think you're saved. It is a commitment to follow Jesus, rain or shine, for better or worse, for the rest of your life. To be devoted to him twenty-four hours a day, seven days a week. The fruits of the spirit should become evident in the person's life. Jesus becomes a part of who we are; I don't see that in you. I'd be lying if I didn't say that concerns me."

"What? Do you see it in Morton?" he snapped defensively.

"No. Morton doesn't claim to be a Christian. Why would I? But you do. I won't marry a man that is not a Christian because you cannot splice wheat and tare and come out with a better seed. I want my children, Lord willing, to be raised in a home with a solid foundation on Jesus. If you can't give me that, then I should leave."

Panic struck like lightning to his chest. His lungs began expanding with his quickened breathing. He had no idea what Audrey was talking about, but he needed to say something to satisfy her enough so they could move on to something else. "I never said I wasn't a Christian. I am. But you know, we have Reverend Cass. I only know what he tells me."

"Nothing is stopping you from reading the Bible for yourself and learning. We need to read the Bible so that when we do hear a false teacher, we can recognize it immediately. We won't be led astray into some lunatic's cult if we read the Bible ourselves. If you've never accepted Jesus as your Lord and Savior, Alan, and I mean for real, then let's pray right now, and you can do so. Then you will know you are saved."

Alan couldn't explain it, but the anxiety inside him began screaming for him to run. He needed to get away from her. "I have to go. I'll talk to you later." he abruptly said and walked away quickly towards town.

Audrey picked Alisha up, set her gently on her back, and tickled her. The little one laughed, exposing her sore gums. The sound of the child's laughter was such a joyful sound that it made Audrey chuckle. She glanced from the swollen gums to the departing man for whom she felt no more attraction. She whispered in prayer, "Lord Jesus. I don't know what to do. If you want me to marry him, I pray you'll give me all the grace and patience you can give me because I'm losing that faith I came here on. I want a child like this one, Lord. And if you don't want me to marry Alan, then I pray you will interfere and not let it happen. Or let me know in such a way that I'll understand. I depend on you alone, Jesus, for all of my life. Marriage, motherhood, happiness, any success, it's all in your good hands. I will trust you."

Chapter 33

Morton moved the paintbrush up and down the vertical boards he was painting. It was a hot day, and the paint was drying relatively fast. He was on a ladder, painting the high areas, while Henry was below, painting the lower half of the tannery.

"Morton, get down here!" Alan shouted as he approached the tannery. The anger he felt growing when he left Audrey had tripled in strength and was directed at the man who betrayed him, his brother, Morton.

"Alan, you sound like you've been hit with a sour stomach. Did Vince make lunch?" Morton joked.

Alan's rage showed no relief by the attempt at humor. "Get down here! You have no business talking to Audrey, and we're going to end that right now!"

Morton paused mid-stroke of his paintbrush and peered down at his angry brother. "Alan, we've already spoken about this. There's nothing left to say. She's engaged to you, so relax."

"Get down here and fight me!" he yelled. Alan pushed the ladder sideways, tipping it over. Morton was twelve feet in the air and hollered as he and his ladder fell and hit the ground with a hard crash, spilling the paint can. Morton rolled across the ground to a stop.

"Are you crazy?" Henry shouted at Alan. He went to help Morton up.

Morton, furious, got to his feet with no help and pushed Henry out of his way to get to Alan. Alan's fists were balled up tight, and his right hand sped from his waist straight forward with a stiff jab to Morton's nose. It wasn't a hard hit but quick, and that speed alone was enough to startle Morton. He knew his brother had lean and fast hands, but he didn't see that blow coming.

The quick jab was followed by a right kick to Morton's groin, that again was unexpected and forced Morton to grimace in pain. He bent over slightly while keeping his hands up to continue the fight. Alan's left leg quickly kicked the outside of Morton's right leg, which didn't hurt, but it was another shot Morton didn't expect. Alan's right arm faked a wide swing, but it stopped short as Morton reacted to block it. A sharp left uppercut snapped Morton's jaw shut and jilted his head back. Alan grabbed his brother's hair with both hands and yanked it down while he raised his right knee over and over into Morton's face. Morton kept his forearms over his face to absorb the blows and limit any damage, but each knee pounding into him weakened him just a bit more.

Henry, wanting to help Morton, wrapped his

right arm around Alan's throat and pulled him backward, forcing him to release Morton. "Knock it off! He's your brother!" Henry seethed.

Alan turned on Henry with a left backward elbow towards his head that missed, but a right elbow to the side of Henry's head connected fully on the ear, which stunned him. Henry released Alan and was quickly hit in the jaw by a vicious right fist as Alan spun towards him. Henry fell to the ground. He jumped on Henry's chest, blinded by rage, and began hitting him with a repeating right fist. Henry's face was quickly a blood-covered mess.

Enraged, Morton dove on Alan to drive him off Henry. The two brothers rolled on the ground, hitting each other wherever the strikes hit, neither hitting effectively while they grappled for the top position to get control of the other. Both men cursed the other as they fought.

Being the stronger and heavier of the two, Morton was able to drop a solid blow that, for just a moment, stunned Alan, but it was just enough for Morton to straddle Alan's chest. Knowing the danger of being pinned under Morton against the ground, Alan straightened his fingers to increase the length of his punch and drove his fingertips into Morton's throat with a hard right. The hit to the windpipe caused Morton to grab his throat and struggle to be able to breathe. He rolled off Alan to his hands and knees, far more concerned about his windpipe being hit than fighting.

Alan wasn't trying to end the fight with the dangerous punch. He did what he had to do to get his brother off him, but the fight was far from over.

Alan got to his feet and kicked Morton in the kidney, followed by a kick to the face.

A gunshot stopped Alan from stomping on the back of Morton's head. He looked over to see Marshal Matt Bannister standing six feet away with his revolver pointed at Alan. Beside him were his deputy Truet Davis and the Natoma Sheriff, Zeke Jones, who appeared to be quite nervous.

"That's enough." Matt said with a hardened expression that revealed he would not hesitate to pull the trigger if Alan intended to strike his brother again.

Alan growled like an enraged animal as he sneered and turned around to kick the ground and scream loudly. He faced Matt again, looking like a madman while his chest rose and fell heavily. He pointed at Matt warningly, "You mind your own business, or you'll get hurt too!"

"Might I?" Matt asked with interest. "Well, you're free to try me."

Alan glared at him with deadly intent and nodded slowly. "We'll meet soon enough. We'll see how lucky you are then."

"I'll see you soon enough." Matt agreed.

Alan pointed at Morton with a vicious snarl. "I whipped you! I whipped you both! I won; she's mine. I won't tell you again to stay away from her; my brother or not, I'll kill you."

Morton moved to a sitting position on the ground. One nostril slowly bled. He glanced up at Alan and gave a half-smile. "You won. Go home and tell her so."

Alan looked at the blood on his hand from Henry. "I will. I don't want to see you anywhere near her tomorrow."

Morton wiped the blood away as he nodded agreeably. "The Sperry Rule is the rule. I give you my word that I won't be near her tomorrow."

Satisfied, Alan peered at his brother Henry who had stood up and held his bleeding nose. His nose and eyes were already swelling. "I didn't mean to hit you, Henry."

Henry laughed scornfully. "It wasn't accidental."

As Alan walked away, Matt asked the two brothers, "Are you two all right?"

Morton stood. "I am. Henry?"

"I'll be fine."

Matt holstered his revolver. "I'm glad I showed up when I did. I was just talking to Sheriff Jones about the stage robbery. Do either of you know anything about that?" Truet kept his attention on Alan as he walked away.

"Nope," Morton said. "You can check with our boss if you want. Henry and I were on our way back from Branson when that happened. You should talk to Alan's fiancé Audrey. She was on it."

"I intend to. That's where I was going next."

"Before you go, can Henry and I talk to you and Truet alone for a bit? You know, in private?"

* * *

Audrey was in the backyard by the garden showing a couple of the children how unique the honeybees that landed on the flowers were. She was trying to explain to Eve and Walter that they didn't need to be afraid of honeybees because they weren't aggressive like a yellow jacket was. She had heard the dogs barking a few minutes before, but she was not expecting to see two lawmen standing in the family room wanting to speak with her when she was called inside. Mattie introduced her to Matt and Truet with a bitter tone that surprised Audrey. The tension in the room was thick, and she had no idea why, but it was clear that there was a deep hostility for the two lawmen in the home.

Matt ignored Mattie's rudeness as it was expected. He spoke to Audrey, "Miss, I would like to speak with you about the stagecoach robbery you were a part of. I'm investigating it and have a series of questions if you have time to speak with me. I like to talk to witnesses privately, so if you would join me outside at my wagon, I would appreciate it."

Vince was suspicious. He knew the marshal had come to their home several times, but he had never come in a wagon. It made him nervous, and he couldn't shake the anxiety that swept through him. He asked Matt, "Don't you usually ride your horse? Why do you have a wagon?"

Matt had a good idea that Vince was involved in the robbery from his uncle Joel's description of the robbers. He squinted his eyes knowingly at Vince as he answered, "I came to arrest some highwaymen as soon as I can identify them. Do you know anything about that robbery, Vince?"

Vince shook his head. "No. I don't know anything."

"Is Tad around?"

Vince shook his head. "I think he's gone to the river."

"Huh. Interestingly, one of the robbers pointed a gun at my uncle and asked if he was coming to marry his grandmother. It's a strange coincidence that this lady here was arriving on the same coach to marry Alan. But that isn't anything more than a strange coincidence. After all, it wasn't Missus Sperry getting married, was it?"

Outside, Matt sat on the bed of the wagon he had rented from the Natoma Livery Stable. He invited Audrey to sit beside him so they could talk in private. Truet had laid his rifle and Matt's shotgun in the wagon's bed earlier. He leaned on the bed rail to keep an alert eye for any trouble.

Audrey told Matt about the stagecoach robbery, and after telling him what happened, she hopped down to go back inside. "And that's all I know." she finished.

Matt patted the wagon bed where she had sat. "Take a seat. I'm not done."

"Oh. Sorry." She sat beside him. "What else would you like to know?"

Matt took a deep breath. "You got me curious. I'm engaged to be married myself. I met my fiancé at a dance hall, and we've been courting for a while. I'm curious, how are the wedding plans coming along? Do you think being a mail bride is working for you okay?"

She shrugged without any enthusiasm. "We're getting married tomorrow."

"You don't sound as excited as my fiancé does.

Her name is Christine, and she's so excited about our wedding that she can hardly contain herself." He rubbed his eye from a speck of dust getting into it. "Why don't I see that with you? Are mail brides always as solemn? It's none of my business, really. I'm just curious about mail brides."

She appeared uneasy. "I'm sure most mail brides are excited to marry the man they agreed to marry. Most mail brides don't marry because they are in love. Most marry for survival, convenience, or loneliness."

"And which one of those defines you?" Matt asked gently.

Audrey took a deep breath. "Curiosity at first, motivated by the fear of never finding a husband, I suppose. I'm not that young, and I want a family before I get too old."

Matt rubbed his beard as he asked, "So, you answer an ad and write back and forth, right? I suppose my first question would be, how do you know if they're lying to you or not? I mean, it takes guts of steel to trust someone's word and move across the country to start a new life as a wife to what could be a false representation of a man that she knows nothing about. That's a scary thought. Did you ever think about that?"

"My first husband did just that." She finished with a tilted head and raised eyebrows, with her eyes on Matt.

"Really? And you tried the mail-order bride thing again? Wow, you do have guts of steel. But it's working out well now, right?" Matt asked while reading her actions carefully.

She nodded halfheartedly while her hands fidgeted with her dress.

"You must love Alan?" Matt asked pointedly.

"I agreed to marry him." She appeared to be getting aggravated by the questions.

Just then, Alan Sperry came out of the house, annoyed. "Isn't the questioning about done? It doesn't take long to say I don't know anything!" he was angry and breathing through his mouth.

"Go back inside!" Truet ordered. His hand slowly reached into the wagon, in case the rifle was needed.

Alan ignored Truet. "Audrey, get inside!" he ordered.

Matt answered sharply, "I'll send her in when I'm done questioning every angle I can think of. Until then, leave! Or I'll take her elsewhere and question her. The choice is yours."

Alan cursed him and went back inside.

Matt hesitated. His friendly and comforting countenance faded as a more severe expression took its place as if he was irritated by Alan's interruption. "It's kind of an odd trait for a devoted Christian lady to marry a non-Christian man, isn't it?"

Audrey's shoulders fell. "He says he is. Wait, how did you know I was a Christian?"

Matt chuckled. "Audrey, do you know why I am here?"

"To investigate the stage robbery." she answered.

"Yes, that's true. I want to tell you something

that is going to upset you. It is going to make you very angry. It is going to break your heart too. But I need you not to react to it as Alan and the others are watching and trying to listen in. Don't react; just listen and remain calm, please. Are you ready?"

"You robbed the stage?" she guessed.

Matt chuckled. "No. I spoke with Morton Sperry in town. Miss Audrey, you have no idea what kind of danger you are in. You were lied to from the very beginning."

"What?" she gasped.

"Don't react. Just listen calmly because it would be safer for all of us. While you were writing love letters back and forth, Alan was in the Oregon State Penitentiary. He knew nothing about you until the day you showed up. None of them did, except for Mattie and Jannie. You were writing to Alan's mother."

The air was sucked out of her lungs abruptly by the news. She blinked multiple times to clear the water that welled in her eyes. "It was all a lie?"

Matt nodded empathetically. "Alan was married before. When he went to prison, some good folks in the community helped her and his daughters escape this hellish home. Alan was a monster to her and would have been to you. He just came home from prison three weeks ago after serving seven years. He was the leader of the Sperry-Helms Gang." Matt paused and looked at the black house. "This family and the Reverend Cass you met are outlaws. According to Morton and Henry, you wanted to get married in the church, so Alan burned it down."

"Morton's an outlaw too?" she asked.

"Morton *was* the gang leader, but he has nothing more to do with it now, to my knowledge. Morton has become a friend of mine and has been trying to change his life for a while now. Miss Audrey, Morton asked me to get you out of this house today for your safety. You would not be allowed to leave here on your own if you tried to, but they can't stop me from taking you. They might pull out their guns, but so can Truet and I, and they know it. So, if you want to leave, this is a good time to do it."

She wiped the tears from her eyes. "I don't have anywhere to go. I don't have any money. Mattie took it when I was sleeping."

Matt offered a warm and comforting smile. "Do you remember that old man from the stage named Joel? He's my uncle Joel Fasana. If he said he'd help you, then he will. You'll be taken care of one way or another, I promise. Let's get you out of here and into a nicer place until we can get you home."

***

Audrey walked into the house, followed by Matt and Truet. She could not believe she had been fooled again, but at least the truth had come out before she married what would have been the worst mistake of her life. She spoke heatedly, "Alan, I hope you enjoy your room. I am leaving here, and I don't ever want to see any of you again!" She almost began sobbing when she looked into Eve's innocent brown eyes.

Mattie's mouth dropped open as the shock devastated her. She shouted, "What? No, you're marrying Alan tomorrow. Marshal, what did you say to her?"

"The truth." Matt answered simply.

Audrey glared at Mattie with contempt. "You're a good writer. But you're a horrible person. I'm getting my things, and I'm leaving. You can keep the money. I don't want it after it's touched your filthy fingers." She walked quickly towards her room, followed by Truet.

Alan sat on the edge of the davenport, breathing in through his nose rapidly as the rage pressurized like steam in a boiler ready to explode. He glared wildly at Matt, who stood near the door waiting for Truet to return with Audrey's large travel trunk. Alan spoke through his gritted teeth, "You ruined my wedding."

Matt adjusted his feet casually to change his positioning. He could tell by Alan's perched body that he was about to attack. "Yes, I did. And I'll do it again if I hear of another lied-to bride."

Alan leaped off the davenport to tackle Matt, but Matt was expecting Alan to do precisely that and spun towards the right, avoiding the tackle and directing Alan's angry burst into the wall head first. The crack of Alan's head hitting the wall could have been heard from the barn. Matt spun him around, grabbed Alan's hair, and dropped his knees to the ground, bringing Alan down and slamming his face into the wood floor. Alan's nose took the brunt of the force and began to bleed. Matt kept the pressure downward on Alan's head, he spun quickly around and drove a knee on Alan's back to face the family, his left hand gripped Alan's hair and pressed his head against the floor. He drew his revolver and pointed it at Alan's head with his right hand to keep him under control and stop any family members from trying to interfere. They were a dangerous family made known by Vince, who had already stood up to help his brother.

"Sit down!" Matt yelled viciously. "All of you stay put. Truet and I are taking Audrey out of here, and if any of you attempt to stop us, you will be shot dead on sight!"

Mattie spat out coldly, "You have no right coming here!" She stood in front of her rocking chair with her hands clenched into two tight fists.

Matt did not hold his thoughts back and spoke harshly, "You have no right to deceive that woman into a life of hell with your son. That is absolutely wicked! I feel sorry for your family. I really do. What a piss poor example of a mother you are!" He turned to look at Daisy, who held baby Alisha close to her heart with a frightened expression on her face. "Be a better mother to your children than she was to you. Do you hear me?"

Daisy's voice cracked, "Yes, sir. I will."

Alan cursed bitterly while Matt's weight pinned Alan against the floor. He began to yell vile threats but was greeted with a whack of the gun barrel against his head and the words, "Shut up!" There was nothing Alan could do. He was defeated, humiliated, and losing his bride as she walked wordlessly past him out of their home. Alan began to scream as he broke into sobs.

Matt let him go and stood. He watched Alan stand up quickly, wiping the blood from his nose and spreading it across his face as he wiped the tears from his reddened eyes that glared dangerously at Matt. "I'll kill you!" Alan shook with rage. "I'll kill you all!"

Matt didn't take the words lightly. He knew exactly what kind of a man he was dealing with. He peered at Alan evenly. "If you step outside this house or follow us, you will be shot dead on sight. That's the only warning I'll give."

Chapter 34

Morton stayed inside the Gregory Hotel until he saw Matt drive the wagon out of Natoma with Audrey sitting beside him on the bench seat. Truet sat on the wagon bed watching behind them while holding a Winchester. Truet raised a hand to wave as Morton stepped out onto the road. He waved back sorrowfully as he watched the woman he longed to have as his own being taken out of town.

Henry put an arm over Morton's shoulders and said in a nasal voice from his swollen nose and eyes, "You should ask her to marry you."

"I don't think she'll ever want to see me again. I didn't tell her the truth myself."

"You did better than that. You sent the U.S. Marshal to take her someplace safe. If she can't appreciate that, then she doesn't deserve you. You should go home, pack your things, and go after her. You just can't bring her back here."

Morton cast a glance at his brother. "And let you support that hoard up there by yourself? It wouldn't feel right."

Henry swatted a fly that landed on his pants. "I can appreciate that, but it isn't fair for you. Morton, you have never, for as long as I can remember, you have never had the opportunity to court a respectable lady. Audrey is a gold mine for you."

Morton snorted slightly. "And I'm fool's gold for her. I have absolutely nothing to offer her, and she'd be a fool to want anything to do with me. But she will be a rich find for the man she finally does marry. It just won't be me. I suppose it won't do us any good to stand here and look at an empty road. Let's go see how angry Ma and everyone is."

"I can imagine. Think they know it was us who told Matt?" Henry asked. He already knew the answer and was prepared to face of consequences of their mother's wrath at home.

"I do. But they'll get over it. We did what was right."

The two brothers started walking toward home. Henry waited until they were out of town when he confided, "I did help Racheal leave our family."

Morton stopped and turned toward his younger brother. "I wish I had been smart enough to help you. Don't tell Alan. Now that Audrey is out of his reach, he'll become fixated on finding Racheal again."

"I've never said a word about it."

***

They entered the house to hear several crying children coming from their rooms. Tad sat on the davenport with a pleased smirk while his younger brother Travis held his side and sniffled. A red welt from the switch was across his cheek. The only other people in the family room were Jannie and Vince; both were very quiet. Their mother sat in her rocking chair, holding her leather-handled switch in her hand. Her expression was colder than a gravestone covered by snow as her eyes burned into Morton.

"What's all the crying about?" Henry asked with concern. He could hear his seven-year-old daughter Mandy sobbing loudly from the back of the house.

Mattie squeezed the switch handle tighter. She shouted, "I should whip you both to the brink of death for what you did! You had no business interfering in our affairs..."

"Affairs?" Morton questioned while Henry walked towards his room to check on his family. "I did what was right. And I don't care what you think about it."

Mattie stood up quickly and raised the switch.

"Ma, if you try to hit me with that, I will take it away from you and break it in half." Morton said calmly.

Mattie fumed, "Audrey was the key to keeping your brother out of prison. He liked her, Morton, and now she is gone. She would have been so good for him, and you ruined it! I'll never forgive you, and I know Alan won't. You just ruined any chance of having a relationship with him. And me!"

Morton wasn't moved. "Ma, you'll get over it, and so will Alan. I won't apologize for having Matt take her away."

"Mother!" Henry yelled from the back of the house. He came quickly to the family room. "Give me that damn thing!" He ripped the switch out of her hand and shouted in her face, "Don't you ever lay your hands on my children again! Don't ever! Mandy's got welts all over her body, Bernice. Even Henry Junior has one!"

"What?" Morton questioned Travis. "What happened?"

Mattie stood sternly. "I whipped them all."

"Vince?" Morton demanded. "What happened?"

Vince answered uneasily, "Ma went a little berserk after the marshal took Audrey away. Matt called her a bad mother, and Alan said he would kill all four of you—Matt, Truet, you, and Henry—for taking Audrey away. Ma started hitting everyone with that switch, even Bernice. Even baby Alisha got struck when Ma lashed Daisy for trying to stop her."

Henry bent the willow switch until it snapped in two and then tossed it at his mother. He sneered, "If you make another one of those, I swear I will use it on you! I'm taking my wife and kids, and I'm leaving this house. Mark has the right idea; the further he keeps his family away from you, the better off they are. I'm taking Daisy and her kids with me. I can't speak for Morton, but I hope he goes after Audrey to make her his wife, and they never come back here. I don't know what words the marshal used, but he's right. You are a rotten, stinking excuse of a mother! No wonder our father left you. Half of

333

your children are too." He pointed at Vince. "You should have stopped her. You!" He walked towards the back of the house to be with his family.

"Go!" Mattie yelled. "Get out of here then. Take your screaming kids and go!" She pointed at Morton. "You too!"

Morton nodded sadly. "Henry's nose is nearly broken, swollen twice its size, and his eyes are nearly swollen shut, black and blue. You didn't even ask Henry what happened to his face. You're just mad about us saving a good woman from you and Alan." He chuckled lightly. "That about sums it up for me. I'm packing my bags and leaving."

"Uncle Morton, can I go with you?" Travis nearly begged.

Jannie slapped him. "You're not going nowhere!"

Morton answered him gently, "Let me get situated, and I'll come to get you."

"No, you won't!" Jannie argued.

"Try to stop me, Jannie. You and Ma treat him like a servant you can beat on while catering to Tad."

***

Half an hour later, Morton had his saddlebags packed and two burlap bags as well. He set his belongings that could be carried on the front porch and then went back into the family room.

His nephew Tad spread his arms across the back of the davenport, puffed his chest out arrogantly, and said, "I guess I'm the new man of the house now. I'll be taking over your room. I might even take the gang over."

Morton's right arm shot forward, grabbed Tad by the hair, yanked him to his feet, pulled Tad's arm upwards behind his back, and forced the boy to the room he shared with Travis. He shoved Tad to the floor and ordered, "Give me the broach you stole from Audrey and the necklace too. Now!"

Tad resigned from arguing, opened a wooden storage box, dug through some clothing, opened a cigar box, and handed the broach and Jane Montgomery's necklace to Morton. "There."

"Where is the knife I gave Travis?" Morton asked pointedly.

Tad opened a broken dresser drawer and pulled it from under some clothes. He handed it to Morton.

Morton put a finger in Tad's face and warned, "If Travis tells me you took his knife or anything of his again, I'll come to take back that rifle I gave you. Am I clear?"

"Yes."

"Good. If you are smart, you will get a job and forget about joining the gang. There is no future in it except prison or death. I don't want to see you do either. I'm not good at saying it. None of us are in this family are, but I love you, kid. I don't want you getting hurt or messing your life up. I'll see you later."

Morton walked out to the barn to get his horse saddled and stopped just inside the door. Alan was sitting in the doorway of his room with his feet dangling over the loft's edge.

"I'm leaving for good." Morton said.

"Just like Audrey, huh? How convenient." Alan said quietly. He jumped down the eight feet to the ground. "You had your friend, the U.S. Marshal, come here to take her away from me because you were not man enough to beat me yourself. It's the Sperry Rule, Morton!" he shouted angrily. "I won fair and square. It must be nice to have friends you can call on to do that for you. How long was that planned? The night we met her? Is that what you two were talking about by the creek? The swing last night? That's quite a plan." He stepped closer to Morton.

"There was no plan..."

"I suppose it all just happened like that, huh? Well, the marshal isn't here to save you this time. But this time, I'm not stopping. Do you want to leave? Good! Your grave won't be found." He swung a hard right fist at Morton's face.

Morton expected it this time and ducked as the wild swing went over his head. He immediately stepped in close and drove his shoulder into Alan to tackle him to the ground. Already in a good position to get control of Alan, Morton wrapped his left arm around Alan's right arm and trapped it fully extended against his ribcage tightly. It left Alan's left hand free, but on the ground, it had limited power to strike effectively. Remembering earlier, Morton was cautious of another extended finger jab to his throat. Alan tried the finger jab immediately, but Morton shifted his upper body to the left and avoided it. When Alan lowered his arm to the ground to coil it for another thrust, Morton quickly trapped the arm under his knee.

Alan was helpless to do anything except scream curses and threats as loud as he could. Morton's right fist was his only weapon, and it was free to pound down on Alan's face, which he repeatedly did, but he couldn't get a full swing or hit with full power while his left arm was pinning Alan's right arm against his body. To get a better swing with more fierceness and power, Morton raised his left leg to elevate his hips off Alan's torso and apply more weight to his punches. He hit with a more solid blow with some power behind it. He hit again.

"Morton!" Vince yelled as he and Henry ran into the barn to break the fight up. Henry grabbed Morton and pulled him off Alan while Vince took a position between the two brothers. "Enough!" Vince shouted. "She's just a woman; you're brothers!"

Alan stood up, quickly ran, jumped onto his ladder, and disappeared into his room behind the blanket.

"It's over." Henry said sharply to Morton. "Get your horse and go after her."

"What's going on here?" Mattie shouted as she entered the barn with Jannie, Daisy, and Tad.

"I'm leaving." Morton said.

Alan yelled from his room, "I won her earlier, Ma! I won fair and square, but he's leaving with Audrey anyway, and he lost! She's supposed to be mine."

"I don't want to listen to this bull crap." Morton

said and started walking towards the horse stall. The blanket flung open, and Alan stepped out of his room with fury in his eyes and revolver in hand. He pointed the weapon at Morton and pulled the trigger. The bullet missed Morton and hit the side of the barn, but the percussion echoed loudly and horrified them all.

Morton didn't have time to be scared, but he knew there would be no reasoning with his brother. Alan intended to kill him like an angry bear, and there was nothing he could do to stop it except react the only way he knew how. He ran towards the opened barn door to exit the barn and reach his weapons on the house's front porch. If Alan intended to have a gunfight, then Morton needed his gun.

"Alan, no!" Henry yelled.

Alan followed Morton with the gun barrel and fanned the hammer twice as Morton reached the door.

Morton cried out painfully as one of the bullets grazed across the upper right side of his back, peeling the skin off his body. He arched his back reactively to the searing pain and then dove to the ground and rolled back to his feet as another bullet whizzed by him.

"Alan, stop!" he heard his mother scream.

"Alan!" Vince yelled.

"He's your brother!" Jannie's terrified voice shouted.

Morton could hear the screaming, but he had only one thing on his mind: reaching the safety of his gun. He ran towards the house, silently cursing himself for not putting on his gun belt.

From the height of the loft, Alan could no longer see Morton once he was outside the barn and knew the time was short until Morton was armed and shooting back. Alan pulled the hammer back until it clicked and leaped from the loft with his finger on the trigger. He kept his determined eyes on the barn door to locate, aim and shoot Morton in the back before he reached the house.

He usually jumped straight down from the loft, but the leap forward increased his momentum and carried him forward after his feet hit the ground. He ran into the opposite barn wall and accidentally pulled the trigger. Alan's wrath refused to take notice of anything except his younger brother's back as he ran towards the house. Within seconds Alan pulled the hammer back and aimed his revolver at the center of Morton's back. His lips slanted upwards into a deadly sneer as he knew Morton would be a dead man. The horrifying scream by Jannie immediately followed a collapsing body in the barn. Alan's extended arm slowly fell as he watched his family react in agonizing terror.

The bullet that was accidentally fired had penetrated the right side of Daisy's chest, tearing through both of her lungs. She collapsed, unable to speak from shock and the lack of air. She tried to breathe, but her lungs were already filling with blood.

"Daisy! Oh lord, no." Mattie cried as she dropped to her knees beside her youngest child. A long thin welt mark was stretched across Daisy's neckline.

"No! Oh no!" Mattie screamed over her child.

Alan stood perfectly still with his gun lowered and loose in his fingers. "It was an accident…"

Henry pushed Tad aside and knelt beside his mother and the others. "Daisy…" He covered his mouth to stop sobbing. "Oh Lord, no…" His body began to jerk with emotion.

"Daisy?" Morton questioned as he came back into the barn quickly. "Oh no! No! No!" He dropped to his knees with the others who were wailing and sobbing.

"I love you, Daisy. I love you so much." Morton rubbed her forehead as she struggled to catch even a short breath. She blurred through the tears that clouded Morton's eyes and fell freely. He kissed her forehead lovingly. He struggled to get his breathing controlled enough to speak, "You know about some supper in Heaven, yeah? Baby sister, I hope you're hungry." his voice cracked as a tear fell from his cheek onto her chest. His jaw clenched to keep from breaking down and wailing.

Daisy's eyes shifted back and forth from Henry to Morton. There was no fear in them, which struck Morton as odd. He had watched many grown men who were tough as nails die with absolute terror in their eyes. Daisy's lips lifted upwards just a touch towards a smile, her finger pointed upwards as a stream of blood flowed from the two sides of her mouth and colored her lips.

Bernice ran into the barn frantically and forced herself between Henry and Mattie. "I'm here."

"My baby…" Mattie wailed mournfully.

Daisy lifted her finger upward again as more blood spilled out her mouth and nose.

Bernice nodded with a broken attempt at a comforting smile while the tears streamed down her face. "Yes, sweety. You are going to heaven. And I'll see you there, little sister. It's okay."

Her gurgling of blood grew thicker and then stopped.

Daisy was gone.

Morton stood and turned towards the wall and hit it with a fist while the ladies and others sobbed and wailed over Daisy's body.

Alan remained where he had stood. He spoke, "It was an accident. I didn't mean to..." he couldn't finish. "I... it was an accident. Morton ran towards her and... It isn't my fault!"

Henry stood and wiped the tears off his cheeks. He glared at Alan dangerously while breathing heavily through his mouth.

"Henry..." Alan raised his hands innocently. The revolver was still in his grip. "It wasn't my fault, she got in the way. It was an accident." There were no tears on his cheeks or a hint of moisture clouding his eyes.

Henry's teeth grit together, and a snarl lifted his upper lip as a rage swept through him like none he had experienced. He walked quickly toward Alan, grabbed the pitchfork leaning against the pigpen, and suddenly rammed it into Alan's abdomen in one continuous motion that happened too fast for Alan to avoid. Henry pushed Alan against the barn wall with the pitchfork and shoved the four tines deeper into Alan until the pitchfork pierced through his body and hit the wall's wood.

Alan gasped in shock as he stared at his brother. The revolver fell from Alan's grasp to the barn floor. Henry's twisted lips revealed his desire to push the tines through the wall if he could.

Morton knew the others were too consumed with grieving over Daisy's body to notice what Henry had done. Morton stepped over quickly, picked up Alan's revolver, and checked the cylinder to see how many shots were fired. Without a word, he aimed the gun at the side of Alan's head and pulled the hammer back until it clicked.

Alan turned his head at the menacing sound and looked Morton in the eyes. His brow lowered questionably. "This is not what brothers are supposed to do." he whispered. A single tear rolled down his cheek.

"No, it's not." Morton said with a barely controlled voice. He squeezed his lips together emotionally, breathed in deeply, and pulled the trigger. Alan fell to the ground, pulling the pitchfork out of Henry's hand while the revolver's percussion echoed in the small barn.

"What did you do?" Mattie screamed in horror. She had not noticed anything happening between her three sons. She ran from Daisy's body to Alan's and wailed with loud screams as she jerked the dirty pitchfork out of her son.

Morton said to Henry, "Now Alan's blood is on my hands, not yours."

"What did you do?" Mattie screamed at Morton.

Her wailing was loud and from deeper within, which can only come from losing two of her children within minutes of each other. "Why?" she sobbed. "Why?" she demanded to know.

Morton yelled, "We did exactly what you taught us, Ma. We fought to the end! Sperry's don't quit, and we don't lose. We keep fighting." He paused to catch his breath. "Damn your Sperry Rule!"

Morton turned away from his mourning mother and gazed at his baby sister's dead body. He walked out of the barn to hear the sound of baby Alisha crying in the house. It tore at his heart. Daisy's oldest son Elliot stepped out of the house. "Where is my mama?"

Morton's breath was expelled by the sudden gasp of an emotional spear sent into his heart. He lifted the little boy in his arms and hugged him. Morton struggled to remain strong enough not to break down sobbing. He offered an attempted smile that fell several miles too short. "Elliot, let's get you in the house. You don't want to go to the barn right now." He held the four-year-old boy tight in his arms and squeezed his eyes shut to fight a losing battle. "Mommy's..." His body began to convulse in short jerks. His voice cracked, "Your mommy wanted me to tell you she loves you so much. So, so much. And everything is going to be okay." He wasn't strong enough not to drop to his knees in the yard and begin to sob. He held Elliot tightly as he wept.

Chapter 35

Matt sat behind his desk, dumbfounded by the story that Morton Sperry told him. "Morton, I'm sorry. I figured Alan would be upset with me, but I never imagined he'd try to kill you. I'm so sorry about Daisy. I never talked to her too much, but she seemed like a very nice young lady."

Morton was broken with grief, which showed in his Sperry green eyes. "The nicest in the family. She had a beautiful heart."

"So, what are your plans now?" Matt asked, having been told by Morton that he left the family and Natoma.

Morton shrugged. "I don't know. I just figured I'd come to see you since I don't know anyone else worth knowing around here. I don't know what I'm going to do. Maybe go to work in the silver mine with my brothers. I plan on talking to Mark later and see if I can stay with him for a while."

Matt had both elbows on the desk as he rested

his chin on his folded hands. "I might be able to help with a job. My uncles own the granite quarry if you're interested in that?"

"I'll take anything at the moment. I'm broke. I don't have a penny to my name."

"The granite quarry is hard physical labor, but it's an honest job. I can talk with my cousin Robert tonight. He's the manager. Do you plan to see Audrey before she leaves town?" Matt asked.

Morton offered a sad attempt at a smile. "It's been five days. I thought she'd already be on her way back home by now."

"No, but she is leaving tomorrow morning. So, if you want to see her, right now might be the best time."

Morton shook his head slowly. "I doubt she would want to see me."

Matt shrugged his shoulders. "Maybe not, I don't know. Maybe I'm wrong, but I got the impression the last time we talked that you were very fond of her. I think she's a pretty amazing lady myself. At the very least, you'd be able to say goodbye to her, or maybe, if you were so inclined, you could talk her into staying for a few days longer. After a few days, maybe you'd want to go with her. I don't know. Just an idea. But she is leaving early tomorrow morning."

Morton rubbed his thick goatee around his mouth. "Ah, heck, Matt. Even if I wanted to, I don't have anything to offer her. Do you know what I mean? You're engaged, so you will understand. Would your fiancé want to marry you if you had nothing, not a job or a place to live? Matt, I am thirty-five years old, and I have nothing to my name except my horse, guns, and a very bad reputation."

Matt raised his brow thoughtfully. "You have everything I had when I came back here. Except, one of these." He opened a drawer and pulled out a U.S. Deputy Marshal badge.

Morton chuckled lightly. "At least you had that and a family you could be proud of. I don't have either."

Matt hesitated. "Morton, I have a very tight budget because I'm still paying Jed Clark's widow his monthly wage. She has children to feed, and I couldn't leave them without. So, I fudge the numbers a bit here and there to make it work. I have three deputies to cover this county and outlying counties when needed. One of my deputies works in the office permanently. He's not a fighter, and he's never going to be one. I've been considering hiring another experienced man because I suspect Truet will eventually marry Annie and move to the ranch."

"Are you offering me a job?" Morton was perplexed.

"I might be if you're interested."

"Matt, everyone knows I'm an outlaw. I led the Sperry-Helms Gang for years. I can't wear that."

Matt raised his brow questionably. "You wanted to change your life, right? You can't get a much broader change than going from an outlaw with a bad reputation to a deputy marshal with a good reputation. If you're serious about wanting to change the direction of your life, then this might be your chance to do so. You'd be working with me, Truet, Nate, and Phillip every day, and we're a pretty good bunch, I think. I need a man who is rough enough to enforce the law but experienced if a gunfight breaks loose. William is a part-time deputy. When I expect a gunfight, I need him the most because Truet is the only deputy I have experienced with that."

Morton wrinkled his nose. "Matt, I have doubts that your deputies would want to work with me, to begin with. Seriously, you don't owe me anything; you don't have to offer me a job. Talking to your cousin about the quarry would suit me fine."

Matt hollered out his private office door, "Truet, Nate, Phillip, come here." When his three deputies crowded around his office door, Matt asked, "How would you gentlemen feel about me offering Morton a position with us? Speak honestly and give me your approval or not."

Truet answered first, "The only concern I would have is his reputation and commitment to the law when confronting his family and friends. Morton, I think you are a very capable man for doing the job, and I think we'd get along fine, but in a life and death situation with your brothers or cousins, you'd have to earn my trust. And I don't know if you want to be put in that situation. That's my only real concern. My answer is… I don't know."

Nate said, "Truet summed my concerns up, but we've worked with Morton before. I say yes."

Phillip hesitated thoughtfully. "I grew up here,

and Morton Sperry is a name most people fear. If he sincerely wanted to change his life around and become a deputy marshal, his name would help keep the peace as much as yours and Truet's do. His family might not want to commit a crime if he joined us. I say, yes."

"Thank you, gentlemen." Matt waited for them to return to what they were doing and closed the office door. "Well, you heard them. The job is yours if you want it."

Morton shook his head. "You heard Truet. I'm a... I don't know. Matt, I already killed my brother. I don't want to have to kill another brother or a cousin, or my nephew. They're outlaws. You're bound to face them."

Matt thought about it for a moment. "The way I see it, what would be a better motivation for them to go straight? They'd know they couldn't hide from you. I won't lie to you, though. We could have a confrontation with your family, but we could whether you're with us or not. But you might be the best option for talking them into surrendering without blood being shed. It would be hard for you to be involved, but it might save their lives or ours. That is where your integrity and loyalty to the badge you wear and to us must become a part of who you are. We're a family here, and you would become a part of it; loyalty is expected. There is no tolerance for betrayals or forgiveness. This job is not physically hard but can be mentally and emotionally exhausting. As I said, I can't promise we won't confront your family, but if we do, I'd rather have you on my side because it's the best outcome for them."

Morton sat quietly with a lowered head.

Matt continued, "Morton, when we first met, I figured we'd be trying to kill each other soon enough, but that isn't what happened. You say you're my friend, and I like to think you are. I believe in giving people a chance to change their lives. Many lawmen around this country were criminals at one time, but they changed their paths and made some of the best lawmen. I'm offering that chance to you. Not because I owe you anything, but because I think we'd work well together."

Morton clicked his tongue and remained silent for a moment. "You have no idea what I've done that can come back and haunt me if I were one of your deputies."

Matt took a deep breath. "I can imagine. The question is, can they be proven in court?"

Morton narrowed his eyes thoughtfully. "No."

"Do you honestly want to start over again with a clean slate?"

Morton nodded. He looked up with tears welling in his eyes. "I wish I never had a criminal past. I wish I could start my life all over again. I wish I had never been born a Sperry."

"Then I have an idea. I'll make you a deal, and we'll leave it up to fate. Take this badge and put it on to see how it feels, and then go see Audrey while you can. Ask her what she thinks about you working for me. Talk to her, and maybe if all goes well, you can encourage her to stay a few extra days to get to know her better. Be honest with her, Morton, and tell her how you feel. Lord willing, at best, she'll cancel her ticket and stay here. At worst, at least you tried. In romance, courting, and love, you have to toss your true feelings out there, or the other person may never know how you feel—knowing somebody's heart can change everything. Put the badge on, go see her, and we'll talk in the morning when you can give me your answer. Here's our agreement, if she stays, you work for me. If she leaves, I'll talk to my cousin and get you a job at the quarry. Agreed?"

"She's leaving tomorrow morning?" he asked with a sniffle.

"On the eight o'clock stage."

"Oh, heck, what have I got to lose? Agreed."

***

Morton could feel his stomach churning with anxiety and tying itself in a knot as he knocked on Joel Fasana's front door. It had taken him some time to find the home as Matt's directions were a bit unclear. He found Joel Fasana's house and knocked loudly.

After a moment, Audrey opened the door wearing an apron over her dress. "Morton? What are you doing here?" she asked with surprise.

He hesitated uncomfortably. He was more afraid of being rejected by her than he ever was of robbing a stagecoach, travelers, or a bank. He was more fearful of being rejected by her than during his first gunfight. He held up the palms of his hands defensively. He found it hard to speak.

"Morton?" she questioned.

"Matt told me you're leaving for California early in the morning, so I'll make this quick. I wanted to return your broach to you. I'm sure Matt told you my family are criminals, and I was too, but I'm not anymore."

She gasped to have her mother's broach back. "Thank you! I thought I'd never see it again. Thank you, Morton." Her excitement to have the broach back lit up her face like a kerosene lamp as she gazed at the rainbow-colored wings of the Butterfly broach while holding it close to her heart. Her eyes moistened with emotion. "The rainbow is God's only visual reminder that he promises never to flood the earth again. My mother gave me this broach as a reminder that God is faithful to keep all his promises. Every rainbow we see in the sky should remind us that God is faithful even when we're not. Thank you for returning it to me."

"You're welcome." Morton said softly. He continued uncomfortably, "I know I should have told you in the very beginning that it was my mother that was writing to you. Alan wasn't anyone you would want to be married to. I... I tried to tell you that in a few ways. He can't spell and has terrible handwriting."

"Ahh, that's why you said to have him write a poem." She leaned against the door jamb.

"Yes. I was going to tell you, but Matt came to town, and it worked out better with him taking you from there. Look, I apologize for keeping that from you. I'm not good with all the romantic things, but Audrey, I really like you. I know you're leaving, but I wish you would consider staying here a few days longer, and maybe we can see if... if... if maybe you might be interested in me? Because I am very much interested in you. Look," he pointed at the badge pinned to his shirt. "I may work with Matt as a deputy marshal and will find a place to live. I don't know yet, but I left Natoma and won't be going back. And if you don't want to stay here, maybe you can give me an address so I can write to you? I'll even write a note now, so you'll know it's my handwriting." He swallowed nervously. "I don't want to lose your friendship, Audrey."

She smiled at his words and how nervous he was. "Morton, I told you I would never marry a non-Christian man."

He fumbled with his shirt pocket and pulled a small square box out of his shirt. He opened it to show her. Inside were two seed heads of different plants that appeared quite similar. He spoke, "The head of wheat has the brown seeds, the head with black seeds is the tare, called Darnel, Poison Darnel or Cockle as I was telling you that day by the creek. This is for you, whether you stay here or not. Jimmy Crawford gave it to me."

"Thank you. They do look similar, don't they?" Audrey asked with interest.

"They do. But they are very different. I'll be honest with you, Audrey, I'm not a Christian, but I will go to church with you every Sunday if you stay here. I will be surrounded by Christians working with Matt and his deputies if I take the job. I won't promise you anything except for this; I won't say I am Christian until I am. Because that tare right there is fake, and you don't deserve a fake husband, whether it's me or someone else."

"I appreciate that, Morton, I do. But my stage leaves in the morning."

Morton's expression grew long. "Audrey, I know I'm not handsome or well-versed in anything. I've been a criminal all my life. I'm not worthy of you by ten miles at least. But for the first time in my life, I would do anything to spend all the time I possibly can with you. I think you are that wonderful, and I enjoy being with you, just talking. You are like a fresh breath of air, or I don't know… a… a… a cold running stream after three days of wandering in the desert. You bring life into my dull world." He continued with a vulnerable pleading in his eyes, "Please, don't go yet. Give me a chance to prove to you that I can be worth something. Audrey, it would break my heart if you left and answered another man's ad for a bride. Because I know how much you are worth and how wonderful you are. I know you're leaving, but I wish you'd give me a chance whether you stay or not. I hope you'll write to me at least because I don't want to lose you."

Audrey's lips narrowed into a smile. "Morton, I'm not going back to California in the morning. I'm going to work at the Monarch Restaurant. I'm a breakfast and lunch cook. But I would love to spend time with you."

His mouth slowly opened, stunned. "Matt lied to me?"

She laughed. "Ask him."

Matt and his uncle Joel stepped into the house's entry behind Audrey. Both men were laughing. "D… d… d… Don't go, plweese." Matt teased with a whining voice as he laughed. "I'm sorry, Morton, but I already knew she would want to see you. I wanted to ensure you came by and poured your heart out before losing her. Well, a deal is a deal; she's staying. You did it! I'll see you in the morning at the office. Oh, there's a room at the Monarch Hotel for the next few nights reserved for you. Just check in and get your key. It's all taken care of, including meals. You have a good night, Deputy Marshal Sperry." Matt said with a wink as he crossed the porch and walked towards the dance hall to see Christine.

"Wait," Morton called, "You sent me on a wild goose chase all over town so you could beat me here?"

Matt nodded with a grin. "See? You're already figuring things out as a lawman should. You bet I did."

"What a creep." He watched Matt walking away. "I like him more all the time. I think I'm going to like working for him."

"Morton," Audrey said gently, "the Crawford family wired the Fasana Granite Works today and ordered a tombstone for Daisy. They are paying for it, and it will be beautiful. That's how I learned she passed away. Matt told us the rest that I didn't know moments ago. I am so sorry that I caused so much trouble for your family. I feel terrible."

His voice was soft, "It wasn't you that caused it. My mother had a terrible plan, and it fell apart, thankfully. My baby sister taught me what real courage is. While she was dying, there was no fear in her, and she pointed towards heaven and even tried to smile despite the pain she was in." He shook his head slightly while he wiped his eyes. "I've seen grown men die, but I've never seen that before. There was something special about her; somehow, I know, she's at that dinner table in heaven that you told me about. I told her she better be hungry. I couldn't finish what I was going to say. I was going to tell her to save me a seat."

Audrey walked out on the porch to sit on the steps. "Let's sit down for a while, and I'll tell you how you can join her at that dinner table. Our seats are reserved; we just have to accept the invitation that Jesus offers. And that peace that Daisy had; you can know it every day of your life until you point your finger towards the sky on that final day too. Morton, I'm glad you're here. I have been praying for you. I think the Lord brought me here for a reason. I was just writing to the wrong brother, but it took all your family did for me to meet you. And I am thankful for that."

Morton's solemn frown couldn't resist growing into an enthusiastic smile as her words reached his ears. "That Matt is one sly dog. He already knew that, didn't he?"

Audrey laughed a delightful sound. "I told him I thought I was marrying the wrong brother. Yes."

"I had that very same impression the moment I met you." Morton's grin faded like a falling tree. "Audrey, tell me more about Jesus, because if he really brought you here to meet me, then I want to know how God could want to bless me with you. Because I'm no one."

Audrey took hold of his hand affectionately. "You're wrong, Deputy Marshal Morton Sperry. God loves you, and that makes you a very important someone. I hope you're ready for your life to change, Morton, because I think it will continue to just get better."

Acknowledgments

First and foremost, I must thank my wife, Cathy, for always being encouraging and supportive. Thank you for always listening. It means a lot. My son, Keith, is the first to read anything I write. I appreciate his honesty, criticism, and suggestions—a few of them I added to this story. His opinion and constant encouragement are greatly appreciated. I am blessed with a very supportive family, Jessica and Chris, Chevelle, Katie and Isaiah—thank you.

I also want to thank Patience Bramlett and the folks at CKN Christian Publishing who work hard to make the Matt Bannister Series not just available, but possible. They have my highest appreciation and respect.

A Look At:
When The Wolf Comes Knocking

Some wolves attack when their prey is at its weakest. Some charge fiercely. Others...knock softly.

When Greg Slater returned home from college for winter break, his whole world changed. After rescuing his high-school sweetheart, Tina Dibari, and helping sentence his best friend, Rene Dibari, to life in prison, Greg fell in love for the first time.

Fifteen years later, life isn't easy, but Greg and Tina are working on their marriage. But an old fear has come back to haunt them...

Rene has escaped prison, and he's thirsty for revenge.

As shocking truths unfold, Greg and Tina face a ripple in their faith and in their home. Tina starts doubting her faith and seeks comfort in a friend with lustful intentions. Meanwhile, Greg struggles to navigate this new unrest in their relationship.

Unfortunately, evil stops for no one, and three very different wolves are after the Slater family.

Will Greg and Tina's love be enough to keep them together, and—more importantly—will their faith hold true when the wolves come knocking?

AVAILABLE ON AMAZON

About the Author

Ken Pratt and his wife, Cathy, have been married for 22 years and are blessed with five children and six grandchildren. They live on the Oregon Coast where they are raising the youngest of their children. Ken Pratt grew up in the small farming community of Dayton, Oregon. Ken worked to make a living, but his passion has always been writing. Having a busy family, the only "free" time he had to write was late at night getting no more than five hours of sleep a night. He has penned several novels that are being published along with several children's stories as well.

Made in the USA
Columbia, SC
23 January 2023